HIDDEN FAMILY SECRETS

THE PAISLEY WOMEN SERIES
BOOK 1

EVELYN HOOD

Boldwood

First published in 1986 as *The Silken Thread*. This edition published in Great Britain in 2025 by Boldwood Books Ltd.

Copyright © Evelyn Hood, 1986

Cover Design by Colin Thomas

Cover Images: Colin Thomas

A CIP catalogue record for this book is available from the British Library.

Paperback ISBN 978-1-80600-177-4

Large Print ISBN 978-1-80600-176-7

Hardback ISBN 978-1-80600-175-0

Trade Paperback ISBN 978-1-80635-389-7

Ebook ISBN 978-1-80600-178-1

Kindle ISBN 978-1-80600-179-8

Audio CD ISBN 978-1-80600-170-5

MP3 CD ISBN 978-1-80600-171-2

Digital audio download ISBN 978-1-80600-174-3

This book is printed on certified sustainable paper. Boldwood Books is dedicated to putting sustainability at the heart of our business. For more information please visit https://www.boldwoodbooks.com/about-us/sustainability/

Boldwood Books Ltd, 23 Bowerdean Street, London, SW6 3TN

www.boldwoodbooks.com

To my mother
Millie Webster Steel

I had a dove and the sweet dove died.
  And I have thought it died of grieving,
  O, what could it grieve for? Its feet were tied,
  With a silken thread of my own hand's weaving.

— JOHN KEATS

PART I

For the third time since they left Beith, Meg's stomach began to rebel at the cart's lurching progress. She tried hard to fight down the queasiness, both hands squeezed tightly against her stomach beneath the shelter of her shawl. But finally she had to twitch at Duncan's sleeve until he moved his blue eyes from contemplation of the farmland to her white, apologetic face.

'Duncan, I'm feared I'm—'

'Not again!' her husband said impatiently. 'D'you want us to take two days to make this journey?'

'I can't help it—' She pressed her hand over her mouth and made to jump from the moving vehicle in her haste to get out before she disgraced herself, and him, completely.

'You'd best stop.' Duncan tapped the driver on the shoulder and he, without a backward glance at his passengers, drew the horses to a halt and waited, back hunched. The animals immediately began to tear at the dry dusty grass fringing the road, twitching their ears and flicking their tails to ward off flies.

With Duncan's help Meg scrambled down from the cart and stumbled over the springy turf. She reached the shelter of a whin bush just in time and knelt on the grass, vomiting miserably and wishing she was back home in the farm kitchen with her family.

It had seemed such an adventure when they first planned it. Duncan, a weaver by trade, was young and ambitious, and in 1745 the flourishing Renfrewshire town of Paisley, some twenty miles away, was the ideal place for a young man willing to work.

Meg was the envy of her sisters. To be a married woman, with a handsome husky young husband like Duncan – she knew herself how fortunate she was. But now the first sweet shyness of marriage had passed and she had begun to realise that this dark confident man was hers, and she his, for the rest of her life. She was bound to follow him wherever he chose to lead. The thought, which had excited her as she danced with him at her wedding beneath the familiar smoke-grimed beams of home, now made her shiver despite the warm May sun above.

What if they didn't fare well? What if she hated Paisley yet had to go on living there, homesick and wretched?

She stood up and glanced at the cart waiting on the track a short distance away. Duncan had stepped down to stretch his legs. The driver, a man of few words, sat hunched on the cart, a sombre figure against the blue sky beyond.

Another spasm dragged her back to her knees. All at once she wanted her mother – though she had been glad enough to escape her sharp eyes a few hours earlier.

'If you have your wits about you, you'll see that there are no babies until you're settled,' her mother had advised as she brushed Meg's hair on her wedding morning. 'You've chosen a wild man – see that he makes enough silver to put food for your belly and a roof over your head before you think further.'

Meg, breathless with loving anticipation, had promised easily enough. She never disobeyed her mother, who was not slow to show her displeasure with a clout on the ear that could send even a full-grown son or daughter flying across the room. But common sense had no chance when she was safely wedded and bedded, and Duncan's youthful passion was sweeping them both headlong on the course they had longed to take since they first set eyes on each other.

When the first signs of nausea and giddiness appeared within a few weeks of their wedding day, Meg had done her utmost to hide them from the older woman, and had eagerly agreed to Duncan's proposal that they join the growing army of people lured by Paisley's expanding linen industry. She had succeeded in her deception, for her mother still had no inkling of her condition.

Meg spat to rid her mouth of a bitter aftertaste, and walked back to the men.

'You took your time, lady,' Duncan greeted her impatiently. 'Early afternoon, I said we'd be there. D'you think we have a whole day to waste on one short journey?'

'I couldn't help it—' she said faintly, apologetically, as he handed her up to her seat and swung up beside her. His round, handsome face was marred by a scowl. Like his mother-in-law, Duncan felt that their first child should have had the sense to wait a little longer for its conception, and he was inclined to blame Meg for her haste.

The driver had lit his pipe during the wait. Meg's insides quivered as a whiff of strong-smelling tobacco drifted back to her, and panic swept over her. Duncan would never stand for another delay! She squirmed into a position that put her tip-tilted nose out of the way of the smoke and sniffed at the grass-scented air with great determination.

Duncan took the slight move away from him as a sign that his wife was annoyed. Compassion flooded his heart as he looked at the soft curve of her cheek and the corner of her kissable mouth.

He loved her in his own irresponsible way, and his spirits rose with every turn of the wheels that carried them to their new life. An orphan, raised by an elderly aunt who cared little about anything but her Bible, he had found Meg's large, noisy family oppressive. He wanted to be independent, to look after his wife and make his own decisions. If he couldn't make his way in Paisley – well, he'd go elsewhere. But wherever he went he wanted Meg by his side.

It was almost two o'clock when the driver raised his whip and pointed.

'There's where you're bound.'

They craned their necks to see. Paisley was tucked snugly below the Gleniffer Braes – the Muckle Riggs as they were known locally. The main features to be seen from a distance were the High Church steeple and the ruins of the abbey, once a great monastic house but now in a state of disrepair.

Smoke from the chimneys smudged the green of the surrounding hills. The River Cart was a shiny ribbon curling through the town, passing beneath the abbey walls.

Duncan put his arm about Meg.

'There's where we'll find our fortune!'

'You think so?' she asked doubtfully.

'I know so! Paisley's growing, and we'll grow with it. We'll have our own place before long, and our own looms – and sons to carry the trade on after me.' His voice was strong, his optimism catching. 'You'll see, Meg – you'll see!'

The fields and hedges blossomed with great stretches of linen as the cart neared the town. These were the bleachfields, where newly woven linen was brought to whiten. Then the first cottages, some thatched and some with slate roofs, appeared on either side of the low rutted road.

Duncan fingered his plain jacket as he looked at the young

men strolling along the pathways of raised earth, stylishly clad in blue and green coats, nankeen britches and flowered waistcoats. Meg's eyes widened as she stared at the women's colourful dresses. Obviously, Paisley was the very place for an ambitious young couple like themselves.

The sound of hammering came to them as they passed through the town's fringes, where new houses were being built. Paisley was growing fast and there was plenty of work for builders – hard work, if they were to keep up with the demand from the constant stream of incomers.

At last the cart jolted into the rutted main street, busy with carts and carriages. Housewives hurried along the footpaths or stood gossiping in tight groups. A crowd of young men laughed and joked outside a howff – and judging by the state of one of them, kept on his feet by his companions, they had been inside sampling the landlord's wares. Bewhiskered businessmen paced solemnly, brushing barefoot children aside like flies, too involved in their own fat-bellied importance to notice their surroundings. Dogs, cats and pigs were amiable company for each other as they nosed among the refuse at the sides of the road.

After the pure country air they had just driven through the travellers found the smell of rotting rubbish offensive, but they knew that they would quickly get used to it. It wasn't any worse than the dungheap that sat just outside the farm door in Beith.

'Here 'tis,' the driver announced. With a final squeeze of Meg's hand Duncan jumped briskly down and rapped at the door of the three-storey building. While he waited for an answer he handed his wife down from the cart and she looked timidly at the buildings crowding in on the narrow street. Had she been alone she would have turned round there and then, and ordered the driver to take her home again, but being a married woman she could only clutch the bag that held her worldly possessions, and swallow hard.

The door burst open suddenly and a small tornado whirled out of it, almost knocking Meg over with the force of its passing. With a squeak of alarm she clutched at the cart for support while the tornado, which turned out to be a red-headed infant no higher than her knees, recovered its balance and headed in determined fashion down the street, skipping nimbly over holes and hillocks.

'Stop that wean!' a voice shrieked from inside the house, and a plump young woman, her own head topped with glowing red hair, came hurrying along the passageway.

'Get a hold of him, quick!' she shrilled, and Duncan, who had been standing open-mouthed, shot off down the street after the child.

'The wee imp!' The woman leaned on the door frame to catch her breath. 'The times I've told these men to make sure the door's not left on the latch! Do they think I've nothing to do with my time but chase after him?'

Then Duncan was back, a screaming kicking bundle of fury held at arm's length before him.

'You rascal, you!' the woman scolded, taking the child and administering an automatic smack on his plump legs. Then she kissed his rosy cheek.

The child stopped screaming at once and settled himself comfortably astride her hip. He rammed a thumb into his mouth and looked at the visitors with round blue eyes. His face was dirty and his head a mass of tangled curls, but even so it was easy to see how beautiful he was.

'You'll be the Montgomerys? I'm Mistress Todd.' The woman transferred her attention to the couple standing before her. 'Come away in – you must be fair worn out after your journey.'

'So am I... am I to stand here all day waiting to get my cart unloaded? I've work to do,' the driver said sourly from behind them.

Mistress Todd's wide green eyes flashed scathingly. 'Poor man, are your arms wasted away, that you can't unload a wee cart by yourself? Well, well, I suppose Mister Montgomery'll help you while we go into the house.' And leaving him at a loss for words she led Meg into the passageway.

'We live above the weaving shop – here it is—' She threw open a door to disclose a large sunlit room, noisy with the clack of looms and the hum of deep voices. Peering over her shoulder Meg could see men working at two of the four looms, swaying rhythmically as they threw the shuttles from side to side.

'I'll not tell you again – the next one to leave the door on the latch gets his ears warmed!' Mistress Todd bawled. 'The wean's wild enough without any help from you!'

Then she slammed the door shut on the shouted replies and went on upstairs, remarking over her shoulder, 'They're not a bad lot, but they need an awful strong hand to keep them in order.'

And a strong hand was what Mistress Todd had, Meg thought as she followed her red-haired guide up the narrow dark stairway and into a large spotless kitchen, fragrant with the smell of home-made bread.

'Sit yourself down and I'll make some tea.' Mistress Todd deposited the baby on a rag rug and handed him a wooden spoon. He immediately began to bang it on the floor.

'That's right, my mannie, you give these lazy men below a good fast rhythm to work to. This is our Jamie – a wild ragtail of a boy if ever there was one. He's for a soldier for sure, unless he finds himself beneath a horse's hooves first,' his mother said cheerfully. 'You've got it all unloaded, then?' she added as Duncan came in.

'There wasn't much to unload.'

Her eyes twinkled. 'Best to start married life light. Not that I did, for Peter's first wife died and I came to a ready-made home when I wed him. He had two grown lads too – now he's on his second family.' She nudged the baby with her toe. 'And Peter says this one's more bother than Matt and Colin put together. You'll have some ale, Mister Montgomery?'

'I wouldn't mind,' he said gratefully, and drained half the tankard in one thirsty swallow when she handed it to him.

The tea was being poured out when Peter Todd himself arrived.

'So you're here already? I'd have been home to greet you, but I had some linen to deliver—'

'—and you got talking.' His wife finished the sentence for him, nodding at Meg. 'They say women enjoy a gossip, but you'll find that in Paisley the men know how to do their share of tongue-wagging.'

Peter Todd let the remark run off his broad shoulders as he studied the couple before him. He was a big handsome man with a head of thick white hair and shrewd eyes of the same vivid blue as his son's.

'So – this my new man, is it? Well, we'll get on together if you're prepared to work. We all work hard in this house.'

'You'll find nobody more willing than Duncan,' Meg said sharply. 'Mister Brodie was fair vexed to lose him.' Then she coloured as Duncan shushed her.

Peter nodded calmly. 'I know that, lass, for Mister Brodie himself recommended your man to me. I see a spinning wheel downstairs – is it yours?'

Now it was Duncan's turn to boast. 'Meg's as good a spinster as anyone.'

'I'll be glad of her help, then, for this wee skelf keeps me away from my wheel often now that he's found his feet.' Kirsty Todd disentangled Jamie's groping hands from her hair and handed the child to her husband. The little boy buried his face in his father's shoulder and Meg watched, amazed. Her father would never have allowed anyone, even his wife, to see him making a fuss of a child.

'This one's going to be a weaver,' Peter boasted. 'Matt chose the army and Colin's a grocer now. He had to give up weaving because the fluff bothered his chest. Mebbe I'll be spared long enough to teach Jamie how to work the loom.'

'Of course you'll be spared!' his wife hectored. 'Show Mister Montgomery the weaving shop while we see to the meal. And you can tell these men down there to stop leaving the street door on the latch!' she shouted after him as he led Duncan downstairs.

As she and Meg got the meal ready, Kirsty chattered on without waiting for a response. She talked glowingly about Paisley, as proud of the place, Meg thought, as if she had built it with her own capable hands.

'Bragging about the town again, Kirsty?' her husband asked dryly when he and Duncan arrived back upstairs.

'That one comes from Dumbarton—' she jerked her head in his direction '—and nothing I say'll convince him that this side of the Clyde's better than the other bank.'

'What's wrong with Dumbarton?' Peter wanted to know.

'Nothing – though you were pleased enough to wed a Paisley woman. I'm Paisley born and bred myself,' she confided to her guests.

'I think they realised that,' said her husband, poker-faced.

After supper Jamie was put to bed in the attic room he shared with his parents and the adults were free to sit round the fire, Kirsty's fingers flying nimbly over a pile of mending. Meg offered to help and soon she too was working busily, letting the men's talk flow over her bent head.

Finally, Peter knocked his pipe out against the chimney head and stretched his arms.

'We rise early and sleep early. And before we go to bed we have a verse or two from the Holy Book.'

His wife put away her mending and rose to fetch the big family Bible from the corner cupboard. Peter took it from her and placed it carefully on the table.

'D'you want to read tonight's passage, lad?'

Duncan's face, flushed by the fire, deepened in colour. He glanced at Meg for encouragement, then burst out, 'To tell the truth, I'm not much of a hand at reading.'

'You can't read?'

'A wee bit – I learned at the school. But I never took to it. Meg sees to that side of things.'

'Learning's a fine thing,' Peter Todd said mildly. 'And there's a lot a man can find in books whether he's a scholar or a weaver.' Then he opened the huge tome and began to read in a slow, clear voice. Kirsty folded her hands in her lap and nodded agreement with the words now and then.

The scene reminded Meg so vividly of the final ritual of the day at the farm that she was homesick and comforted at the same time.

When the book was closed and put away again, Peter and Kirsty stood up.

'Goodnight to you,' he said with grave courtesy. 'We rise at five o'clock.' Then the Todds departed up the winding staircase that led to the attic.

In their own bedroom, a tiny apartment that had little space for anything but the bed, Meg snuggled up to Duncan's warm body, but resisted his attempts to make love to her.

'Sssshhh! They'll hear!'

'But we're wed! I'll be quiet as a mouse – come on, lass!'

But she couldn't bring herself to make so free of their new employer's bed on such short acquaintance, and Duncan was finally forced to turn over, grumbling to himself.

Meg lay wide-eyed. The room was very dark, and all at once she was grateful for Duncan's presence, protecting her from the ghosts and bogles of the night. She lifted herself onto one elbow.

'Duncan?' she whispered. 'Duncan – I'll learn you to read, then when we have our own house you can read from the Book every night like Mister Todd. It's easy.'

He heaved himself over onto his back and she felt his fingers tangle themselves in her soft loose hair.

'My wee Meg—' His voice was already thick with drowsiness. 'You're a good lass, Meg. You'll see – we'll have a fine home, and our own looms. I'll look after you, Meg.'

Wrapped in his arms she slept at last, certain of the fine future they had mapped out for themselves.

2

Meg and Duncan were quickly caught up in the rhythm of Paisley life. There were two other weavers in Peter Todd's shop besides himself and Duncan – one was an irrepressible young man who saw humour in everything, the other a studious man who kept a pile of books by his loom and loved to hold forth on any subject under the sun. The men's tongues worked as swiftly as their looms.

Each morning Meg and Kirsty saw to the housework, baked, visited the market, and looked after red-headed Jamie, a day's work in itself. Any spare time they had was spent spinning coarse thread for the looms. Their wheels were placed close to a trap-door that allowed communication between the kitchen and the weaving shop below. When the trap was open the women could join in the conversation, and the pirns or reels of spun thread could be passed down to the weavers as they were needed.

When Jamie tired himself out with his continual toddling around and his occasional forays into the street when the door was left open, he was lifted into the big wooden cradle, then

Kirsty slipped her foot into the rope looped to one rocker, and rocked him as she tended her wheel.

As well as domestic duties, Kirsty and Meg, as the women of the household, were responsible for the upkeep of the long garden at the back of the house. It was stocked with sweet-scented flowers for the benefit of the bees in the two skeps, and there were plenty of bushes where the washing could be spread out to dry.

Meg was happy with the Todds, but she longed for a home of her own, where she and Duncan and their coming child could be a real family. Kirsty was sympathetic.

'I mind when Jamie was on the way – Colin was still living here and I was fair fretting for him to find a place of his own, the soul. Not that I ever let on to him or to his father.' She deftly guided thread onto the spinning wheel as she spoke. 'Then he and Lizzie wed and moved into the rooms behind the wee grocer's shop. I sometimes think he'd have been better staying here with us.'

Then she bit her lip and added swiftly, 'Not that it's any of my business. He chose Lizzie, and if he's content that's all that matters.'

* * *

Colin Todd, the grocer, had his father's good looks, but was of slighter build and had none of the older man's vitality. Soft fair hair helped to give him a fragile air, but when he smiled, which happened rarely, his thin face lit up and Meg was charmed.

When she first met his wife Lizzie she found it hard to understand why Kirsty, one of the most generous women she had ever known, disliked the girl. Colin's wife was mouse-like, quiet-voiced, her brown hair tucked beneath a clean white lace cap, her eyes lowered.

It wasn't until Peter and Kirsty held a gathering for their friends that Meg saw the other side of Lizzie's nature; then she knew why Kirsty had her doubts about Colin's choice of a wife.

When she worked in the shop Lizzie wore a grey dress, high in the neck and long-sleeved. But for the social evening she appeared in a white cambric dress sprigged with yellow, red and blue flowers. It was cut low enough to reveal the swell of surprisingly full breasts, and her slim arms were bare. Long brown hair, stylishly curled, fell about her shoulders, and for the first time Meg noticed, and envied, Lizzie's tiny waist. The head that was usually lowered was now held proudly on a long slender neck and her eyes, smoky grey with an almond shape to them, were raised boldly to Duncan's handsome face when they met.

'You don't take snuff, Mister Montgomery?' Even Lizzie's voice was different now, self-possessed and attractively husky.

Duncan looked puzzled. 'I don't.'

'That's why we haven't met before. The women and bairns are in and out of the shop for provisions every day, but the men only come in if they want snuff.'

'Mebbe I should think of taking the habit up,' he said with clumsy gallantry and Meg, hovering by his side, felt a flicker of unease run through her.

'You'll do nothing of the kind, Duncan Montgomery – we've enough to do with our money as it is!'

The smoky eyes left Duncan's face and flowed over Meg. It was as though Lizzie was seeing her for the first time, and assessing her.

'I hear you're anxious to find a place of your own before your bairn comes.' Her gaze moved to rest, briefly, on Colin, who hovered by her side. Somehow she managed to make him look insignificant and frail in his brown coat and plain vest. 'We have no family – yet. All Colin's energy goes into caring for his shop.'

There was calculated malice in the remark. Colin flushed and Duncan looked puzzled. Then, mercifully, Kirsty interrupted them and the moment was gone.

As the evening wore on the children were carried to the attic bedroom to sleep, packed tightly together on the Todds' bed, until their parents were ready to go home. The men went downstairs to talk around the fire in the loom shop and the women stayed in the kitchen, most of them with knitting or sewing in their hands.

Meg noticed that Lizzie reverted back to her mouse-like nature once the men had gone. She retired to a seat in a shadowy corner, her face hidden by a curtain of hair, her fingers toying with the looped earrings in her small lobes.

She brightened noticeably when the menfolk came stamping back upstairs for the musical part of the evening. She stood in the centre of the room, eyes bright and cheeks glowing, and sang in a sweet, strong soprano. Meg turned to look for Duncan and caught him watching Lizzie with a frown tucked between his brows, as though he was trying to decide what to make of her.

Suddenly uneasy, Meg made a small movement towards him, and was relieved when he turned his head and slowly smiled at her as though wakening from a dream.

'Are you content with me, Duncan?' she asked later when they were in bed together.

His hands explored her body tenderly. 'What a thing to ask, and us wed these four months past. Of course I'm content with you!'

'I wish I could sing like Lizzie Todd – and look like her.' She waited for his reaction, holding her breath, but he only laughed.

'I'd not have you any other way – my bonny Meg,' he

murmured into the valley between her breasts, and Meg was
happy.

* * *

Two days later Lizzie Todd, busy at the shop counter, looked up
from a list of figures as the door opened. She took in the
newcomer at a glance then went on totalling prices. Neat as a
sparrow in her grey gown and white cap, she completed the list,
took money from wee Tommy Burns's hot fist, handed change
over, and bundled parcels into his arms.

'Mind that money,' she said automatically as he went out.
Then she smoothed her skirt and tilted her chin to survey the
customer who stood, hands planted on the counter, awaiting her
attention.

A faint smile curved the corners of her mouth and gave added
lustre to her smoky eyes. 'And what can I do for you, sir?'

'I was thinking—' said Duncan Montgomery '—that I might
buy myself some snuff.'

* * *

Matt Todd, Peter's eldest son, came home on leave from the army
soon after the Montgomerys arrived in Paisley.

Tall and broad and handsome, he was very like his father,
with Peter's boundless energy and extroverted nature. Even Meg,
who knew that Duncan was the handsomest man in the town,
felt a flutter of excitement when she first set eyes on Matt in the
tartan plaid and blue feathered bonnet of the Fusiliers.

His coming was the signal for one gathering after another.
Everyone wanted to hear of his adventures, and Matt was more
than ready to entertain them. His tales of the life a soldier led

had the men roaring with delight and the women blushing. When a story became too embarrassing, Kirsty would reach up to slap his curly head and order, 'That's quite enough of that – you'll not be bringing any more of those lies into my house, thank you!'

'Lies? Lies?' Matt's blue eyes opened wide and as often as not he swept Kirsty off her feet as though she was a child. 'Would one of His Majesty's brave soldiers tell his little old mother lies?'

Then Kirsty, struggling in vain, would shrill, 'I am not your little old mother – I'm only six months older than you. And you're still young enough to get a slap on the ear if you don't put me down this instant!'

It was then that Meg was most aware of Colin, sitting quietly in a corner, smiling at the fun, but outside it. Lizzie, too, was quiet when Matt was around, which surprised Meg more than a little.

It was Matt's idea that he and Colin should ride in the annual Silver Bells horse race, due to take place in a few days' time.

'Man, it's a grand event!' he enthused one night when the Todds and Montgomerys were together in the kitchen above the weaving shop. 'Everyone comes to the Silver Bells race – in the old days the three of us used to ride in it.' His eyes blazed blue fire. 'We could all enter for it again—'

'Not your father,' Kirsty said at once. 'He's not as young as he once was.'

'Aye, my day's past for racing,' Peter agreed reluctantly. 'It's a sport for younger men.'

To Meg's relief, Duncan declined to take part. He was no horse rider, but she was well aware that although he was now a married man, soon to be a father, there was still a reckless, restless side to his nature and for a moment she had been afraid that he would take up Matt's suggestion.

'Then it's you and me, Colin – just like the old days, eh?'

'No!'

They had almost forgotten Lizzie was there, sitting silently beside Colin. Her chin was up and she was glaring at Matt.

'Risk your own neck if you want to – but leave Colin alone!' she said with startlingly open antagonism.

His face was suddenly stiff. 'I didn't realise you cared so much for your man's safety.'

Lizzie shot him a look of pure venom. 'Colin's got responsibilities. He's not a thoughtless fool!'

'Then he can speak for himself,' Matt said coldly, and turned away from her. 'What d'you say, Colin?'

Meg saw Lizzie's hands clench on her lap. Colin's eyes flicked over his wife's face, then lifted to Matt.

'I'll ride with you,' he said, and Lizzie's hiss of rage was almost drowned by Matt's triumphant: 'Good for you, man – we'll bring the Bells home!'

* * *

The town's looms clattered late into the night before the Silver Bells race, so that the weavers could take the next day off. Long after she was in bed, Meg could hear the faint thump of the shuttles racing to and fro and she pictured the men, red-eyed and weary, working in the lamplight. When Duncan finally came upstairs he was asleep as soon as he crawled in beside her warm body.

Matt had hired two horses from a local farmer, and had invested enough money in wagers to ensure that if either he or Colin were among the first riders home, he would not be out of pocket. Kirsty and Meg scrubbed the spotless house in readiness for the gathering to be held there after the race.

'I hope you've plenty in for our guests,' Peter said anxiously and his wife tossed her red head.

'When have you ever known this house to lack refreshments? Well I know the celebrations you'll have whether your own lads win the Bells or not, and there'll be plenty for everyone, never you worry.'

As she walked with Duncan and the Todds to Love Street, where the race was to begin and end, Meg felt the festival atmosphere stirring her blood. Children ran through the thick crowds, squealing like piglets in their excitement, men congregated in groups to place wagers on the outcome, women wore their best and brightest clothes.

Street vendors had set up stalls at the Cross, strangers flocked into the town from miles around – it was as if the whole of Scotland had congregated in that one small town for the Silver Bells horse race. The council members massed importantly at the starting point, bearing with them the wooden casket which held the silver bells that gave the race its name.

Duncan held Meg's arm as they picked their way carefully down the street, skirting refuse heaps. Peter was well known and had no difficulty in finding a good spot for his party, where they could see the start and finish of the race.

Many Fusiliers were home on leave like Matt, and their uniforms added an extra splash of colour to the scene. The local gentry were in attendance, gazing loftily over the heads of the crowd from their fine carriages.

Kirsty nudged Meg's arm. 'There's the Laird of Dundonald,' she murmured, indicating a richly dressed young man. 'A wild, wild laddie – they say there's nothing to be done with him at all.'

'Too fond of fighting and womanising,' Peter added bluntly. 'And he's taking a lot of Paisley's lads on the same track as himself.'

Colin and Matt were already at the starting post. Their father eyed their mounts critically.

'Fine animals. You've still got a good eye for a horse, Matt.'

The soldier grinned. 'There'll be no stopping us.' He leaned from the saddle to thump his brother on the shoulder. 'A pound says I'll cross the finishing line afore you.'

Colin's thin face was flushed and handsome, the fragile air gone. Even his voice was stronger, more confident, as he said, 'You'll lose your money!'

'Not me!'

'Pride goes before a fall,' Kirsty reminded Matt, hoisting Jamie more securely on her hip. 'Just you do your best, my bonny soldier, and don't be so sure you're always going to be a winner!'

Colin laughed and nodded agreement, then his eyes moved beyond Meg's shoulder, and she saw a cloud come over his face. She turned and saw that Lizzie had arrived, demure in a white linen bonnet and russet gown. The girl's lips were set in a thin line and splashes of colour in her cheeks matched her short scarlet cloak. She looked at her husband unsmilingly, then turned away to scan the crowd. Colin's shoulders slumped for a moment, then he straightened in the saddle, his mouth as firm as Lizzie's.

Nobody else seemed to have noticed the angry, wordless exchange between husband and wife.

Colin should have found someone better, Meg thought, and realised that she shared Kirsty's misgivings.

The senior bailie raised his hand and the crowd hushed at once. The riders jostled their mounts into position, the town officer bawled, in a surprisingly high thin voice for such a brawny man, 'Mind these bairns! Clear the way, now!' Then the signal was given and the horses were off, their riders yelling like savages, the crowd screaming encouragement.

Meg had a brief final glimpse of Colin sweeping past, mouth open in a full-throated roar, eyes glowing. Matt followed, crouching over his horse's neck. There was a mad flurry of hooves and noise, and the riders were gone, plunging in a tight-packed bunch down the narrow thoroughfare and round the corner into St James' Street. From there they had to go onto the Shambles Road, then circle back to the Love Street starting point.

'My certies, what I wouldn't give to be one of them!' Peter boomed as the last horse swept out of sight and the yells of the crowd in St James's Street drifted back to them.

'No doubt, but it's time you realised that you're too old for such ploys,' Kirsty said mercilessly.

'But not too old for everything, eh, lass?' Her irrepressible husband slid an arm about her shoulders and she fended him off with a scandalised: 'Peter Todd – will you mind where you are?'

He took out a small box and helped himself complacently to a pinch of snuff. 'I'm at the Silver Bells horse race – and the Bells'll belong to the Todd house tonight. It's grand to be the father of sons, Duncan. Before we know it, Jamie here'll be riding for the Bells.'

Kirsty rubbed her chin against her son's head. 'Mebbe, for he's as wild as you and Matt ever were. But there's time enough, is there not, my wee mannie? You'll not be in a hurry to grow up.'

'Don't cosset him, Kirsty,' Peter cautioned, but Meg, feeling the child in her womb flutter at that very moment, knew what the other woman meant. She longed to hold her own baby in her arms, and when that day came she would be in no hurry to see him – or her – grow up and away from her.

Small boys – as often as not inarticulate with excitement – deftly stitched their way through the crowds, carrying the latest news.

'Will Robb in front – Gordon Ogilvie's horse went lame on him – Matt and Colin Todd are well up—' The messages were passed from mouth to mouth and Peter almost danced with anticipation, craning his neck to see the end of the road, where the first riders would soon appear.

The full-throated roar was a dull rumble at first, swelling as it swept nearer. Even Lizzie was caught up in the tension, standing on tiptoe to see the winner come in. Peter scooped Jamie from Kirsty's arms and held him high; Meg gripped Duncan's arm as she heard someone shout, 'Here they come!' Then the ground shook beneath her feet as the horses pounded back into Love Street, their red-faced riders clinging on for dear life.

Lumps of dried mud sprayed up on either side as they galloped past the line, a huge bay in front with three others fighting for second place behind it.

'Pat McGregor – it's Pat!' a man yelled as the winner, a jovial Paisley cobbler, whooped and threw his bonnet in the air.

Peter Todd stood aghast. 'Would you credit it? They're not there – not a sign of them! What the blazes do they think they're up to, the pair of knuckle-headed, clumsy—'

'Now, now, Peter,' his wife, admonished. 'It's only a race. They did their best, I'm sure.'

'Not a very good best—' he was beginning, when one of the bailies came hurrying over, an urchin at his heels.

'Peter, this lad says there's been an accident just round the corner. One of your boys – they've sent for a physician—'

But Peter was already shouldering his way through the throng. Kirsty thrust Jamie at Duncan and followed, snatching at Lizzie's wrist as she went and towing the girl along behind her.

'Duncan—?' A chill had taken hold of Meg's limbs.

'Come on, lass, we might be needed.' He put his free arm about her and helped her along, stumbling through the dense crowd, pushing against the flow of people, for everyone else was flocking to the winning line.

They rounded the corner and found a knot of men standing

in the middle of the road. Some horses, steaming after their frantic gallop, were being held by wide-eyed gawping boys.

In the middle of the group Matt knelt beside Colin, who lay in a careless, oddly boneless heap as though a giant hand had picked him up then tossed him aside. His eyes were closed and his fair hair was bloody over one temple.

As the Montgomerys arrived Kirsty dropped to her knees and lifted her stepson's head onto her lap. Peter's hands moved carefully over Colin's limbs. Lizzie stood looking on.

'I'd not move him too much, lass,' Peter said quietly. 'It looks bad.'

Matt rubbed both hands over his paper-white face. 'It – it happened so fast.' He stumbled over the words as though the language was new to him. 'We were out in front and he'd just shouted to me that he'd take the Bells for sure. Then his horse must have put its foot in a hole – the daft gowk, why couldn't he have been watching out for it?' he added in a burst of anguished fury. 'He went over its head and landed – on his back – on the dyke.'

They all looked at the low wall, at its hard, sharp stones.

'God help us!' Kirsty whispered, stroking Colin's bloodied hair.

Jamie, sensing that something was wrong, began to weep and punch at Duncan's shoulder. Meg took him, clasping the wriggling little body close for comfort.

'It was so quick—' Matt said again, then reeled back as Lizzie broke out of her trance and flew at him, her hands clawing for his eyes.

'It's your fault!' she screamed at him. 'It's always you! Why did you have to come back here and spoil everything, Matt Todd? Why did you have to come back?'

3

Colin Todd survived the accident that marred that year's Silver Bells race, but his back was broken and he was paralysed from the waist down. In the space of a few seconds he had become a ruckle of skin and bones lying on a cot in the kitchen behind the grocer's shop.

Peter and Matt were ghosts of themselves, weighed down by guilt.

'Colin's a grown man after all,' Duncan protested miserably to Meg during that bleak time. 'He made up his own mind to race. It's wrong of Lizzie to blame Matt for encouraging him, but the woman's out of her mind with grief.'

But instinct told Meg that Lizzie's claim on Colin was possessive rather than tender. The attack on Matt had been prompted, she felt, by fear of what would become of Lizzie herself if anything happened to her husband. And it went deeper – she was quite sure that Lizzie harboured a bitterness against Matt Todd that went beyond any consideration she might feel for Colin's welfare. But she kept her thoughts to herself. This was no time to air them, even to Duncan.

Colin had heard the physician's verdict quietly – indeed, he scarcely spoke at all. But his eyes held a look of trapped anguish that tore at Meg's heart each time she saw him. She and Kirsty did what they could to help, sitting with Colin to let Lizzie have a rest, making delicacies to tempt the invalid's appetite, helping in the shop. But both Colin and Lizzie seemed to have locked themselves away behind set, pale faces and tight lips.

When Meg called in at the shop the day before Matt was due to rejoin the Fusiliers she found Janet, the girl who had been brought in to attend the counter, dealing with a handful of customers.

The kitchen beyond was empty apart from Colin, lying in the box bed. His head was turned away from the door and he made no move when Meg went in. Quietly she put her basket down and took her cloak off. She was reaching up to hang it on the nail hammered into the door that separated the kitchen from the 'best room' when she heard voices from beyond the wooden panels.

There was no mistaking Matt's deep tones – 'You'd expect that of me, you slut?' – or Lizzie's voice – 'Why not? D'you think I'm going to spend the rest of my life like this, with a man who's no use to any woman? You weren't ashamed to touch me before, Matt Todd!'

The voices came clearly to Meg, but it was a moment before she glanced at the bed and saw with sick horror that Colin was awake, his blue eyes fixed on the ceiling, his fists gripping the blanket that lay over his useless legs. She took a step towards him as the door to the inner room was swept open so hard that it crashed off the edge of the dresser.

Matt stood in the doorway, eyes blazing in an angry face, his move into the kitchen checked as he saw Meg. Lizzie's face bobbed round his arm.

Cold anger, the first intense rage that Meg had ever experienced, gripped her.

'Have you no shame?' she asked Matt. 'Have you no feeling for the man at all?'

His eyes immediately went to the bed and she saw the colour drain from his skin.

'Colin! Colin, lad, it was a misunderstanding—' He stumbled over to take his brother's hand in his own. 'I would never—' His voice died away as Colin looked at him, a look that made Meg shiver and sent Matt stumbling from the room.

Lizzie stepped cat-like to the bed and Colin's eyes moved to meet and hold hers. But the gaze that had destroyed Matt held no fears for her. She matched it until his eyes closed against the sight of her and he turned his face back to the wall.

Then she gave Meg her attention. 'You wanted something?' she asked flatly, as though attending to a customer in the shop.

'I came to sit with Colin—'

'I can see to him.' Lizzie's voice was cold, dismissive.

The anger that gripped Meg gave her courage. 'I came to help. I didn't expect to find you and Matt—'

'You never know what you'll find in life,' Lizzie cut through her words. 'I went looking once, and I didn't find what I wanted. You'll learn.'

'Not your way, Lizzie Todd!' said Meg, and walked out before her fingers gave way to an impulse and buried themselves in Lizzie's neat brown hair.

She avoided Matt until he left Paisley; it was a relief to her when she knew that he was away. She couldn't even bring herself to tell Duncan what she had seen and heard, and he began to worry over her pallor and her depression.

'It's been the shock of Colin's accident,' Kirsty told him. 'What she needs is some good country air.'

When he suggested that Meg should go back to Beith for a few days, she seized the idea eagerly, longing to escape for a while from Colin's misery and Lizzie's cold, secretive face. Duncan travelled down with her on a cold, drizzly day that gave them an excuse to cuddle together under a plaid rug as the cart carried them away from Paisley.

'I'll miss you,' he whispered, and she hugged him.

'I'll be back soon. You'll keep at your reading while I'm gone?'

He sighed but nodded. Meg had been a hard taskmaster since that first night in Paisley, but her bullying was paying dividends and Duncan's reading and writing skills had greatly improved.

Meg fell back into the ways of the farm with surprising ease. It was comforting to be a daughter again, ordered about by her mother, giggling with her sister Mary, treading blankets in the big tub in the farmyard.

In Paisley, Duncan eased his loneliness by spending most of his free time with some of the young married weavers. He hadn't realised before how interested the Paisley men were in world affairs and he learned a lot from listening to them.

He had the sense not to join them in the howffs, for he couldn't afford to spend hard-earned money on drink, but he went with them on their long walks, argued with them, bowled with them, and on more than one occasion fought beside them when they had differences of opinion with men from other districts. Their cheerful rowdiness appealed to that part of him that hadn't yet resigned itself to marriage and its limitations. He enjoyed the life of a bachelor once again; it was only at nights, alone in bed, that he hungered for his wife's soft, warm body, her willingness, her loving.

'It's time for Meg to come home,' Kirsty said shrewdly one evening when Duncan had gone out to meet Davie. 'It's not natural for a young man to be parted from his wife for too long.'

Lizzie, sitting in a corner of the kitchen with her sewing on her lap, looked up from under pale eyelids. The quiet older weaver who worked in Peter's loom shop had offered to sit with Colin and free her for a while.

'Meg'll be back soon enough,' Peter said easily. 'I've no doubt she's missing Duncan as much as he's missing her.'

Lizzie's long fingers folded the material she had been working on. 'I'd best get home,' she said.

* * *

Duncan, bored and restless, was wandering home when he turned a corner and bumped into Lizzie. The books in her arms would have gone flying if he hadn't caught them deftly.

'I'll carry them for you,' he offered. She said nothing, but let him take the rest of the books from her.

'How's Colin?'

'No different.'

'It must be hard for you.'

She lifted her head for the first time and looked fully at him. 'It's not easy. But folk don't seem to understand what it's like to be young and wondering what's to become of me for the rest of my life!'

Taken aback by the bitterness in her voice he stammered something, but she ignored him.

'Just because I say little they think I don't bother – but I do, I do!' she went on fiercely. 'Night after night I lie there, beside him, and I look into the future, and I'm frightened—'

Her voice broke and she clenched her hands into small, knotted fists. They came to a pothole in the roadway and Duncan took her elbow to steer her safely round it. A strong tremor seemed to run through Lizzie's body and into his hand. He snatched his fingers away as though they had been burned, then slowly, deliberately, took her arm again and guided her along the rough road as though she was made of fine china.

She said no more until they reached her door, then she turned and took the books from him, tilting her chin defiantly. 'I've shocked you.'

'No, no—!'

'Aye, Duncan Montgomery, I have.' Her voice had taken on a soft lilt. 'I've shocked you and I'm not sorry for it. You're mebbe the only one who can understand how I feel. I had to speak out to someone. Meg's far away in Beith – you know as well as I do what it's like to lie alone at night, wanting – hurting—' The words hung in the dusk between them. 'I'm not ready to finish with life yet,' she added, low-voiced. 'Not yet! Thank you for listening. I'll not ask you in.'

And with a nod she was gone.

Duncan walked home slowly, thinking over her words. His final thoughts before he fell asleep that night weren't of rounded, loving Meg, but of slender, pale Lizzie with her brilliant eyes and her lilting voice.

He wondered if she was thinking about him at that moment as she lay awake beside her silent, crippled husband.

* * *

Lizzie Todd was as intoxicating as strong drink. She haunted Duncan's mind over the next two days. He avoided the shop but on the third day, his work finished and a lonely afternoon before him, he met her in the street.

Her grey eyes held his. 'I'm going to the moors for a breath of air – mebbe you'd like to accompany me,' she said softly.

He hesitated, but only for a moment. 'I was thinking of going there myself,' he said, and allowed his hand to brush hers as he turned to walk by her side.

The grass on the moors at the foot of the Muckle Riggs was short and springy and warmed by the sun. They found a little hollow sheltered by bushes, and Lizzie picked daisies and made a chain while Duncan watched her, drinking in each movement she made. She slit the final stem with sharp fingernails, tucked a daisy head through it, then put the completed circlet on her hair and smiled up at him.

'What do you think?'

'You look bonny. Like a queen.'

Her almond eyes laughed at him. 'I never thought to hear such a compliment again.'

'It's the truth.'

'You're a fine-looking man yourself, Duncan Montgomery.' She reached out to take his hand in hers and again he sensed that tremor flowing between their fingers. It tingled through him, exciting him, and at the same time warning him of danger.

'We should get back.'

Lizzie shrugged, then let herself fall back on the grass, her eyes mocking him. 'It's early yet. Are you scared of me?'

'Mebbe I should be.'

She laughed. Strands of her hair fell across the tiny white flowers that starred the grass beneath her. Her teeth gleamed white and sharp between parted lips. His body burned with his need of her.

'Then why don't you take to your heels and run home, where you'll be safe?' she suggested silkily.

He knew well enough that he should do just that – run over the moors and back to the streets; run all the way to Beith and to Meg. But he was infected by Lizzie. He couldn't rest until he possessed her.

'You know why—' he said hoarsely, and caught at her shoulders, raising her up to where he knelt above her, bringing her mouth to his own hungry lips.

Her kiss excited him, made him want to take her swiftly, fiercely – and yet he must delay the moment of taking as long as possible, because with Lizzie there were so many delights to explore first. She twined her fingers in his hair, then she was writhing like a wild thing against him, her mouth warm and moist, as he bore her down again onto the springy turf.

* * *

They had three further meetings before word of Meg's return reached him.

The letter lay in Duncan's hand like a stone. Meg's goodness and love, and her trust in him, shone from those few scrawled words. Like a handful of icy water thrown into his face, they brought him back with cruel haste to his real purpose in life – making a home for his wife and his child.

He felt weak, like a man who had just recovered from a consuming fever. His burning lust for Lizzie ebbed away as he read the letter again, and in its place came a longing to hold Meg in his arms once more. The illness had almost been fatal, but now he was cured. Then he remembered that he still had to face Lizzie, and his limbs trembled anew.

Mercifully, she was alone in the shop when he went in. She looked sharply at him when he stepped through the doorway.

'What's amiss?'

'Meg's coming home – tomorrow.'

Her eyebrows lifted slightly, her eyes mocking him. 'And you'll go back to being the perfect husband. Is that it?'

His mouth was dry. 'I must. Lizzie, it was never meant to last – we needed each other for – for comfort, that was all.'

'And after tomorrow you'll have no more need of me?'

He swallowed, and longed for a mug of ale. 'You knew as well as I did that there was no future to it.'

A strange light flared into the grey eyes that surveyed him, and he braced himself to face her rage, then the look was gone, and she shrugged. 'So we'll just have to make the most of this afternoon?'

'No!' His voice was so emphatic that she frowned and put a finger to her lips.

'Ssshhh! The girl's in the kitchen with Colin.'

'I'll not see you this afternoon, Lizzie. It's finished.' He hadn't meant it to sound so blunt but he didn't know what else to say. For a moment her lips parted to speak, then she shrugged again.

'Please yourself. There's other men,' she said deliberately. The contempt in her voice stung, but Duncan welcomed the cleansing, absolving pain of it. He walked out, towards the nearest howff. It was over.

* * *

As the time for her baby's birth approached Meg became happier than ever before. Shortly before Christmas, she and Duncan were able to move round the corner from the Todds' home into a two-roomed ground-floor house in Lady Lane, scantily furnished, but a palace as far as they were concerned.

Duncan kept well away from the grocer's shop, and didn't see Lizzie at all as the weeks passed. It seemed that their affair had only been a passing dream – then at the very moment when he began to let himself relax he was summoned one night to Peter Todd's house.

'Is there something wrong?' Meg asked anxiously when a boy knocked at their door and delivered the message. 'Should I go with you?'

'No, it's probably to do with the loom shop.' Duncan shivered as a handful of rain spattered against the window. 'You stay here, by the fire. I'll be back soon.'

But when he walked into the warm kitchen and saw Lizzie, wild-eyed and bitter-mouthed, he knew that his shameful secret was out. His knees dissolved and he had to catch at the back of a chair to keep himself upright.

'No doubt you know what this is about?' Peter asked in a harsh unfamiliar voice.

'Did you have to bring them into it?' Duncan asked Lizzie, indicating the Todds with a jerk of his head. Her eyes narrowed, no longer luminous and inviting.

'I wanted them to know what their fine new weaver's brought to their door!'

'That's enough!' Peter's face was old and drawn, and Duncan was reminded of the day the man had looked down at his son, bloodied and unconscious in the mud. 'What's done can't be cured by harsh words. We have to think of what's best for... the child.'

Duncan cursed himself for a fool. He might have known that their passionate loving would bear fruit. Hadn't Meg fallen pregnant right after their marriage?

'Meg mustn't know—' he said automatically.

'Oh – so Meg mustn't know?' Lizzie mocked shrilly. 'She'll know all right! You've got me with child and now you'll have to acknowledge it! You'll have to set up house with me!'

'Leave Meg for you? But I-I love her!'

'You should have thought of that before you gave Lizzie a

child!' Peter made a move forward and Kirsty put a restraining hand on his arm.

'I wish to God I had! But I'm thinking of it now – and I'll not leave Meg! I'll pay for the child's keep, Lizzie, but I'll not leave my wife!'

Lizzie made for the door. 'We'll see what she thinks when she's heard about it—'

Duncan's hands caught her shoulders and spun her round. He shook her until her head flopped on its long neck.

'You dare to go near Meg – you dare to say a word to her, and I'll kill you—!'

'For God's sake, man!' Peter dragged him away and Kirsty pushed Lizzie, spitting defiance and threats, into a chair.

'It's you and me'll have to sort this out,' she told her husband bluntly. 'These two hadn't the sense to leave each other alone, and they've not got the sense now to decide what's best.'

'I'll not leave Meg!' To his horror Duncan heard his own voice thicken with the threat of angry, frightened tears. He had never wanted or needed Meg's loving arms more than at that moment. 'I'll see you right for money, Lizzie, but that's all. I'll take Meg away, back to Beith. I'll tell her that I can't settle in Paisley—'

'And you'll get out of it that way, will you?' Peter almost snarled at him. 'What about my son? God – this'll be the finish of him!'

'And what about me?' Lizzie screeched. 'A child I don't want, no man to look after me—'

'Wait a minute.' Kirsty's quiet authority cut across the girl's rising hysteria. 'It's too late to start blaming each other. What's done's done, and we're here to decide how to make some sense out of it. Lizzie, how far on are you?'

'Eight weeks,' the girl said sullenly, and as another gust of

wind drove rain against the house walls, Duncan recalled those
sunny afternoons in the little hollow. In the weeks since then he
had known more contentment with Meg than ever before. He
would have plunged a knife into his heart willingly if he could
only obliterate his affair with Lizzie.

'A few weeks here or there wouldn't make much difference,'
Kirsty thought aloud, swiftly. 'The child could have been
conceived just before Colin's accident. It could be his.'

'It's not!' Lizzie almost screamed at her. 'It's his!' One long
finger stabbed at Duncan.

'I'm saying that for all anyone knows – for all Colin knows –
you could be further on than you are.'

'You'd let Colin think he'd fathered another man's child?'
Peter asked, aghast. 'I'll not have it!'

'Now listen for a minute before you say another word,' his
wife ordered. 'Colin's always wanted a family, and the poor soul's
never going to father children now. Would it be such an unkind-
ness to let him think it's his?'

She watched her husband's face, and saw understanding
dawn in the blue eyes.

'But there's me to consider – what about my wishes?' Lizzie
said sourly.

'You might as well face up to it – Duncan's admitted responsibility but he'll not leave Meg for your sake,' Kirsty said flatly.
'You'll either be alone with the child or you'll let Colin think it's
his and have a roof over your head. And I daresay Peter would be
willing to pay Janet to stay on and see to the shop for you. Eh,
Peter?'

'You think I'll be content with that?' Lizzie sneered.

'I don't see that you have much choice, Lizzie. It's that, or
manage on your own with a child to birth and raise. Is it worth

breaking Colin's heart? Surely the poor man's got enough to contend with.'

'I'll not agree to it!'

Peter caught his daughter-in-law's wrist with strong fingers. 'You'll do what's best for Colin – whatever that might be!'

Kirsty let out her breath in a sigh, eyes bright with relief as she realised that her husband, at least, was beginning to give her his support. 'This is the way I see it,' she began with a new briskness.

Lizzie wrangled for another hour before she accepted that Duncan wasn't going to leave his wife for her sake. Then she sulkily agreed to Kirsty's plan, and slammed out of the door and down the stairs.

For a moment the three left in the room were silent, then Peter said, 'You're mad, woman! It's a daft ploy – the whole town'll see through it!'

'Not unless Lizzie tells them,' Kirsty argued. 'And a crippled husband's better than no man at all to the likes of her. Pay her well and she'll hold her tongue.'

Duncan straightened and felt his joints creak. He was certain that he had aged twenty years since leaving Meg by the fireside.

'I'm sorry, Mister Todd.'

'Well you might be! Colin lying helpless and your own wife carrying her first child, and you—'

Duncan's face drained of colour, then flamed. 'You can't say anything to me I haven't already said to myself.' He picked up his cap, twisted it tightly in both hands. 'And now I've to face Meg.'

'Poor lass – does she have to know about Lizzie? It'll kill her, Duncan,' Kirsty said, her mind already busy with another scheme.

'She'll never know about that, for it's my guilt, not hers. I'll tell her—' He swallowed, thinking of her pride in their first proper home. 'I'll tell her I can't settle here. I'll tell her tomorrow.'

* * *

'And they'll go back to Beith and you'll lose a good weaver,' Kirsty said as they listened to Duncan's footsteps, slow and heavy, stumbling down the stairs.

'There's other weavers.' Peter's voice was hard.

'But Duncan's better than most, is he not? Admit it, Peter, he's more like a son than an employee already.'

'You see more than your fair share – and talk more than your fair share too!' he said angrily, but she shrugged the reprimand off.

'And there's Meg, too – they both fit well into Paisley. You're angered just as much by the way Duncan's betrayed your trust as by the way he's betrayed Colin.'

'Kirsty, I've never raised my hand to a woman before, but if you don't guard that tongue of yours—' her husband howled, goaded beyond endurance.

'Let them stay, Peter.'

His jaw dropped. 'Let them stay?' he repeated incredulously. 'Let him stay in the same town as Colin after he and Lizzie... after they—'

'Just hear me out before you go jumping around as if you've met up with a flea.' She put a firm hand on his arm. 'It's over between Duncan and Lizzie – you must see that for yourself. The lad's got a good future here. He'll never make a fool of himself again, that's for sure.'

'Keep him on in my employ after—' Peter made for the door. 'I'm going to my bed.' Then he swung round and snatched his jacket from the back of his chair. 'No, I'm going out for a drink.

You're the one that should be going to your bed. It's late, and your mind's addled with all this trouble!'

'Peter, if Duncan suddenly goes it'll cause more talk than if he stays. And you'd not want Colin to wonder at his going, would you? The poor man's crippled, not stupid.'

'D'you think I could go on working with Duncan Montgomery, knowing the truth about him and... and—?'

Kirsty took the jacket from his hands. 'I think you're an honest, just man, Peter Todd. I think you've got a good heart. And if you'd just give yourself a chance to ponder over what I'm saying you'd know I'm right.'

There was a long pause, then Peter said, 'I'm away to my bed.'

'Do as the Book says, Peter—' Kirsty said as he touched the latch. 'Cast your bread on the waters. As far as Duncan Montgomery's concerned, it'll come back to you. You'll see.'

He went out without speaking or looking at her. Kirsty listened until she had satisfied herself that he was going up to the attic and not down to the street, then she went about her duties with hands that shook very slightly, making sure that the room was tidy and putting oatmeal to soak for the morning's porridge.

When she went into the attic bedroom he was sitting on the bed staring into space.

'Mebbe you're right,' he said gruffly. 'Mebbe I'll talk it over in the morning with Duncan.'

Kirsty beamed at him. 'Mebbe you should, Peter.'

'That's not to say he'll stay.'

'I think he will.' She didn't tell him that she, too, would have a word with Duncan.

'But I'm damned if I know why I let you talk me into things against my better judgement, woman,' Peter grumbled.

It was only then that Kirsty allowed herself to believe that her plan was going to work out. Duncan and Meg would stay, Colin would have his child, Lizzie would hold her tongue. Slowly, aware of his eyes on her, she untied her white lacy cap and released her fiery silken hair from the pins that confined it by day. Then she went to sit by her husband, her arms about him, her lips against his face.

'Because I'm always right,' she said demurely.

4

Meg's son was born one January afternoon just as the last of the grey daylight was ebbing and the weavers were setting tapers by the looms so that they could continue their work. Kirsty, summoned that morning when the pains began, had ordered Duncan off to his loom as usual.

'A first baby can take a while, and you'll just be in the way,' she'd said, pushing him out of his own street door. 'I'll let you know when you can come back.'

All day he blundered through his work, and when word finally came for him to go home he jumped to his feet, almost knocking his taper into the loom.

'Will you watch what you're about!' Peter roared at him, then added, as he looked at the knotted threads Duncan had been trying to unravel for the past half hour, 'Ach, mebbe you'd be as well to burn the lot after all!'

But Duncan was already away, his boots clattering along the passageway then skidding on the hard-packed, ice-rimed earth of the footpath.

The kitchen was warm and peaceful when he burst in; Kirsty

was putting on her cloak and Meg lay in the wall bed, her face radiant when she saw him.

'There's food on the table, and I'll look in later,' Kirsty said briskly, and went out as Duncan stared down at the baby, plump and smooth-skinned, with a thatch of dark hair.

'He's like you,' Meg said contentedly. 'Give him to me.'

Duncan lifted the warm, solid bundle from the cradle, balanced it carefully in his two hands, and settled it in the curve of his wife's arm. Then he hid his face in Meg's warm, soft shoulder.

'I promise I'll be a good husband to you for the rest of my life,' he whispered into her hair. 'I'll take such care of the two of you—'

Surprised by the damp touch of his tears on her skin, she reached up to stroke his face.

'But Duncan,' she said, puzzled, 'you've always been good to me.'

* * *

Robert Montgomery took to life as a weaver's son without any misgivings at all. Each day Meg scooped him into a shawl and took him out and about with her, and wherever they went people responded to his lopsided, toothless smile and his large blue eyes.

Everyone, that was, except Lizzie Todd. If Meg was helping Lizzie in the shop or about the house, she tucked Robert in at the end of Colin's truckle bed and the invalid, now propped up on cushions, watched over him. But Lizzie ignored the child and Meg wondered uneasily what sort of mother she would be to her own baby when it arrived.

'She's such a cold creature,' she fretted to Duncan. 'A wee one needs love—'

He got to his feet abruptly, pleasure in his own fireside suddenly gone. 'D'you have to talk so much about Lizzie Todd?' he asked sharply.

Hurt, Meg kept her thoughts about Lizzie to herself from then on. But it was hard, especially when Lizzie's baby was born in May. The girl went into labour after a fall from the stepladder in the shop and had a long and hard labour before William was born, a frail, passive little boy.

'He's dark, like you,' Meg said cheerfully when she went along to visit mother and child. Lizzie, still confined to bed, shrugged, then shook her head and drew back when Meg bent to give the child to her.

'I can't be doing with his crying – put him in the crib.'

'In a minute.' Meg straightened, reluctant to put down the tiny mite that nestled against the curve of her breast. 'A crib's a lonely place for such a wee thing.'

Colin called from the parlour, where he lay on his cot. As she went in he held out her arms. 'Give him to me—'

She handed William over and watched as Colin stroked the small face gently with one finger.

'He'll strengthen fast enough,' Meg assured him. The difference between William and her own chubby, healthy child, now four months old, was frightening.

'I know. I'll keep him by me for a wee while, Meg.'

Going back into the kitchen, looking at the woman who lay like a ramrod in the bed there, Meg was glad that Colin and his son had each other for warmth.

* * *

Further north, and almost in another world as far as Paisley was concerned, the Jacobites and the government troops were locked in a struggle to the death.

On the whole the Paisley folk supported the king and disapproved of the hot-headed clansmen and their loyalty to a young man who, when all was said and done, was 'more a Frenchie than a Scot, and not the man for the crown at all,' in their view. The packmen kept them abreast of the latest news, and where two or more people met there was always some lively argument going on about the situation. Often Kirsty got so caught up in a disagreement with the men in the shop below that her spinning wheel almost whirred right off its mounting, and Peter would be goaded into bellowing up at her, 'Ach, why don't you content yourself with pots and pans and bread making, woman, and leave the opinions to the menfolk?'

To which Kirsty, face crimson, would yell, 'If you wanted some mealy-mouthed skivvy who'd keep her mouth shut and your belly filled, Peter Todd, you should have stayed in Dumbarton and not come to a place where the women have minds of their own!'

Then she would kick the trap shut and, eyes gleaming and red curls bouncing, say triumphantly, 'That's one argument he's lost, big man that he thinks he is. Never let them have the last word, Meg!'

After a while Peter would bang on the hatch, Kirsty would open it and, with a sweet smile, pass down the old top hat that she kept the loaded pirns in – and the argument would be forgotten, until the next time.

Matt came back home, his old vigorous self again, spilling over with tales of the Battle of Falkirk a few months earlier. Seated in his father's kitchen, a pipe in his hand and Jamie asleep on his knee, he held court to a crowd of wide-eyed listeners, chilling their blood one minute, throwing them into laughter the next with a malicious and hilarious word picture of poor John Renfrew, who in the noise and confusion had dashed straight into a hedge and stuck fast.

'We'd not have bothered with him, but he was the colour-bearer, and we weren't going to let those Highlanders get their hands on Paisley's standard.' He winked at the ring of faces. 'Man, you should have seen Johnny – head on one side, fat rump on the other, bellowing like a stuck heifer – and his hands clamped round the banner all the time with a grip like death itself. It took three of us to pull him free.'

Meg noticed that Lizzie didn't attend any of those gatherings. The only time she appeared in the Todds' kitchen was when Matt went along to see Colin.

A terrible suspicion began to form in Meg's mind. She could say nothing to Duncan or even to Kirsty, so she had to keep her thoughts to herself until one day when she had to work at home because Robert was teething and too fretful to take out.

Duncan had arranged to call round for the finished pirns, but when the door opened Meg saw Matt's tall figure outlined against the light beyond, his head stooped beneath the lintel.

'I told Duncan I'd fetch the pirns,' he said and she felt warmth rise in her face. She hadn't been alone with him since that day in Colin's kitchen.

'They're in the corner there.'

He closed the door behind him, shutting out the street. 'You've got a fine home since I last was here.'

'Aye,' she said shortly, eyes on her wheel, willing him to go away. Instead, he sat down opposite her.

'Meg—'

Reluctantly, she slowed the wheel and looked up at him – to

be stunned by the lost look on his handsome, normally confident face.

'I have to talk with you – about Lizzie.' He put out a hand as she started to speak. 'Listen to me! I know what you think about her and me, but you're wrong! We walked out together before I went into the army, but I had no thought in my head then but soldiering, though it turned out that Lizzie had her heart set on marriage.'

His big, capable hands knotted into fists as he spoke. 'God, she had plenty to say when she realised that I was set on going away. She flew at me like a she-devil and near tore my face open with her nails. But I went all the same so she set her cap at Colin instead. When I came back they were wed. And from that day I've never treated her as anything other than my brother's wife.'

'You can say that to me, when I heard with my own ears—'

'What you heard – and, God forgive me, what Colin heard – was Lizzie's doing, not mine!' Matt spoke with a sudden surge of energy. 'I wanted to crush her as if she was a flea on my arm – I still do. It would please me if I was never to set eyes on the bitch again. I've done enough to Colin, making him ride with me that day. D'you think I'd do more?'

'And William?'

'As God's my witness, Meg, he must be Colin's, for he's not mine!'

She studied him for a long moment, then nodded. 'I believe you, Matt.'

Relief lit his handsome face. 'I'm glad that's settled between us. I'll take the pirns to Duncan,' he said, then hesitated at the door.

'Meg, will you keep watch over Colin and the wee one?'

'We'll all look after them—' Meg broke off as the baby started to cough. She went quickly to the cradle, and Matt, whistling, left for the loom shop. Walking up and down with Robert muttering fretfully in her arms, Meg thought of Lizzie and those strange grey eyes of hers, the way they changed when they looked on men such as Matt and Duncan—

She stopped, and Robert squeaked a protest as her arms tightened. Meg kissed his sweat-damp hair and rocked him soothingly, her thoughts in sudden turmoil. As Lizzie and Duncan's names linked in her mind panic caught at her heart, then she forced herself to calm down, to be sensible.

Lizzie looked at all men, other than her husband, in the same way. It meant nothing, particularly to a man as sensible as Duncan. Besides, he never looked the road Lizzie was on, never even encouraged Meg to talk about her.

'You've got a silly mother,' she said shakily to Robert, and made up her mind once and for all, as she laid the baby back in his cradle, that never again would she allow such foolish ideas about Duncan to enter her head.

* * *

By the time his son reached his first birthday Duncan had joined the Society of Weavers, and he and Meg had become members of the Baptist Church, attending meetings in the Abbey Close.

To Meg's intense pride Duncan was even invited to speak at a church meeting, an occasion fraught with nerves for them both. Duncan's hands gripped the lectern before him, his face red with effort; Meg sat in the front row, her lips moving in unison with his, leaning forward to prompt audibly if he faltered. When the ordeal was finally over, she almost split in two with pride.

A month after Robert's birthday his sister Margaret was born, and six weeks later Kirsty Todd gave birth to a daughter, Kate. In June, when the tiny white flowers were beginning to star the grass on the moors, the whole town was rocked by a piece of scandal.

The gossips were out in force at once, eyes gleaming, tongues wagging. 'Lizzie Todd's run off wi' a farm worker! Have you heard about it? That poor man – and that poor bairn!'

* * *

Meg, who heard the story at the marketplace, hurried at once to Kirsty's kitchen, Margaret tucked into her shawl, and Robert running alongside as fast as his fat little legs could carry him, complaining breathlessly.

'It's not true!' she said as she burst into the kitchen.

Kirsty, rocking in her chair with Kate in the crook of one arm and William in her lap, was stony-faced.

'It's true. Hell mend the woman, for she's done a terrible thing this day!'

'How's Colin?'

Kirsty shook her head. 'Determined to fend for himself and the boy, though there's no way he can run the shop. There's room here for them both, and food enough, but he's being that thrawn about it – Peter's near out of his mind.'

At that moment an idea came to Meg, such a daring idea that it caught the breath in her throat. She said nothing to Kirsty, or even to Duncan, but the thought stayed with her. When she couldn't stand it any longer she called on Colin, still living in the rooms behind the shop, though Kirsty was looking after William.

The woman waiting to be served eyed her with open curiosity as she went round the counter with a brief nod to Janet. She heard their voices buzzing as she closed the house door behind her.

Already there was an air of neglect about the place, though

Kirsty had been in that morning, Meg knew, to see to the house-work. But there was something undeniably depressing about a house without its proper housewife.

Colin was propped up on a pile of pillows, staring at the opposite wall. His face, gaunt since his accident, was no more than skin stretched over sharp bones, his eyes, when he glanced up at her, were sunk in their sockets, without any hope in them at all.

'I'm in no mood for visitors – or sympathy!' he said harshly.

'I'm not a visitor. And I've more to do with my time than pity you.' She sat down on the chair by the bed and stared at him defiantly. He glowered back at her, then turned his face to the wall.

'Go away, Meg – leave me be!'

She steeled herself, recognising his frustration, his despair, his desperate need to be whole in himself.

'We have things to talk about, you and me. Colin, I want the shop,' she said bluntly, and saw his head turn, the grim set of his face slacken with sheer surprise.

'You what?'

'I want the shop. I've worked in it often enough and I managed fine. I could run it with Janet's help. But I'd need this house as well.'

Anger flared in his eyes, and she was glad to see it there.

'And I just take my son and move out to suit your convenience? By God, Meg Montgomery, you know how to take advantage of a man's misfortunes to line your own nest!' He almost spat the words at her. 'I'll chain myself to the grate before I'll move from here!'

Meg tucked her hands beneath her shawl in case Colin saw how they shook. 'Tuts, man, d'you have no sense in your head at all?' She had to speak loudly to quell the tremor that conveyed itself from her fingers to her voice. 'You can't manage the shop by yourself. But I can, if Duncan and me move to these rooms where I can see to the children and the counter at the same time. I'm offering to run the place for you, with financial gain for us both.'

'And what about me and William?'

'You've got brains, Colin. Use them,' she rapped back at him. 'Peter has a storeroom across the passageway from the weaving shop. I'm sure he'd let you turn it into a room for yourself and William. Kirsty can keep an eye on the two of you and you can help Peter to sort out wages and accounts. You could mebbe teach some children their letters too, if you had the time.'

'And what do you get from this daft idea?'

'A home, rent-free, so that we can save up and build our own house one day. And something of my own to do. It's not such a daft idea, Colin, if you'll just think of it.'

She leaned forward, enthusiasm giving weight to her argument. 'I like working in the shop – I like it more than anything else. Ever since I came to Paisley I've wanted to be part of the place in my own way. Now I can be.'

'What does Duncan say?'

'He doesn't know. If you refuse I'd as soon he didn't hear about me making a fool of myself, and if you agree you can help me to persuade him that it's a good idea.'

There was a short silence, then to her surprise Colin laughed, a genuine peal of amusement. 'God, Meg, but you're a breath of fresh air!' he said, and it was settled.

With Colin won over, it was easy to persuade Duncan to give his approval. Within two weeks Colin and the baby were settled in the Todds' former storeroom, under Kirsty's eye, and the Montgomerys had moved into their new home.

With Janet to help her in the shop, Meg was able to combine the roles of shopkeeper and housewife efficiently. The dwelling house was adequate, and there was a garden where she kept bees and grew vegetables. It was as though Lizzie, with her final act of betrayal, had somehow bestowed the gift of peace on those who had known her.

* * *

Meg was too busy to travel to Beith, so her parents came to Paisley to see her new home and her little daughter.

'I don't know how you can live in such a crowded place,' her mother said nervously as she picked her way along a footpath.

Meg laughed and skipped nimbly aside as a passing cart sent water flooding up from the rutted road. 'You get used to it.'

'I never could!' the older woman said with feeling. But she was proud to see the recognition Meg received as they walked along. A gentleman standing at the door of his establishment, resplendent in knee britches, tall hat and tail coat, bowed to them and Meg, pink with pleasure, whispered, 'That's Mister Robertson – one of the biggest cloth manufacturers in the town.'

'Imagine!' gasped her mother and stepped into a puddle in her excitement. Then she stared. 'Mercy – who's that?'

A crowd of young men, some dressed in the height of fashion and others in weavers' working clothes, stood on the opposite path. In their midst a good-looking young man held court.

'That's the Earl of Dundonald – a rapscallion, they say. The council are always complaining of the disrepute he brings on the town.'

Her mother tutted disapprovingly. Like most people of her class she was willing to give the gentry their place, but only if, like the working people, they had the sense to keep in it. Rowdies were rowdies, be they lords or apprentices, and she had little time for them.

* * *

Meg was secretly shocked at the relief she felt as she watched her parents clamber aboard the cart for Beith at the end of a week's stay. Despite her new-found maturity she was still wary of her mother's sharp tongue, and to her secret annoyance she had reverted a little during the visit to the role of submissive daughter. Confidence flowed back as she watched the cart jolting away, and she hugged Duncan's arm tightly as they turned back into the shop.

She had chosen her path, and it was one that more than pleased her.

5

'Will you hold still, you wee scamp? Duncan, get out the back this minute and bring Robert in. He'll be black as the devil by this time, and us supposed to be at Kirsty's long since! We'll be the last there, and I promised I'd give her a hand before the other guests arrived!' Meg lamented, holding on to Margaret with one hand and wringing out the flannel with the other.

'But I'm—' Duncan stopped, sighed, and made for the back door. Let his shirt be unbuttoned and let his slippers get wet. There was no arguing with Meg when she was in that mood.

His son was at the bottom of the garden, as usual, and climbing the apple tree – as usual.

'Out of it!' Duncan ordered, and grabbed at Robert when he reluctantly slid down the trunk. 'Your mother'll skin you alive!' he fretted, brushing leaves and bark off the boy's jacket with a large but gentle hand. 'Get into the house quick, before she comes out here after the pair of us!'

Robert gave him a gap-toothed conspiratorial grin, and scuttled up the path. Duncan fastened his shirt as he followed. It seemed only yesterday that he had been the wildest boy in

Ayrshire, and now his own son was a four-year-old miniature of himself.

Time was moving on, he thought as he stepped into the kitchen. The first dusting of grey could be seen on his dark temples and his waist had that slight thickening that tells of prosperity and contentment.

'I'll have to let out your trousers soon,' Meg said at that moment with uncanny perception.

He patted his stomach defensively. 'A man needs a bit of muscle.'

'There?' She poked him in the midriff, then squealed as he swept her off the floor and kissed her. 'Duncan! The wee ones are watching!'

He let her go, grinning down at her laughing, pretty face. 'Ach, a show of affection'll do them no harm.'

Margaret toddled after him as he went to fetch his jacket, her eyes huge after her afternoon sleep. He held his arms out and she rushed into them.

'Now don't get her into a mess,' Meg cautioned. She scrubbed at Robert's rosy face and he stood uncomplaining, knowing that if he opened his mouth to protest it would be filled with wet flannel.

'And you didn't even see the bonny flowers, did you?' Duncan was asking Margaret, who had slept in his arms all through their afternoon walk in the Hope Temple Gardens.

Meg smiled to herself as she recalled their promenade round the flower beds, the pleasant moist warmth within the glass enclosure, the snug fit of her new leather boots, the way the senior magistrate's wife had bowed to them when they met. The memories gave her such pleasure that Robert's features were almost scrubbed off his face.

'There – you'll do.' She released him and he rushed to join his father and sister, who were romping on the box bed.

'Keep tidy, now!' Meg called automatically, and went into the shop to make sure that everything was in order. The outer door was closed and bolted, the floor swept clean, the sacks tied tightly, the scales shining. She stood for a moment, one hand on the counter, and inhaled the rich smell of meal.

She had been in charge of it for two years, and had enjoyed every minute of it. She and Duncan had just put down the first payment on a piece of land on the west fringes of the town. There, in a few years, they would build their own house. She smoothed her skirt, letting her palms linger for a moment over the bulge caused by the coming baby, then called Duncan and the children, and put her cloak on for the walk to the Todds' house.

* * *

The place was in a turmoil when the Montgomerys arrived. Kirsty, crimson-faced from the heat, was stirring a huge pot of broth while trying to soothe John, the baby. Kate, Jamie and Willie were chasing each other up and down the stairs, and Peter could be heard from the bedroom, demanding to know where his best shoes were.

'I'm glad you're here!' Kirsty greeted Meg. 'I'm in a right pickle – would you take the wee one for me? Duncan, keep an eye on that broth. And as for you—' she swooped on the older children and deposited them on a settle by the fire '—sit there and hold your tongues for two minutes while I see what that handless man wants. Where are your best shoes always kept?' she yelled as she vanished. 'Seven years, and you still don't know where to look for them!'

By the time she reappeared a minute later, tucking a stray wisp of glowing hair beneath her cap, Meg was setting the table, the baby whimpering fretfully on her shoulder.

'He's not so grand today.' Kirsty took her son and rocked him. 'He's been coughing since morning. I'll try to settle him down before the others arrive.'

She stroked the child's flushed cheek with one finger and John moved his small head against her sturdy arm. By the time he was in his cradle the visitors had begun to arrive, and the kitchen was soon filled.

Duncan and Billy Carmichael, the packman, carried Colin upstairs and put him on a chair by the fire and William, a quiet little boy, immediately climbed onto his father's knee and fell asleep, one thumb jammed into his mouth and his head nestled under Colin's chin.

After supper all the children were taken to the attic where they were packed into bed like sardines to wait for their parents. Billy took his fiddle from his pack, and the evening got off to its proper start.

In an hour or two the house was bouncing with music and the babble of voices, yet the sound of a child in distress broke through the noise easily. First one woman, then another, fell silent, listening to the dry, painful coughing from up in the attic room, fearful in case they recognised their own child. It was the sound of croup, that lung-torturing illness that dogged infants in Paisley's low-lying, damp atmosphere.

Half a dozen anxious women followed Kirsty upstairs. When she came back to the kitchen she carried John, his face crimson, his little lungs crackling and wheezing as he tried to suck in air.

Someone put a kettle on the fire to make steam to ease his labouring lungs, someone else heated a blanket to wrap him in, then they all gathered their children and left. The party was over,

and Kirsty would probably be up all night with John, waiting for
the attack to pass.

* * *

Duncan had scarcely left for the weaving shop the next morning
when he was back, white-faced.

'Kirsty needs you. I'll fetch Janet. She can see to the bairns
and the shop today.'

Meg didn't stop to ask what was wrong. She didn't need to. In
a few minutes she was in the Todds' kitchen which was no longer
the warm, noisy place it had been only a few hours earlier.
Instead it was frighteningly silent and Kirsty sat huddled by the
fire, oblivious of Peter's arms about her and the bewildered faces
of the children who hadn't yet learned to understand the
meaning of sudden death.

While Peter went off to make the necessary arrangements for
his little son's burial, Meg fed the children and sent them down to
Colin's room, then made tea and wrapped Kirsty's cold, stiff
fingers about the cup before setting about the housework. The
kitchen had to be spotless, and there was baking to do in prepara-
tion for the people who would start arriving as soon as word of
John's death spread.

Kirsty sat motionless, scarcely heeding the visitors. She didn't
even pay attention to Mistress McKenzie, one of the first callers.

'The Lord giveth and the Lord taketh away,' that lady
announced almost as soon as her foot was over the lintel. 'Your
bairn's been chosen to reside with his Maker, Mistress Todd, and
it's not for poor mortals like us to question or to lament. I'll try
one of these scones, Meg.'

'Are you trying to say that Kirsty should rejoice?' Meg heard
herself say in a strange, hard voice.

The black ribbons on Mistress McKenzie's bonnet rustled dryly with the force of her nodding.

'Just so. Children belong to the Lord, not to us. It's an honour when one's chosen from among our number. It's not for us to question the ways of the Lord.'

Meg swallowed hard and glared at the woman who sat with her skirts hitched up to let her heavily veined legs soak in the fire's warmth.

'It seems to me that if the Lord knew more about the work that goes into caring for a baby, and the mortal love that goes with it, He'd have a bit more compassion for mothers!'

It was the other woman's turn to gape, and a half-chewed chunk of scone almost escaped past her teeth. She gulped, choked, and muttered something about Baptists knowing no better.

Meg set her lips over an angry retort. This wasn't the time to quarrel.

'But I could have taken her by the hair and dragged her out of the kitchen and down the stairs,' she stormed to Duncan when she was home again. 'The besom! Her with no children of her own – talking about honour and rejoicing!'

And she hugged Margaret so tightly that the little girl's lower lip began to tremble.

* * *

A few days later Kirsty and Peter saw John's tiny coffin buried in the churchyard, then they went back home and set about their usual day's routine.

There was little time to spare for mourning in a thriving town like Paisley. Water had to be fetched from wells, bees had to be tended and living children cared for, and thread had to be spun for the ever-hungry looms that beat out a steady rhythm for the townsfolk to live by.

As the time for her own baby's birth drew near, Meg found it more and more difficult to cope with all her duties. Janet was a dreamy girl, not to be trusted in the shop alone if there were more than two customers. At times Meg longed to shake the girl hard, just to see if there was any life behind that vacant face. Her temper grew short, and it was as much for his own sake as for hers that Duncan suggested asking her sister Mary to help with the chores until the baby arrived.

Mary arrived within a few days, delighted with the opportunity to leave the farm. With an ease that stunned her older sister she familiarised herself with the shop routine and her happy nature and pretty face, with its sparkling brown eyes and its frame of dark curls, made her a great success with the customers. She even had an impressive effect on Janet, who began to take an interest in her appearance and her work.

'How did you manage to waken that ditherer?' Duncan demanded to know one day after he had found Janet, neat and tidy, chatting animatedly with Mary as they restocked shelves.

His sister-in-law leaned across the table and wiped crumbs from Margaret's chin. 'She just needed a firm hand. Nobody's ever encouraged her to take an interest in the way she looks, that's all.'

Mary was the beauty of the family. Meg was plump and maternal, but Mary was slender and elegant. They had the same dark hair, but Mary's was glossy. Her manner was confident, her bearing almost regal. Somehow she managed to make even the plainest dress look stylish.

The town's young bachelors flocked to the shop and the snuff jar had to be replenished once every day; but to Meg's astonishment her sister wasn't interested in romance.

'A wee flirtation can be entertaining, I'll grant you,' she said carelessly. 'But I'm not interested in marriage.'

'What else is there?' Meg asked, and Mary threw a scathing glance at her.

'Plenty!'

She was fascinated by fashion, and always willing to take the children to the Hope Temple Gardens where she could study the ladies' clothes. She bought silks and ribbons and made her own bonnets, and on Meg's first outing to the Baptist rooms after her baby, Thomas, was born, she wore a hat made by Mary's nimble fingers.

Duncan's eyes shone when he saw his wife's rosy face framed by the new bonnet. 'You'll be the loveliest woman in the place!'

Meg laughed and blushed. But it was true. Nobody else had such a fine hat.

'Though it's wicked to think such vain thoughts in the Lord's House,' she whispered to Mary, who whispered back, dimpling, 'Mebbe the Lord's too busy admiring my fine bonnet to notice the vain thoughts underneath it.'

If the Lord did admire the hat, He wasn't the only one. Within a short time quite a number of the townswomen, including Mistress MacLeod, wife of one of the town's councillors, had asked Mary to make bonnets for them, and the little spare time she had was spent surrounded by ribbons and lace.

One day she came back from delivering a bonnet to Mistress MacLeod with shining eyes and an extra bounce to her light step.

'Meg, it's the grandest place I've ever been in – we sat in the parlour, but she calls it a withdrawing room, and the maid served tea just as if we were two ladies visiting! And I'm to make another bonnet for her!'

She seized Meg's hands and whirled her round. 'And she's going to pay me more money than I would have asked for myself!'

It was fortunate that Meg was back to her former energetic self, for Mary became too busy to give much time to the shop. The kitchen was a riot of colour as she stitched away at her bonnets by day with the children, festooned in ribbons, playing happily beside her. At night, when Duncan and Meg needed the peace of their own fireside, Mary worked in her tiny room.

When the time came for her to return to Beith, she announced that she had decided to settle in Paisley.

'But—' Meg looked helplessly at Duncan. The house behind the shop was already crowded and Mary's millinery was taking up more room than they could afford.

Mary's sharp eyes saw the look. 'You've nothing to worry about. I'm going to set up a wee shop at the Sneddon and live on the premises. It's all arranged between Mistress MacLeod and me,' she swept on as Meg opened her mouth to protest. 'We talked about it today, when I delivered her new bonnet. I'm to be a milliner!'

'Hold on there, Mary—' Duncan finally made himself heard. 'It's all very well talking of wee shops, but where d'you expect to find the money for all this?'

She gave him a withering look. 'D'you think I haven't thought of all that? Mistress MacLeod's going to pay the rent of the place, and pay me to work for her. And I'll see she gets her money back as soon as I can give it to her. The woman's got more money than she knows what to do with, and it'll pleasure her to help me. At least she'll not be throwing her silver away.'

'What about the farm?' Visions of angry parents swooping down on her and accusing her of tempting Mary away from her proper place in life floated before Meg's eyes.

'I'll see to that – and I'm not going back, whatever they say!' Mary tossed her sleek dark head. 'I was never afraid of hard work, but I'd as soon be doing something I want to do. And I know now that it's got nothing to do with farm work!'

There was no arguing with her. Mary had found her vocation in life, and within the next few weeks she had scrubbed out the Sneddon shop and the rooms behind it, and had settled in. From then on she was often to be seen tripping about the town with a box in each hand, delivering wares to her customers. Almost every time Meg called in at the shop, there was a carriage waiting at the door. Mary, like Meg, was a born businesswoman, and her shop thrived.

'That sister of yours has a good head on her shoulders,' Kirsty approved when she and Meg were spinning thread together.

Meg sighed. 'I suppose she's right when she says farm life's not for her. But I wish she would take a husband.'

Kirsty snorted with laughter. 'Why should she? She's managing fine on her own. It was a good day for Paisley when the Montgomerys arrived, Meg. There's you seeing to Colin's shop for him, and Mary doing the same for Mistress MacLeod. And Duncan's the best weaver Peter ever employed. You're all making your mark on the place.'

Meg said nothing, but she smiled at the thread smoothly winding itself onto the pirn. She wouldn't have changed places at that moment with the king himself.

* * *

Working silently beside her, Kirsty marvelled at her own words. The ugly wound caused by Duncan's affair with Lizzie had healed. She had been right to persuade Peter to keep Duncan and Meg in Paisley.

Colin was content, and nobody could wish that William, a

quiet and lovable little boy, had never been born. For his part, Duncan had learned his lesson and would never stray again; she was sure of that.

It's an ill wind, Kirsty thought to herself with a trace of justified smugness as she added another loaded pirn to the old top hat by her side.

PART II

6

The grocer's shop in New Street was Margaret Montgomery's whole world, and she loved it.

True, there was more world outside its doors – narrow muddy streets, carriages and horses and people, rutted footpaths to walk on, houses leaning above her in friendly curiosity, the weaving shop where her father worked – but the grocery was the main part of her existence.

She loved the thick dusty smell of meal, the way the rough sacks tickled her palms, the exciting sensation of grain shifting and yet resisting when she punched the sacks with small knotted fists. She loved the counter, though at five years old she was still too small to see over it and all she knew of it was the feel of its flat surface beneath her fingers and the sight of raw grained wood at eye level. She loved the way her mother's voice changed from loving or irritable to brisk and efficient when she was waiting on customers.

Everyone came into the shop, thus proving what Margaret already knew – that it was the hub of the town. So she loved the customers too, because the shop gave them a reason to exist.

With the open-hearted trust of one who had never been betrayed, she loved the ladies with their rustly clothes, the house-wives with their ready laughter, the deep-voiced, snuff-buying men, the children struggling with large unwieldy baskets and reciting sing-song lists dinned into their heads by busy mothers. She even loved old Mister Lyle and his dog – and not many people loved them. They both smelled, and she had heard people calling Mister Lyle an old rascal, no better than he should be. Whenever he came in for his groceries Margaret deserted her post by her mother and slipped out to stroke the dog, waiting patiently by the door for its master.

When Mister Lyle came out, he smiled at her and patted her on the head with a dirty hand. A lot of people would have found the smile terrifying, a drawing back of cracked lips to reveal gums and a few black teeth, but Margaret saw only its gentleness and its friendship. Then Mister Lyle would go off down the street, his dog at his heels, the two of them old and stiff and unloved by anyone else but Margaret.

Her capacity for affection was vast. It even included her brothers, though Thomas, still a baby, could be a great trial and Robert bullied her if she gave him the chance.

There were times when she could do nothing with Robert. Today was one of those times, she realised wretchedly as he dragged her along the crowded High Street, ignoring her pleas.

'I want to go home!' she repeated again and again, each time raising her voice a little more. But there was such a crush and noise about them that her voice made little impact. She had never known the street to be so busy, and the forest of legs and skirts she was being towed through unnerved her. She dragged back, but Robert merely tightened his grip on her hand and forged ahead, towing her behind him.

Margaret hadn't wanted to go out that day; she had burrowed

into her mother's skirts and whined to stay in the shop, but Meg had pushed her at Robert and ordered her in a new, sharp voice to stop being a nuisance and do as she was told.

'You're supposed to be taking me to Aunt Kirsty's house!' Margaret pointed out, but Robert only jerked harder on her hand and she yelped with fright as she almost lost her footing.

William Todd, on her other side, steadied her.

'It's all right, Margaret, I'll look after you,' he whispered, and she squeezed his fingers in gratitude. William wasn't like Robert or Jamie – he was kind, and she felt safe with him. She often wished that grey-eyed, brown-haired William was her brother.

'Come on!' Robert's face glowed with excitement and he plunged into the thick of the crowd, dragging poor Margaret along.

The atmosphere reminded her of the fair days, though this wasn't one. Voices clanged in her ear or whizzed past and vanished, leaving half-finished, confusing sentences for her to puzzle over.

'Going to the hanging... the hanging... hanging—' The word was on everyone's lips. She had heard her parents mention it that very morning.

'Today's the hanging,' her father had said and Margaret, supposedly asleep in the truckle bed that by day was pushed beneath her parents' big bed, opened one eye to see him put an arm about her mother.

'Don't cry, Meg – there's nothing you or me can do about it.'

'But, Duncan, he's an old man! And all he did was take some kail from someone's garden—'

'It wasn't his only theft – or his first. You know that, Meg.'

'But he doesn't deserve—' Her mother pressed the back of a hand against her lips to stop the words.

'Why don't you close the shop for once and take the children to the braes for the morning?'

'No!' Her mother's voice was unusually sharp. 'The shop'll be open – though no doubt most of the customers'll be off for some entertainment instead of going about their lawful business!'

Then they had seen that she was awake, and had said no more. She and Robert were hurried through their breakfast and bundled out of the shop with orders to go round to Aunt Kirsty's at once. Instead they had met up with Jamie and William and now, like it or not, Margaret was on her way to the Cross with most of Paisley's population.

Jamie's red head acted like a beacon ahead of them, but they didn't catch up with him until they had reached the site near the river where the stalls were set up on market days. He and Robert burrowed their way to the front of the mob with Margaret and William following.

Margaret felt a little better when she found herself at the edge of a big open space with the bulk of the people behind her. Now the only legs in front belonged to the militia lining the open area. Beyond them stood a queer wooden arrangement of ladders and platforms that she didn't recall ever seeing before. She was trying to puzzle out what it could be when a cart was driven into the empty square, and an expectant sigh rustled through the crowd. The cart drew up before the wooden structure and a group of men clambered out.

Margaret eyed them idly, then her attention was caught by the figure in the middle. She tugged at Robert's sleeve. 'It's old Mister Lyle. What's wrong, Robert? Is he ailing?'

Mister Lyle was being helped along by two of the men. His old legs seemed to have lost their strength, and he lurched against his helpers, almost falling twice. He was escorted to the wooden contraption, then the men began to help him up a ladder.

'Robert, why are his hands tied? Is it a game?'

Ignored by the three boys, Margaret ducked down to peer between the legs of the soldier standing directly before her. While the crowd buzzed with anticipation, the old man was heaved onto a small platform. A plump man in a long black coat was hoisted up the steps in his turn, but with his hands free, then he began to talk long and earnestly to Mister Lyle, as though scolding him. The old man stood abjectly before him, a pathetic, defeated figure.

Something grimly purposeful about the rest of the men on the platform, something helpless and shrunken about Mister Lyle's stance, struck an uneasy chord in Margaret's mind. She reached out to William, her only ally.

'I want to get out of this place! I want to go home!'

But the crowd's excitement gripped William fast now. He spoke hurriedly, without taking his eyes from the scene before him. 'Ssshhh, Margaret, we'll go home in a minute—'

Fear began to whisper in her ear. She closed her eyes then opened them again as the rumble of a drum cut across the babble of voices behind her.

The man in the long black coat had stopped talking to Mister Lyle and had stepped back. Then someone else looped a rope about the old man's neck. Completely bewildered, Margaret craned her own neck to see what happened next.

To her horror the platform beneath Mister Lyle's feet broke and he dropped through the hole, to be caught before he touched the ground by the rope about his throat.

His legs kicked and he swung to and fro like a doll. The crowd hushed for a second, then moaned, a sound that reached eerily to the sky. But nobody went to help Mister Lyle. Appalled, Margaret watched him swinging, kicking, choking – while the militia, the crowd, and everyone on the platform just stood and watched. Her hands went up to her own chubby neck in an instinctive effort to relieve the hempen grip on the old man's windpipe. His body swung right round then lost momentum as the legs stopped kicking.

Margaret, too, spun round, gripped by unspeakable horror, searching the faces behind and above her for some sign of compassion. But they all bore a look of rapt fascination, like babies watching a toy dangle before their eyes.

'Robert—' She tugged frantically at her brother's sleeve. 'Robert, what's happening to Mister Lyle?'

He watched the old man's last gyrations on the end of the rope. 'He's hanging, Margaret.' His voice was filled with awe. 'He was a bad man.'

'He wasn't!'

'He was so!' Jamie Todd interrupted her sharply. 'That's why he had to be hanged. He was a bad man – and now he's dead!' There was no mistaking the satisfaction in his voice.

'Dead?' Margaret whirled back to the scene in the middle of the empty square. She suddenly realised that Mister Lyle would never again walk on the ground that lay a tantalisingly short distance below his shabby boots. He would never come into the shop again, never pat her head or walk along a footpath with his old dog again. The enormity of it descended on her like a threatening cloud. She felt a sudden terrible need to get home to her mother—

Her dash for freedom brought her up against one of the soldiers lining the square. The man, almost thrown to the ground by the impact of her sturdy little body against the backs of his knees, caught her shoulder.

'Lassie, what are you doing in a place like this? Someone take the bairn away!' he appealed to the crowd. Margaret, seeing his tall uniformed figure stooping over her, feeling his hand on her arm, took his interest as a sign that she was to be the next victim.

'I'm not bad – I'm not for hanging!' she shrieked with the full power of her lungs, and flailed her arms until she managed to wriggle free. Then she eeled round and dived into the crowd before any of the boys could catch her.

Screaming for her mother she fought her way along, bumping painfully into knees, tripping over feet, half-mad with terror and convinced that at any minute a rope would slip about her neck.

When the ground dropped away and left her feet kicking in mid-air as Mister Lyle's had done, she shut her eyes tight and redoubled her screams.

'Here, here, lassie, no need to take on like that.' Billy Carmichael the chapman wrapped his arms about her to still her struggles. 'It's Margaret Montgomery, isn't it?'

Margaret refused to open her eyes. 'They gave Mister Lyle a hanging and I don't want one!' she bawled, kicking and punching at the hands holding her. Then she felt herself carried swiftly along while a deep warm voice rumbled overhead.

'Nobody's going to hurt you, lassie. See, I'm taking you home. You mind me, don't you? Say hello to me like a good wee girl—'

When she finally prised her eyelids open and recognised him she threw her arms about his neck and demanded loudly to be taken to her mother at once.

'We're going, lass, we're going, for this is no place for you. I'd just be grateful if you'd neither smother nor deafen me on the way,' Billy said, and fought his way through the people pressing forward for a glimpse of the still figure swinging on the rope.

Margaret quietened down once she realised that they were leaving the crowd behind and heading for home, but at the sight of her mother and Mary in the shop, her terror and outrage returned in a fresh well of tears.

Meg sank down in a chair, clutching her weeping daughter, while Billy explained.

'The hanging? Oh, my poor wee lamb! And I thought they were safe at Kirsty's. Wait till I get a hold of Robert—!'

'And Mister Lyle's hands were t-tied and he fell and no – nobody would help him,' Margaret roared. 'And Robert said he'd been b-bad and it was a hanging, then the soldiers took me for the hanging t-t-too—'

'See now, Margaret, wee lassies don't get hanged.' Mary's practical voice broke through the noise. 'They might get smacked if they need it but they never get hanged. The soldiers wouldn't do a thing like that to anybody.'

Margaret raised her swollen red face from her mother's shoulder.

'They gave Mister Lyle a hanging,' she retorted with as much sharpness as her aunt. 'And he's dead!'

'Aye – well, I'll grant you that, since there's no sense in denying it. Now listen.' Mary lifted her niece from Meg's lap in time to avert a fresh outbreak of sobbing and stood her on the floor, kneeling to wipe Margaret's streaming eyes and nose. 'I'm going to wash your face and then we're going to deliver a new hat to Mistress Black's house. Would you like that?'

Margaret nodded, her body still racked by great tearing sobs.

'But you'll have to stop crying first. Mistress Black'll mebbe have a nice bit cake for you if you're a good girl.'

The sobs were replaced, after a massive effort on Margaret's part, by sniffs and hiccups.

'There's my brave lassie,' Mary said briskly. 'Now come with me and we'll clean your wee face.'

Five minutes later, soothed and washed and brushed, Margaret waited for Mary, one thumb jammed comfortingly into her mouth, the other hand stroking the familiar grain of the shop counter. Billy's voice washed over her as he talked to her mother and helped himself to snuff from the big jar that was always kept on the countertop.

She felt as though she'd had a terrible nightmare and had wakened to find herself safely tucked up in her warm, soft bed. Idly she watched the light catch the thick bottom of the snuff jar as it was lifted up.

Then the jar thudded onto its accustomed place again and Billy's large hand with its square-cut nails rested on the scarred wood, just level with her eyes as she stood on tiptoe, her nose pressed against the edge of the counter.

The significance of what she had just witnessed burst on Margaret in a shower of stars. She stood gaping, open-mouthed, then let out a delighted roar. Meg swung round, startled, and Billy inhaled snuff the wrong way and exploded into a huge sneeze. Mary, emerging from the room behind the shop, stopped short with one hand half in and half out of its glove.

Margaret stood behind the counter, her hands white-knuckled on its edge, her blue eyes wide as they peeped over the top.

'I can see!' she crowed. 'I'm not a wee bairn any longer – I can see over the counter!'

'Did you ever see such a change in a lassie? She's forgotten the hanging already,' Meg said with relief when her daughter had skipped out of the shop with Mary.

'Aye.' Billy had his doubts about that, but he didn't voice them. 'You've got a bonny family.'

'Come early tonight and see them all before they go to their beds.' She knew how much children meant to Billy. A big, easy-going man, he had been a cobbler before his wife and three young children were struck down by fever.

Left alone, he had taken to the roads, joining the band of men who peddled their wares from town to town.

'I'd like that. I hear there's been changes in the town since I was last here.'

'Aye.' She folded her hands over her apron, soothed by the everyday comfort of a wee gossip. 'There's always something going on. The new grammar school's open now, and the flesh market in Moss Row too.'

'And the council's put a tax on beer and ale, I hear. Bad news travels,' he said wryly.

'The money's needed to deepen the river and put up more new houses, so Peter says.' Meg spoke with all the earnestness and pride of a true citizen. 'You'll have heard that they've made Peter one of the directors of the new town hospital? Kirsty says he's hardly ever at home these days. And Colin's as cheery as ever I've seen him.'

Billy's head came up quickly at mention of Colin. 'I heard news of Lizzie Todd last month, up by Dundee,' he said, and a cold hand clutched at Meg's heart.

'What of her?'

'She was living near there with that man of hers until recently. Things haven't been going well for them.'

'She's only got herself to blame!' After more than five years, Meg still couldn't think of Lizzie without deep uneasiness. 'You'll not tell Colin?'

The big man shook his greying head. 'It's best left unsaid.'

'Aye.' Meg took up a cloth and rubbed the spotless counter hard. 'That's all over and done with. Best forgotten.'

* * *

The town dismissed old Hector Lyle from its memory almost as soon as Jamie, William and Robert stopped smarting from the punishment they received for going to the public execution. Margaret's pain was buried deep, and everyone thought it, too, had been forgotten, although she had bad dreams for the next six months or so.

Winter closed in and Duncan, now Peter's right-hand man, had extra work to handle when his employer took to his bed with a heavy cold that refused to go, but lay on his chest for weeks.

'You might as well admit it, man – the fluff's got into your lungs. Either that or it's all these meetings you have to attend,' Kirsty hectored. 'I told you, did I not, that you should have stayed home and looked after that bad cough when it started instead of going out till all hours in the chill air. Remember, you're not as young as you used to be.'

'Away with you, woman!' Peter scoffed. But he couldn't disguise the fact that the illness had left him breathless and unable to climb stairs easily.

The cold weather at the end of 1755 took its toll of young and old alike. One of its most disreputable victims, an inmate of the new Poor's Hospital, went carousing in a bothy with cronies one January night then stumbled homewards in a blizzard. He was found the next morning, frozen to death yards from the hospital door.

Mary's benefactress, Mistress MacLeod, succumbed to a severe chill brought on by a charitable visit to the hospital on a cold wet day.

'She should never have gone out – and her with a cough that's said to have drowned out half the High Church service two days before,' said Mary sadly to Meg.

'What'll become of your wee shop now?' Meg trailed covetous fingers over a fanciful creation on Mary's counter.

'Nothing, for I've already repaid a fair piece of the money to Mistress MacLeod.' Mary looked about her little shop. 'I called on Mister MacLeod to pay my respects, of course, and while I was there we had a wee talk about the rest of it. He's content to take the payments month by month, just as it was when his wife was alive.' Mary's fingers flew among ribbons as she worked on another hat. 'Poor man, he's bad with the rheumatism, and only a parcel of servants to see to him in that big house. He'll miss his wife sorely. I don't know why it's the best of us that get taken every time.'

* * *

Spring came at last, and brought with it the realisation of a dream for Meg and Duncan. By the time May brought warm sunny days to replace April's showers, plans for their new house at Townhead had been drawn up, and the house itself was finished in the early spring of 1756.

After the workmen had downed tools for the last time, toasted a job well done and departed, Meg ran from room to room gazing out of the small windows, peering up chimneys, opening and shutting doors. The children clattered noisily about and Duncan basked in the glow felt by a man of property.

'I told you we'd do it one day, lass.' He caught Meg's hand and drew her to him when they found themselves alone in the kitchen, across the passageway from the loom shop.

She beamed up at him through tears. 'I never doubted you.'

The memory of a woman with almond-shaped grey eyes came fleetingly to Duncan, but he pushed it away.

'I'll not have my own looms yet, of course. But the shop's here and the looms'll come in good time.'

Meg slipped her hand into his and they stood dreaming for a

moment before she shook herself and said briskly, 'Time to get back to the shop.'

'Janet can manage fine without you.'

'I'm not so sure, now that new weaver of yours has put stars in her eyes. Young folk in love can be right stupid at times.' Meg shook her head primly, then blushed like a girl when Duncan laughed.

'You're right there. I mind as if it were yesterday the time you got into trouble with your mother for dropping a basket of new-collected eggs – all because you saw me passing by in the road!'

* * *

'Mary, you can't!' Meg stopped sweeping the hearth and stared up at her sister, her eyes wide with shock.

'And what's the "can't" for, Meg Montgomery? Just because you didn't have a hand in arranging the match, does it follow that I'm not allowed to get wed?'

'But – Mister MacLeod! Mary, he's an old man! Besides,' she floundered, seeking words to express her dismay, 'his wife's not that long in her grave!'

Mary sighed and began to remove her gloves. 'The man's been widowed for more than eighteen months – and he's crippled with the rheumatism and scarcely able to move out of his house half the time. And here's me, back and forth between my shop and his house this past year and more, trying to see to him – for what good are servants when a man's ailing? It's the wisest thing to marry him, then I can see to him properly and save my legs a lot of running.'

'Have you accepted him, then?'

Mary stared. 'What do you mean, accepted him? There was no accepting about it. I just told him plump and plain – if you've any sense in your head, I said, you'll marry me and save me all this toing and froing.'

Meg's apron was thrown over her horrified face. 'Have you no shame in you at all? You mean that you proposed marriage to a gentleman twice your age and as rich as a lord? D'you know what they'll be saying about you in the streets?'

'They can say all they like and it'll not stick in my throat,' her sister said calmly. 'His age doesn't come into it, and neither does his money. If he didn't have it he'd be welcome to come and live in my wee room behind the shop. As it is, I'll move into his house and have more room for my work. And don't start that again,' she added ominously as choking sounds came from beneath the apron. 'I'll keep my shop and my independence. Nobody'll be able to say I married Andra MacLeod so that I could be a lady of leisure. Indeed, it's going to be hard work seeing to it that those lazy servants of his earn their keep for a change.'

Meg's flushed face appeared for a moment round the apron. 'D'you want to shame me entirely in this town?' she squawked. 'Rich men's wives don't keep shops!'

'This one will – for no doubt I'll outlive Andra, poor old soul, and I'll need something to keep me occupied in my own old age.'

'Would you not have a word with Duncan first?' Meg appealed.

'What has it to do with him? No, no, Meg, it's all arranged, and a date set. Not that the minister was entirely happy at first, but I soon pointed out that it was a Christian thing I was doing, and he agreed with me – eventually.' Mary got to her feet. 'And next week I'm taking Andra down to Beith to tell my mother and father.'

'I forgot about them!' Meg moaned. 'Oh, Mary, what are they going to say?'

'Leave them to me. I don't think they'll make half the fuss you have. Anyone would think I was disgracing you, Meg Montgomery. Take my advice and pay no heed to wagging tongues – or tell them to come and wag at me. I'll soon sort them out.' Mary looked round the cosy kitchen as she drew her gloves on again. 'It seems to me, Meg, that the two of us have come a long way since we used to tread the blankets together down on the farm.'

'Mary, are you sure that you're—'

'You'd best see to Thomas,' Mary said from the window. 'The wee scamp's asking to get himself stung, plunging round the bee skeps waving a stick.' And she escaped in the ensuing domestic panic.

* * *

'You're talking as if Mary's going to bring disgrace on us, instead of marrying with one of the most respected men in Paisley,' Duncan argued when he came home that night to be met by an agitated wife.

'But the scandal!' Meg almost wept.

'Tuts, woman, we both know well enough that she's not after the man for his money, so what does it matter what anyone else says? Even if she was, she's earned it, the way she's tended him since his wife died. There'll be no more weeping over Mary's plans in my house,' he ended firmly, and Meg had to leave matters at that.

* * *

Mary married her elderly husband in the Laigh Church, with a gathering in Andrew MacLeod's house afterwards. Andrew was a tall, lean man, stooped and twisted by rheumatism, but retaining some of the good looks he had once had. Quiet and shy, he obviously doted on his vigorous new wife. His home was a big two-storey building on the hill behind the High Street, looking down on the ruined abbey with the River Cart slipping beneath its walls.

Mary, taking on the role of mistress of the house as though born to it, sat in the parlour dispensing tea for the ladies and something stronger for the men, and supervising the servants with an ease that made Meg and her mother gasp.

The children were less intimidated by the place than their elders, and explored enthusiastically. Margaret's eyes were round when she returned to her mother.

'It's a castle! How many folk live in it?'

'Just Mister—' Meg stopped, blushed, tried again. 'Your new Uncle Andra and your Aunt Mary and the folk who look after them.'

'But this house is too big for them!' Margaret was outraged. 'Half our street could live in it. Why do they need so many rooms?'

Meg hushed her, glancing guiltily round the room. 'Uncle Andra's got a lot of money, so he can afford a big house. Stop your questions, for any favour!'

'But why should rich folk have houses that are too big for them, when—'

'They just do!' She refastened Margaret's jacket and tidied her hair. 'Run and find the boys; there's a good lass.'

Margaret did as she was told, but as she scurried along the big dark hall, hung with paintings, a rebellious inner voice that was to be heard many times during her life continued to ask, *Why should the rich have so much space when the poor have to crowd together in hovels?*

7

Mary turned her predecessor's sewing room into a workshop, took on an assistant, and was a devoted wife to Andrew MacLeod. The fact that she now met most of her wealthier customers on a social basis in the evenings made no difference to her business dealings with them during the day.

'But I'll admit, Meg,' she confessed with a dimpling smile, 'that I have a wee chuckle to myself when I go to one of those grand gatherings and see that most of the bonnets in the room were made by my own fingers.'

She also took on the charitable duties expected of the more well-to-do women in the town, fitting them into an overcrowded day without visible effort. The gossips who had predicted that she would play the fine lady and not bother with anything else soon found themselves proved wrong. Busy as she was, Mary involved herself just as much as ever in other people's lives.

It was she who found a replacement for Janet when the girl married a local stonemason and gave up her work in the shop. Mary promptly produced a capable widow with a family to support and talked Colin and Meg into taking the woman on as a shop assistant and letting her have the empty rooms behind the grocer's shop. Then she organised the task of converting the rooms, now used for storage, back into a home.

She swept into the shop dressed in practical working clothes and festooned with cloths and pails. Robert and Thomas, who were unfortunate enough to be there at the time, were despatched to fetch water.

'And go right to the well, d'you hear me? You needn't think you'll take the lazy way out and climb the wall to get to Mistress Pearson's well.'

She handed them each a stoup to carry the water in. 'That bad-tempered old devil of a man of hers can still run, and he'll keep these if he gets the chance. Now then, Meg, tuck your skirts up out of harm's way, for we've a lot of scrubbing to do. It's a bad deed that benefits nobody,' she added as she set to and scrubbed until drops of water flew from her brush. 'You'll not regret taking the widow woman on, for she's a hard worker and an honest soul. But I think Janet's made a mistake. That new husband of hers is a shiftless creature that broke his first wife's heart.'

Meg sat back on her heels and nodded, brushing a tendril of hair back from her face with one wet fist. 'For once I agree with you.'

'Just because her sweetheart jilted her,' Mary puffed. 'If you ask me she's gone out and thrown herself at the first man she saw to prove to us all that she doesn't care. I don't know why women have to be so set on marriage! And if you say one word about me proposing to Andra, Meg, I'll empty this bucket of water about your ears, for that's not the same thing at all!'

* * *

As time passed it became clear that Peter's bronchitis had become chronic. Duncan took on most of the responsibility for the loom shop, though Peter kept an eye on everything from his big armchair by the kitchen fire.

Duncan was soon trying to persuade him to let one of the looms go over to the manufacture of silk gauze, a new material that was selling well in London. Some of the town's manufacturers were trying it out on their looms, and Duncan saw it as part of Paisley's future.

'Linen isn't going to keep us going forever,' he argued. 'The town's growing – we need to try new ideas if we want to grow along with it.'

'He's right.' Colin nodded, fingering the sample Duncan had brought in. 'This is a cloth the gentry'll want to buy, Father. The weaving trade can't afford to stand still.'

'Humphrey Fulton's contracting weavers to make it for him.' Duncan was referring to another man from Beith, who had become a successful manufacturer. 'He sees a good market for it – and he knows what he's about. We have to keep up with the times, Peter!'

'Ach, you're new-fangled, both of you,' Peter grumbled, but his eyes were shrewd as he in turn took the material, rubbing it through his fingers. 'Well, go ahead – but if it doesn't pay its way it comes off my loom, mind!'

'Aye, aye, I hear you,' Duncan agreed cheerfully, and went on to prove that silk gauze was a paying innovation.

The restlessness that had led him into the affair with Lizzie was channelled into his work and his plans for the future. He was a man of property, mellowed and content with his life. He rarely thought of Lizzie now; Duncan was one of those people with a talent for closing their minds against memories that shamed or angered them. Not even the sight of William reminded him of that dark secret in his past. The boy and Colin were devoted to each other, and Duncan always thought of the youngster as Colin's son.

* * *

When he was summoned to Mary's shop late one afternoon it didn't occur to him that there might be something wrong. He hovered in the doorway, waiting until her customer had gone, uneasy in this feminine haven. When the woman left, he stepped out into the street to let her by, and re-entered the doorway to see his sister-in-law whisk a cloak about her shoulders.

'I'll not be long,' she told her assistant, and hurried Duncan back onto the footpath.

'What fine new idea have you got in your head now?' he asked indulgently.

'None, as yet – but I wish I had, for it's going to take brains to get us out of this pickle,' Mary said crisply. 'I was at the Poor's Hospital two hours since, and I met a woman there who claims to be Colin Todd's wife.'

'Lizzie?' Duncan stopped short and she almost bumped into him. A hand caught at his heart and began to squeeze it painfully. He felt the colour ebb from his face. 'You're certain?'

Irritation touched her voice. 'I spoke to her. She told me enough to make me believe her, for all that I've never set eyes on the woman myself. In fact, she told me more than I'd like my poor sister to hear, Duncan Montgomery!'

A red mist clouded Duncan's vision and he wondered if he was going to succumb to apoplexy. 'Oh God! Dear God!'

'Well might you call on Him for help – though I doubt if it'll do you a lot of good.' His sister-in-law's eyes raked his face. 'No need to ask if she was telling the truth or just trying to make mischief between you and Meg. The guilt's written on your face for anyone to see. Duncan, Duncan – who'd have ever thought you'd be such a fool!'

'What does she want?' he asked, sick with apprehension, his thoughts filled with Meg and the need to keep this from her.

'She has it in mind to take back her old position as Colin's wife. She arrived late last night, it seems, with nothing but the rags on her back. She's in a sorry state. Lucky for you she went to the hospital instead of going straight to Peter's house.' Mary wagged her bonneted head. 'A right hornets' nest she'll stir up if she gets her way. But I got her to promise that she'd stay where she was for the moment – if I bring you to see her.'

'The bitch!'

'I told her that Peter's ailing and the shock of seeing her's like to kill him. I said nothing more. Not a word about Colin or the laddie. Not that she asked about them – just about you. I don't care how you do it, Duncan, but you'll have to get that woman away from Paisley before Colin finds out about her.'

The Poor's Hospital was a large building not far from Mary's shop. Homeless and penniless townsfolk found refuge within its walls; the children were schooled, the women set to wash and cook and keep the place clean, and work was found for the men and the older children whenever possible. Duncan shivered as he followed Mary through its big doors and across the hall, past faces blank with misery and despair.

The mistress greeted them in a small bare room on the ground floor. She raised an eyebrow when Mary asked to see Lizzie, but said nothing. Fortunately, she was a comparative stranger in the town, and it didn't occur to her to connect the new inmate, who gave her name as Lizzie Todd, with the prosperous and respectable Paisley family of that name.

Duncan paced the small room, four steps one way, four steps

the other, while he waited. He had thought that Lizzie was out of his life forever, had never dreamed that after all this time she would return to haunt him like a malignant ghost.

Mary sat motionless on a hard upright chair, watching him but keeping her own counsel.

'You're thinking of the terrible thing I did, betraying Meg,' he blurted out at last.

'Men can do awful daft things. I take it that she never knew the truth of it?'

He shook his head. 'And she never will, supposing I've to—' He broke off as the door opened, the colour leaving his face then rushing back as he stared at the woman standing before him.

Lizzie came into the room slowly, eyes downcast and hands clasped in the same pose she used to adopt when standing behind the shop counter. Then she looked up and he saw that her once pretty face was gaunt, her hair lifeless and threaded with grey, her almond eyes set deep in shadowy sockets. She was a cruel parody of the girl who had lain beneath him among the little white flowers on the moors. But her boldness, as she looked him up and down, was unchanged.

'Well, Duncan Montgomery? You're a welcome sight.'

'It's you right enough, Lizzie. I never thought to set eyes on you again.'

'Oh? So it was good riddance to bad rubbish, was it?' Her laugh was harsh, mocking. 'Are you not glad to see me after all those years?'

'I never wished to look on you again, Lizzie – and well you know it!'

'Mebbe – and mebbe not.' She twitched a shoulder in a faintly coquettish gesture he remembered. It was as though some ragged crone was slavishly copying the mannerisms that had belonged to the young, vivid Lizzie. It was grotesque, and Duncan's skin crawled.

'I hear Peter's unwell.' Neither of them paid any attention to Mary, who stayed where she was, silent for once, watching this reunion of former lovers with bright, unblinking eyes.

'He is, and you'll do him no good at all by turning up again. Besides, Kirsty would scratch your eyes out of your head for what you did to Colin and the bairn.'

Her tongue flickered over cracked lips. 'I'm still Colin's wife.'

'Stay away from him, Lizzie! He's happy now – he's more of a man than you ever let him be!'

'Since he's become a man, let him speak for himself!' she flared at him. 'And there's my son. I have a right to see him, have I not?'

A churning, sick feeling stirred in Duncan's belly. 'You cared nothing for him when he was little and helpless. Why should you see him now?'

'Because he's nearing an age when he can go out and work for his own keep.' Mary spoke for the first time, and Lizzie whirled on her with a movement full of grace despite the rags she wore.

'I have the right to take him away with me if I choose!'

'You have no rights!' Duncan's voice was a low hiss. 'Colin raised that boy, not you. He's the one to say what becomes of William.'

Lizzie's teeth, discoloured and broken, showed in a sneer. 'So he thinks. Mebbe it's time he learned that it's you and me that have the say in the lad's future, not him. After all, it was you and me that made William, Duncan!'

Her shoulders were brittle beneath his hands. Even in his anger he was careful not to grip her too tightly, aware that he could so easily crush and snap those fragile bones beneath his fingers. Instead, he shook her hard.

'You ever say that again to a living soul, and by God, Lizzie Todd, I'll spill your blood! If you try to see Peter or Colin or the boy, I'll take you out onto the moors where it all started and wring your neck! Who's to care if you're found lying in a burn one morning?'

She swayed within his grip, her eyes wide and bright, her open mouth uttering little whimpering sounds. But she didn't try to break his hold on her. It was Mary who caught at his wrists and tore him away from the other woman.

'For any favour, Duncan, d'you want to get yourself hanged?'

He let go and Lizzie almost fell. She recovered her balance by catching at the back of a chair, the faint little enigmatic smile he remembered playing round her thin mouth.

At the sight of it, and the gleam in her knowing grey eyes, despair choked Duncan. She had won. Now he must pay for the years of foolish complacency. If the two women hadn't been there he might have sunk down on the floor and given way to tears.

'Why don't you go ahead, Duncan?' Lizzie asked, her voice suddenly young and sensuous, with a provocative lilt to it. 'Why don't you put me out of my misery and get yourself hanged? I'm not the only one who betrayed folk, am I? You're no better than I am, if the truth be known!'

'God damn you, Lizzie Todd!'

'He's done that already.'

'Lizzie, what would you take to keep your mouth shut and leave Paisley?' Mary asked briskly, and the other woman laughed.

'You'll not get me away as easy as that. If it was money I wanted, d'you not think I'd have asked for it long since?' Lizzie mocked. 'It's been a long lonely road for me. I want companionship. I want to be cared for. I want Colin – or the boy – or you, Duncan. It's up to you to decide which it's to be.'

If Mary hadn't stood her ground between them, he would

have killed Lizzie there and then and be damned to the consequences. Instead, he stood helplessly by, fists knotting and unknotting, while Mary forced a reluctant promise from Lizzie to keep her mouth shut and stay where she was until the next morning. Then Duncan was hustled out into the street where he gulped the fresh evening air in.

'She's safe until the morning, and we've got time to think about what's to be done. Say nothing and do nothing until you see me again,' Mary ordered. 'There has to be a way out of this without breaking innocent hearts.'

'You heard her – you saw her! The woman's evil! She's hell-bent on destroying lives the way hers has been destroyed.' He ran a big hand over his face. 'I'll have to go with her, out of the town, then—'

'Leave her body in a ditch and end up swinging from a rope? You've not got the sense to escape a hanging,' his sister-in-law said scathingly. 'Listen to me – I'll visit the woman again first thing in the morning, and it's my guess that by then she'll be willing to take enough money to keep her for a while and get out of the town. Away home, Duncan Montgomery, and not a word of this to Meg. Come along to the shop first thing tomorrow and we'll see what can be done. Go on, now!'

He went, shambling along the street instead of walking with his usual confident gait. Watching him, Mary sighed and shook her head.

* * *

Duncan couldn't face Meg right away. He wandered into a howff near the Cross and sat alone in a corner with only a jug of ale for company. By the time he was accosted by a well-known voice, the level of the jug had lowered considerably and he was finding it hard to focus. He peered blearily up at Matt Todd through the howff's smoky atmosphere.

The soldier lowered his big frame onto a stool at the other side of the table. 'Everyone's round at our house having a grand wee gathering. I told Meg I'd look for you.' He winked. 'She's none too pleased because you never came home from your loom.'

Duncan tried to say something but the words came out as a slurred mumble.

'By God, she'll have something to say when she sees you like this—' Then Matt took a closer look and his expression changed. 'Come to think of it, I've never seen you in such a state myself. What's amiss, man?'

Duncan couldn't keep his misery and worry to himself for a moment longer. His tongue seemed to start wagging of its own accord while one part of his brain, the sober part, stood by, unable to stop the flow of words.

As Matt heard him out, one expression after another moved across his face, but Duncan was too steeped in his own misery to notice the other's reaction.

'What in God's name am I to do?' he finished wretchedly. 'How am I to tell Meg?'

'Listen to me—' Matt leaned across the table, his voice low and urgent. 'You're in no fit state to do anything tonight. Go on home and I'll see to Lizzie for you.'

'But I must tell Meg before—'

'You tell Meg and I swear I'll give you a hiding from one end of the town to the other! Do as Mary says and hold your tongue until you see her tomorrow. Come on, I'll help you on your way.'

Duncan shook his head. 'I can... I can manage to walk to my own door,' he said with dignity, heaving himself to his feet. Then he clutched at the table as his knees sagged.

Matt dragged him upright again and half-carried him outside, where the fresh air set Duncan's head reeling. With some difficulty the two of them made their way to Townhead, and Duncan was snoring loudly almost as soon as Matt dropped him into his bed.

The soldier looked down at him thoughtfully. 'Man, Meg'll go berserk when she sees you!' he murmured, then let himself out of the house again.

It was still only mid-evening when he presented himself at the hospital and asked for Lizzie. When she found him waiting for her in the little ground-floor room she stopped abruptly in the doorway, her almond-shaped eyes widening.

'So – you're home, are you?'

'Aye. You didn't think to see me, did you, Lizzie?'

She smiled faintly. 'No more than you thought to see me. I'm glad you came—' she looked about the room and the smile deepened mockingly '—calling on me.'

'Do you have to stay here?' The place depressed him, made him feel shut in.

'We can go out, unless it shames you to be seen with me.'

He ignored the teasing lilt in her voice. 'I know of a place where we could talk in peace.'

She shrugged, then fetched a worn cloak and they went out into the darkening streets together. Silently he led her to a tenement building by the river and she waited by his side as he paid the landlady for the use of a small room. He left Lizzie there and went out to buy some ale. When he returned she had managed to light the fire and was huddled beside it, fingers spread out to the flames.

'It's cosy in here.' She reached for a mug with a work-roughened hand and drank greedily.

'Duncan tells me you want to see Colin.'

Lizzie tossed her head. 'I'm still his wife.'

'You're no wife to him, for all the church service you went through together. You gave up the right to call yourself wife the day you walked out on him – a helpless cripple! It damned near killed him – do you know that?'

She smiled, her lips wet with ale. 'Did it? So we both nearly killed him, didn't we, Matt?'

The force of the blow threw her off her chair. She sprawled on the floor, one hand to her face, staring at him. He stood where he was, making no move to help her, and at last she got up and poured out more drink to replace the ale that had spilled.

'D'you think I'm not used to that sort of treatment? It makes no difference, Matt,' she said vindictively. 'You and that horse race took my man from me, and I couldn't settle after that. I'm not the sort of woman who could love a cripple.'

'Because you've never cared about anyone but yourself, you evil bitch!'

Lizzie's eyes flared, then dulled. 'Think that if you want.'

'What else is there to think? First you tried to tempt me, then you fastened on poor Duncan. You'll not cause any more mischief in this town, Lizzie. Leave them alone!'

She laughed, emboldened by the warmth of the drink in her belly. 'What can you do to stop me?'

'You're not dealing with Colin and Duncan now,' he said quietly. 'I'm not a gentleman – so be warned.'

She spat a sulky curse at him, drained the mug and made for the door. He reached it before her.

'Get out of my way, Matt Todd!'

'No, Lizzie!' He grabbed her arm, swung her bodily away from the door and against the damp wall. 'I've had a debt to settle with Colin since the Silver Bells race and now's my chance to pay it. If you try to see him, or get word to him that you're in Paisley, I'll kill you, Lizzie.'

'You're the second to make that threat today.' Her voice was scornful, but a tensing of her body and a sudden heat in her smoky eyes told him that she was keenly aware of his nearness as he held her against the wall.

'I could scream for help.'

It was his turn to mock. 'Lassie, in this building, who'd pay any heed to you? The folk who live here have no wish to call the militiamen's attention to their doings. They know when to turn a deaf ear.'

He was right. In the ramshackle hovels by the river, pimps and prostitutes and thieves plied their trades in safety. Nobody would pay attention to a woman's screams, and Lizzie knew it. She let herself go limp and he caught her as she slipped down the wall, holding her to him with an arm about her waist. She tried to push away from him, then suddenly her clawed hands were in his hair, her thin body pressed against him with an animal urgency.

'Matt! Oh, Matt—' she said breathlessly. 'Before Colin, and all the time I was married to him, it was you. It was always you I wanted, Matt!'

'Damn you!' said Matt, and released her. She held on fiercely, wrapping her arms about him, pressing herself against him.

'Kill me, if that's what you want to do! Kill me and get it over with! I'd as soon die at your hand as live without you!'

He gripped her arms and she gasped as his fingers bit deep. He looked at the gaunt face just below his, and was suddenly, painfully reminded of the lovely, tantalising girl he had courted long ago, the girl he had left behind when he joined the army.

There was a tense pause, then 'Will I never be free of you, you

Jezebel!' groaned Matt, and dragged her down onto the floor with him.

Their coupling was vicious, an act of hate instead of an act of love. On Lizzie's side there was a deep thirst to be quenched, and revenge for the bitterness of his rejection years before: on Matt's there was all the resentment man had ever felt against woman's ability to tempt and wreak havoc.

Daylight was trying to force its way through the grimy little window before the two of them fell away from each other and slept, exhausted, on the rough wooden planks.

8

When Lizzie opened her eyes the fire was a pile of cooling ashes and Matt was dressing quickly and silently.

'Where are you going?' She raised herself on one elbow, pain stabbing through her bruised body.

'Out of this place.'

'Take me with you—' She began to scramble to her feet. 'I'll follow the regiment – I don't care where. I'd be true to you, Matt, only you—'

But he shook his head vehemently. 'I'd as soon walk with Old Nick himself as with you. And you'd best mind what I told you – keep away from my brother and from the Montgomerys!'

She caught at his sleeve. 'Matt, don't go!'

His face was bleak as he looked down at her. Overnight, new lines had chiselled themselves downwards from the corners of his mouth. 'You wanted me to lie with you when your own man was helpless. You left him and went off with someone else. You're a whore, Lizzie, and last night I used you as a whore. I used you because I wanted to show you what you are. And if you go near Colin or anyone else in Paisley, I'll see to it that they all know what happened between us in this room.' There was triumph mingled with contempt in the look he gave her. 'Colin might have taken you back yesterday – but now he'd not dirty his hands on you!'

Without realising what she was doing she reached up with one broken-nailed hand and drew her torn, dirty gown about her throat in a defensive, feminine gesture. 'That's why you brought me here?'

'Just that. D'you think it gave me pleasure to touch you?' he asked bitterly. 'I felt sick! But I had to do it for Colin's sake.'

Her mouth writhed, cursed him, spat on him. He dug into his pocket and tossed some coins on the floor at her feet.

'I'm a generous man – I pay for favours received.'

Silenced, her venom spent for the moment, she gathered the money then straightened again, her eyes fixed on his face. He hesitated at the door, then stripped his jacket off and tossed it at her.

'It's cold outside,' he said, and went out.

* * *

The chill morning air struck through Matt's shirt sleeves as he strode away from the building without a backward glance. Deep in his body a familiar pain gnawed. It was a hunger that had wakened in him when he first began walking out with Lizzie all those years ago, a wanting that only her sensuous, insatiable body could ease. But the military way of life had also demanded his attention, and it had won.

During all the time Lizzie was his brother's wife, Matt had subdued his desire. Now, when it should have been sated, it burned within him. No other woman had ever been able to rouse him as Lizzie could. Even now, dirty and half-starved as she was, he wanted her. But because she was his brother's wife, and because of what she had done to Colin, he must turn away from her and suffer his own torment in silence.

He hunched his shoulders and walked to his father's house, his eyes fixed on the ground as he went.

* * *

By the time Mary called at the hospital, Lizzie was back.

'Now then – I've been thinking about you, Lizzie, and it seems to me that you'd be better taking charge of your own life than hanging on to some man's coat-tails—' the milliner began briskly, and was interrupted.

'You can forget about the sermon, Mistress MacLeod.' Lizzie sneered the name. 'I've decided that I've no more wish to live among the self-righteous mealy-mouthed Paisley folk than I had before.'

Mary gaped, taken aback for once by the sudden change in Lizzie, then noticed the good warm jacket, several sizes too large, about the other woman's shoulders.

'I've seen that before.'

Lizzie gathered it protectively about her. 'It's mine!'

'Oh aye?' Mary asked dryly, then got down to business. 'You've decided to go back to the man you went away with the last time?'

'Him?' Lizzie spat out a curse. 'I'd die before I'd go back to him!'

'So you've finally found the way of the world? Women are daft if they let their happiness depend on a man.'

'From what I've heard, you managed to find a prize for yourself.'

'Andra's a good husband.' Mary refused to be baited. 'But I

had my independence long before we wed, and I can look out for myself if need be. Any woman with her head fastened on properly can do the same. Look at the way you worked in the shop – you could turn your hand to shopkeeping again, could you not?'

'If I had to,' Lizzie admitted grudgingly, her eyes suspicious.

'Tuts, it's not a case of having to, it's a case of wanting to. You've no need of Colin or William to buy your bread for you, and you know that fine. You can earn your own living.'

'With nothing to my name but these?' Lizzie indicated the clothes she wore.

'You've got two good hands, and a brain of your own. I started my business with the help of Andra's first wife, and with a lot of hard work on my own account. If you're willing to put in the work I'd mebbe be prepared to put up some money – as a loan, just.'

It was Lizzie's turn to gape. 'And what's to stop me making off with your precious money?'

'I'd set the militia after you if you did. But I doubt if you'd be that daft. Listen to me – Andra has good business friends in Dumfries. If I was to give you a letter of introduction to them, and some decent clothes and money to get you there and give you a start, you could take a wee shop and set up in business for yourself. Mind you, I'd be looking for my money back. But if you put your mind to it there's no reason why you shouldn't pay off the debt in a few years, the same as I did myself.'

It was a gamble, but during the long night, while Lizzie and Matt writhed together on the floor of the dingy room by the river, Mary had carefully thought over everything she had ever heard about Colin's wife, and had gradually uncovered a pattern similar to her own nature.

True, Lizzie had been selfish and cruel, but Mary recognised her intelligence and determination, and felt that it was high time those qualities were appealed to.

She waited patiently as doubt, suspicion and bewilderment chased each other across Lizzie's drawn face.

'You're willing to risk a lot just to buy safety for Colin and your sister's man.'

'I'm not overly concerned with them,' Mary scoffed. 'I'm thinking of what's best for everyone, including you, for you'll not let anyone here rest easy until you're settled, Lizzie. If you agree to my proposition we'll go right now to my house and I'll give you a decent breakfast. Then we'll go to Glasgow to buy some clothes and get a legal acquaintance of mine to make out a proper business agreement between us. But if you're set on going to hell in your own way—' Mary rose and went to the door '—I'll bid you good day right now.'

She put a hand on the latch.

'Wait—' Lizzie said from behind her. 'I'll come with you.'

'I knew you were a woman with a good head on your shoulders,' said Mary, and led the way out of the little room.

* * *

Duncan's head pounded from the night's drinking and from the tongue-lashing Meg had given him when he finally woke, wincing as daylight splintered into his eyes. Although he hazily remembered promising to see Mary before doing anything else, he hurried along to the hospital as soon as he could escape from Meg.

His blood ran cold when he discovered that Lizzie had gone. He recalled meeting Matt the night before and telling him about Lizzie and her threats. What if the soldier had killed her to protect his brother?

With visions of Lizzie floating in the River Cart passing through his befuddled mind, Duncan ran to Mary's house. She came into the entrance hall to talk to him, closing the parlour door carefully behind her.

'Get back to your loom and hold your tongue,' she ordered before he could speak. 'The matter's settled and there's no need for you to stay here.'

'But—'

Mary almost pushed him out into the street. 'Duncan, will you go away? Lizzie and me are coming to an arrangement. She'll be out of Paisley shortly, when she's broken her fast.'

'You mean she's here?' he yelped, suddenly realising why the parlour door had been closed so firmly behind Mary.

'Aye, she's here. Now – you can either stay and ruin all my hard work or you can get back to your loom and thank the Lord you've got a friend like me with all her wits about her. I'll tell you about it when I've got the time.' And she shut the door with a decisive slam.

Totally confused, but weak with relief, he slunk back down the hill to the loom shop. He had to wait until late in the afternoon before Mary came to the High Street house and gave him a brief outline of her talk with Lizzie, ending with: 'So she's away, fed and clothed and looking more like her old self already, the poor soul.'

'It's not right that you should have to put your hand in your pocket on my behalf. I've some money put by that Meg knows nothing about—'

'Tuts, I didn't just do it for you! There's Colin to think of, and Lizzie herself. And if you're able to put anything by without my sister's knowledge then she's failing in her proper duties,' Mary said dryly. 'Don't you go offering me a penny of it or I'll feel bound to tell her you've got it.'

She went to the door, paused, and returned. 'Duncan – you

didn't go back to the hospital last night to talk to Lizzie on your own, did you?'

'D'you think I could have faced her again? No, I got as drunk as a lord and Matt had to help me home,' he admitted, embarrassed.

'Matt?' Her voice sharpened. 'Did you tell him?'

Duncan's shame deepened. 'As I mind it, I did. But you've no need to be feared of Matt. He'd never speak a word of this to Colin or anyone else.'

Mary's face was suddenly blank. 'I'm sure you're right. See that wee bit of money you were bragging about a minute since? Mebbe you should use it to buy Matt a new jacket. Something tells me he could do with one,' she said, and opened the door.

'Eh? Jacket?' Duncan spluttered, but Mary had gone.

Women! he thought. He'd never understand them, especially his wife's sister.

***

Duncan's prediction that silk gauze would become an important industry in Paisley came true, but Peter Todd only lived to see the first hint of it. One April night in 1760 he died in his sleep, and was laid to rest in the family plot beside his first wife and his infant son.

Colin was a rock for Kirsty to lean on in the first grief of widowhood. Often, after the children were in bed at night, she took to sitting in the downstairs room with her stepson, soothed and comforted by the calm presence that reminded her so much of Peter.

Matt was like a lost soul the first time he came home after his father's death.

'It's as though the heart's gone out of the town,' he told Meg miserably. 'Everywhere I look I expect to see him. But there's nothing – nothing.'

Duncan, much as he yearned to get looms into his own shop, agreed to stop on and run the Todds' weaving shop for Kirsty. Jamie had finished school and had become an apprentice at the looms, though Duncan confided to Meg that the boy wasn't cut out for the work.

'He's more like Matt than anyone. He's restless. He only started his apprenticeship to please Peter. Mind you, I think he'll see it through for Kirsty's sake, but he'll likely be off as soon as he can.'

'Kirsty's got more sense than to hold him against his will, surely?'

There was no reply.

'Duncan!' She tweaked a corner of the newspaper clutched in his fists. 'Come out from behind that paper and let me have a proper talk with you! You've surely heard all the news already?'

The Paisley men usually stopped work and got together to read the paper as soon as it went on sale. Items from all over the globe interested them deeply; in Paisley they knew more about the world's affairs than most working folk in Britain.

'I like to go over it again when I'm on my own.'

Meg laid her sewing down in her lap. 'Do you indeed? And are you not glad I bullied you into learning how to read all those years ago? Where would you be without me – tell me that?'

'Aye, I suppose I didn't get a bad bargain the day I picked you,' he said casually, then yelled as the paper was whipped out of his hands by his exasperated wife.

* * *

Paisley became the acknowledged centre of silk gauze manufacture. The town's weavers could match anyone when it came to texture, quality and cost, and by the end of the year it was quite common for the local people to hear English voices in their streets as more and more London merchants sent representatives north to open up new branches. There was work for all, and the looms in the surrounding villages were pressed into service for the Paisley manufacturers.

Over the next two years Duncan at last got his own looms installed. For Kirsty's sake, he continued to spend most of his working day in the Todds' shop, employing a reliable weaver to supervise the looms in his own shop.

Robert and William both put in a year at the new grammar school, then were apprenticed, Robert to a weaver, William to a cobbler. Margaret and Thomas were attending the English School, where they learned to read and write, and were taught grammar and geography.

Thomas, who in his mother's words 'soaked up learning like a cloth in a bucket of water', found his schooling quite inadequate, and persuaded his father to let him have extra tuition from Colin.

Although the space left by Peter's death was never quite filled they all adjusted, and life continued smoothly.

'We're like a sack of barley,' Margaret said to William. 'Poke your finger in it – if my mother isn't looking – and when you take your hand away the grain flows back into the space as though it had never been there at all. We do that. We smooth over things and it's all the same again. Well, almost.'

'Except that my grandfather wasn't a finger in a sack of barley,' he said stiffly, then relented. 'But I know what you mean.'

She smiled at him. William was different from the others. He never laughed at her high-flown ideas or belittled her. She slid her hand into his and squeezed his fingers affectionately.

The sense of injustice she had first known when she demanded of her mother at Mary's wedding, 'Why do rich people have houses that are too big for them?', strengthened as she grew older.

Margaret could never accept a system that decreed that some folk lived in poverty while others enjoyed wealth, and as she grew into her teens she was often to be found at the town hospital in Sneddon Street, taking the inmates scraps of food saved from her own meals or warm clothing that she and her brothers had outgrown. Her parents approved of her sense of responsibility towards others, but they had to draw the line when her enthusiasm reached the stage where both shop and house were being raided regularly.

'Colin'll be wondering what's happening to his profits,' Meg protested.

'And if much more goes from this house you'd be as well to move us all to the hospital so that we can enjoy our own possessions,' Robert added scathingly. So Margaret had to rein her generous nature in a little, though she continued to beg and coax unwanted items from all her friends. Margaret always knew of some poor soul in need.

When one of the young hospital inmates was expelled for giving birth to a bastard child, it was Margaret who fought on her behalf, storming into the building to confront the hospital mistress and master.

'I found Jenny in the street, crouched against the side of a house!' she accused them, while the shamed girl wilted beside her, clutching her baby. 'You can't just put her out like that. Where's she supposed to go? How's she to care for her baby?'

'The lassie's sinned in the eyes of the Lord and the community. Forbye, she tried to hide the truth from us. It's a hospital rule that she can't stay here!' the master said coolly. 'You've got a good heart, child, but it's a trifle misguided.'

The baby began to wail and Jenny's white, tear-streaked face crumpled. But Margaret was made of stronger stuff.

'Come on, Jenny.' She put an arm about the girl and marched to the door. 'We'll go to where folk care about other folk!'

Outside the big door she hesitated, baffled. A light patter of rain was falling, and Jenny did her best to pull a tattered shawl over the baby's head.

'We'll go to see my Aunt Mary,' Margaret decided, and the two of them made for the milliner's shop and a lukewarm reception.

'There's times when you vex me sorely, Margaret!' her aunt scolded. 'I might have had some lady in here buying a hat!' She covered her ears as the hungry baby's wailing filled the little shop.

'All the better,' said her unrepentant niece. 'The lady might have had a conscience and taken Jenny in. Since there's nobody here but you, Aunt Mary...?' She paused hopefully.

'You needn't think of my house, for Andra's not at all well at the moment and I'd lose the servants if I walked in with a crying bairn. Why not bother your own mother instead of me?'

'Because my father warned me the last time that there was to be no more of it, and it's too soon to change his mind. Please?' Margaret beseeched her.

Mary sighed and shook her head. 'What am I to do with you, girl?'

'It's what you're going to do with Jenny that matters,' Margaret rapped back at her.

'Well – Mistress Brown's a decent widow woman who's fond enough of bairns, and she could probably do with a hand in her wee shop,' said Mary, and so a refuge was found for Jenny and her child.

Not content with her success, Margaret dared to face one of the hospital directors in the street and take up the matter with him. The shocked man called on Duncan to complain about his daughter's impertinence.

'If we were all as irresponsible and as soft-hearted as your daughter, the hospital would end up as a refuge for all the feckless poor in the town!' he protested.

Duncan eyed him thoughtfully. 'Is that not what it was built for? She's mebbe hasty at times, and for that I apologise to you. But a wee bit of compassion for a young mother and her blameless child isn't entirely out of place, surely.'

The director's face flamed. 'It seems that you have no notion of the right way to care for paupers!'

'Mebbe not,' Duncan said shortly, suddenly sickened by the man's manner. 'I only know how to care for folk – and it's the same with my daughter. Now, sir, if you've said your piece, I've work to do.' And he pressed his foot firmly on the treadle and set the loom into noisy action, turning his broad back on the visitor.

When he went home later, he soundly rebuked Margaret for her impudence towards a member of the hospital board.

'I wasn't impertinent – I asked him in a civil manner how he'd feel if his own daughter had fallen like poor Jenny and was in need of compassion,' she protested.

'Mercy!' Meg's apron flapped over her reddening face. 'Margaret, how could you speak to a respectable gentleman in that fashion?'

'See here, Margaret, if you're going to defend folk, you'll have to learn to do it with a smile and a soft word,' Duncan said patiently. 'That way you'll get more out of others without them realising it.'

He was soon to regret his words, for she took them to heart from that day on and redoubled her efforts to help others. When she left school she worked in the shop and helped Meg in the house. She was a deft spinner, and as thread was sorely needed to fill the eight looms under Duncan's care she persuaded him to employ some of the hospital women as spinners.

'She's a nuisance at times, but apart from that,' said Mary smugly, 'the girl's got a lot of my nature in her.'

Duncan sighed and nodded. 'That's what worries me,' he said – but he said it very quietly, so that his sister-in-law couldn't hear him.

* * *

Margaret bustled down the length of the hospital sickroom, her blue eyes scanning each bed as she passed. She stopped here and there, to pull a blanket round someone's shoulders, to soothe a fretful child, to hold a cup of water to dry lips.

She reached the end of the room and was about to turn back to the door when her attention was caught by a man tossing in a corner bed.

'Billy? Is it you, Billy?'

She approached the cot cautiously, wondering if she was only imagining a resemblance between the big, cheerful chapman who visited her parents each time he was in Paisley and the flushed, delirious creature twisting and turning between coarse grey sheets.

The sick man looked at her without any recognition for a moment, then his glazed eyes managed to focus and his lips twisted into a faint smile.

'Wee Maggie Montgomery! Lassie, it's good to see a friendly face.' His voice was harsh with fever. 'Would... would you fetch some water? I could drink the Cart dry if I just had the energy to crawl to it.'

The jug by his cot was empty. Margaret sped out of the room and was back in no time with water, then she supported Billy's shoulders while he drank greedily. Her hands felt scorched by the heat from his big body. When he had slaked his thirst she helped him to lie back on the mattress.

'What brought you to this place?'

Billy's head moved fretfully from side to side. 'Just a foolish chill that wouldn't leave me. A few days' rest and I'll be right again.'

Margaret looked about the cheerless room, listened to the cries and moans of the sick. 'This is no place for a man who wants to recover.'

'Where else would I go? No use staying at my usual lodgings if I can't fend for myself. All I need's a bed and shelter till the fever breaks—'

A fit of harsh coughing tore at his chest and Margaret took a linen square from her pocket and wiped the sweat from his face. Then she waited patiently while he struggled to get his breath back.

'So now it's you tending to me?' he said hoarsely when he could speak again. 'The years go by too fast. Mind that day I found you down at the Cross, out of your mind with fear, and I carried you back to the shop on my shoulders? Remember it, Maggie? The day your brother took you to see that old man's hanging.'

'I remember.' It had been buried deep in her mind, only surfacing occasionally in nightmares. She forced her mind to reject memories of the sight she had seen at the Cross that day, and concentrated instead on the kindness shown to her by the man lying in the cot. 'I remember, Billy,' she said gently.

'By God, you near burst my ears with the noise you were

making.' He managed a faint chuckle. 'I wish my lungs... were as good as... yours were that day—'

His eyes closed and his voice died away. Margaret stared down at him, troubled.

When she left the hospital, William was waiting for her outside, as he often did. She poured out Billy's story as the two of them walked through the busy streets, ending with: 'I think he's awful sick, William!'

'I'll ask Aunt Kirsty to visit him tomorrow. She'll know what's best for him.'

'Yes – do that,' she said with relief, smiling up at him as they stopped outside her parents' door. Margaret was quite tall but William was a good head taller, lean and lithe and always dependable. 'He looks awful sick.'

He had an attractive, crooked grin that lit up his grey eyes. 'Don't fret yourself, just leave things to her. Will you go walking on the braes with me tomorrow?'

'Come to the shop when you're finished work, and if I can be spared I'll go. But don't be hammering any more fingers, or your work'll never get done!' She indicated his left hand with its bandaged index finger. He was learning his trade the hard way, and the number of times he arrived home with bruised fingers made him the butt of everyone's jokes.

The grin widened. 'Jamie says it's because I'm a dreamer. He says I'm handless.'

'You will be if you go on like that,' Margaret told him, and slipped into the house.

'Out with William Todd again?' Robert greeted her as she hurried in. Thomas sniggered, then turned it into a cough as he met his mother's eye.

Margaret looked down her nose at her brothers. 'I was at the hospital, as you well know. William walked home with me.'

'He always seems to walk home with you,' Robert scoffed. 'I'll wager he asked you to go up the braes with him – and you know what that means.'

Margaret flushed scarlet, and this time Thomas couldn't disguise his snigger. The braes beyond the town were popular with courting couples.

'You've got a bad mind, Robert Montgomery!'

'That's enough, the lot of you!' Meg ordered as her husband came in. 'Sit at the table and mind your manners!'

* * *

Later that night, when Meg and Duncan were getting ready for bed, she said thoughtfully, 'He's a nice lad, William Todd.'

'He's civil enough,' Duncan agreed.

'Margaret could do worse than marry with a decent young man like him.'

Duncan stopped in the act of taking his shirt off, his back to her. After a pause he said carefully, 'What nonsense is this you're talking now, woman?'

'It's not nonsense! They've always been fond of each other, William and Margaret – and it wouldn't be the first time childhood friends wed.'

'Are you serious?'

'You'd have noticed it for yourself if you'd taken the trouble to look,' Meg said with unfair scorn, for she herself had only just begun to wonder about a future romance between the young people.

'You're letting your thoughts run away with you!' Duncan said vehemently, and rolled into bed.

'Are you so old that you've forgotten what it's like to have an eye for a bonny lass?' she teased, but he hunched himself up, turning away from her.

'Margaret's too young for that sort of thing!'

'I didn't mean they were crying the banns already. There's plenty of time – but she's old enough to start thinking of her future.'

'Then she can look elsewhere, for I'll not have her throwing herself away on the likes of William Todd!'

'Duncan! He's an upright, honest lad who comes of fine stock!'

'He's not the right one for our Margaret!' His voice was muffled.

'But—'

'For God's sake, will you blow the lamp out and get to sleep!' he barked at her. 'I've got work to do in the morning, and no time to lie here and listen to your nonsense!'

Furious, she put the lamp out and thumped down onto the mattress with her back to him. She was soon asleep, but Duncan lay staring into the darkness, mortally afraid, not only for Meg and himself, but for his daughter. When dawn's grey fingers probed into the room and Meg stirred beside him, he had only slept fitfully, and had been plagued by bad dreams.

Swinging his feet to the cold floor, rubbing eyes that felt as though they were filled with dry grit, he swore to himself that from now on he would keep an eye on Margaret. And if necessary he would act to put a stop to her growing friendship with William Todd before things went too far.

9

Billy Carmichael's eyes lit up Kirsty arrived at his bedside on the following morning.

'It's good of you to come and see me, lass.'

Her eyes scanned his fever-ravaged face. 'I'm doing more than that,' she said flatly. 'I'm going away right now to arrange for a cart, then I'll get you well wrapped up and take you to my house till you're well again.'

"Deed you will not! You've got enough to do without taking a sick man into your home—'

'Wheesht, Billy,' she ordered. 'The matter's all settled. I'd not let a good friend like yourself stay here while there's room for you in my own house.'

His protests were ignored. Within the hour he was jolting painfully in the back of a cart to the High Street house. Between them Kirsty and Duncan managed to get him upstairs and he was soon in bed, with Kirsty spooning hot broth down his throat.

His recovery took longer than any of them had imagined. His feverish chill had already turned to pneumonia, and Kirsty had her hands full caring for him and tending her family. Thanks to her careful nursing he passed the crisis and found himself on the road to recovery, though as weak as a kitten. By the time he was on his feet again winter was coming in, and Kirsty steadfastly refused to consider his return to the road.

'D'you think I nursed you back to health just so you could get soaked through and catch another fever?' she wanted to know, hands on hips. 'Make up your mind to a winter spent under this roof, Billy, for you're not fit to go back on the road yet.'

He was secretly happy to give way to her, for the weeks spent under her roof had been a warm reminder of the domesticity he had known before the fever deprived him of his wife and children.

To pay for his keep he returned to his old trade as a cobbler, working in a corner of the weaving shop. At night he sat companionably on the opposite side of the fire from Kirsty, in Peter Todd's old chair, or spent long hours downstairs talking to Colin.

Kirsty was equally content with their arrangement. 'It's good to have a man about the house again,' she confided to Meg.

'No doubt. How's Kate faring?' Slim, red-headed Kate had just started work in a dressmaker's shop.

'She's doing fine. Time flies, does it not? I mind the day your Robert was born as if it was yesterday – and now they're all going out into the world. There's only Thomas left at school.'

'Aye – Thomas!' Meg laughed and shook her head. Still as round and rosy as he had been since babyhood, Thomas seldom had his nose out of a book. Most of his spare time was spent at Mary's house, where he was allowed to browse through Andrew MacLeod's library. His parents marvelled over his scholastic bent, while Robert and Margaret openly thought of him as the 'strange' member of the family.

'Margaret, now – she's a different problem altogether,' Meg went on slowly, and Kirsty saw a sudden shadow passing over her friend's face.

'What's amiss?'

Meg shrugged and drove her wheel faster. The two of them were alone in the Todds' kitchen, spinning thread for the looms below.

'It's Duncan. I don't know what's amiss with the man. He's like a cat on hot bricks every time he sees Margaret and William together – and you know as well as I do what close friends they've always been. What harm could it do if they decided to wed?'

Kirsty's hand, deftly guiding the strand of thread, stilled for a moment.

'Wed? You're not serious, Meg! Margaret's only just sixteen and William's less than a year older!'

'They're old enough to be thinking of marriage. I wouldn't be surprised if they came to the idea one day. They're fond of each other, and what would be wrong with a marriage between them? William's a fine lad. I can't think why Duncan's suddenly so set against him and Margaret seeing each other. He's started to go on at her, and the two of them are having terrible quarrels over the head of it.'

'That's the wrong thing to do,' Kirsty admitted. 'If Duncan's set against William, Margaret's just the sort of lassie to defy him.'

'That's my own view.' Meg shook her head. 'But why should he be opposed to the boy? William's never done anything amiss in his life – he's a credit to yourself and Colin. I don't know what's got into Duncan at all. He won't talk to me about it.' She sighed, her normally happy face clouded. 'I tell you, Kirsty, it's got me fair worried. I don't know where it's all going to end!'

* * *

Duncan himself came to Kirsty a few days later. He closed the trapdoor then paced the kitchen, his brows knotted with worry.

'Kirsty – I don't know how to begin. The Lord knows I've no wish to rake up the past—'

'Is it Margaret and William? Meg told me,' she said as he gaped at her. 'She can't understand what you've got against the two of them having an innocent friendship.'

'And she'll never know, please God.' He threw his hands out helplessly. 'It never entered my head until I heard Robert teasing her about him, then I realised that they're always together, these two.'

'They always were. It's no more than that, Duncan, and mebbe it'll never be anything else.'

'I can't take that chance, Kirsty! And I can't let them know the truth.' He slammed one fist into the other. 'If I'd had any sense at all, I'd have seen to it that they were kept apart from the beginning!'

'You couldn't have done that. All the bairns went about together.'

'I wish I'd never set eyes on Lizzie!' said Duncan for the hundredth time.

'Then you're wishing William away, and that's wrong, for he's a fine boy who's made Colin's life worthwhile.'

She paused, then said slowly, 'If you really think the pair of them'll have to be kept apart, Duncan, Colin must be brought into it.'

'No!'

'Have some sense, man! You know your Margaret as well as I do. Forbid her to see William and she'll fall in love with him just to spite you. And you'll have Colin thinking that his son isn't good enough for your daughter. You'll need his help, can you not see that?'

'It'll kill him!'

'Not now,' said Kirsty. 'He's strong enough and wise enough to take the truth and not let it make a whit of difference to the way he feels about William, at least. Leave it to me – I'll see to it.'

'It's my place to—'

'I know how to talk to him,' she said firmly. 'It has to be done right. How would you like to hear plump and plain from another man that he's your son's real father?'

'Don't make me feel worse than I do already, Kirsty!' he groaned.

'I doubt if anyone could do that.' Her tone was matter-of-fact, but her heart recognised his torment and wept for him. 'Now it's time you got back to your work, for it seems to me that there's more clacking from the tongues than from the looms down there. Go on with you, and leave Colin to me.'

* * *

Kirsty turned at the kitchen door to look at Billy, dozing by the fire, a newspaper in his lap. A faint smile touched her lips as she closed the door gently. It was good to see a man by the fireside again. Then the smile faded as she made her way downstairs. She had no stomach for what she must do now.

Colin was working by candlelight when she went into his room, transferring a finished design from rough paper to design sheet. A box of colours stood by his elbow. He looked up and smiled.

'Come away in and sit down. Give me a minute to finish this.'

Before him lay the design paper with a black-leaded page over it. On top he had laid the paper with the design sketched on it, and he was carefully going over the outlines with a blunt steel point. In spite of the furrows that his accident had engraved on his face, he was still youthful in appearance and his mop of fair hair was as thick as ever. At last he straightened up and grinned at her, a boyish grin that made him look very like his father and brother.

'I'll colour it tomorrow, then pass it over to Duncan.'

She looked at the simple but delicate pattern of leaves. 'It's bonny.'

'It's a special order. How's Billy coming on?'

'Well enough. He's talking of going back on the road now the weather's turning.'

'You'll miss him,' he said shrewdly, and she flushed.

'I suppose I will.'

He leaned across the table and put a hand on hers. 'Take my advice, Kirsty – keep him with you. Billy's a good man. He'd look after you.'

'Colin Todd!' she blustered, confused and embarrassed. 'I never thought to hear you black-footing like an interfering old woman!'

His grin widened. 'Black-footing's resulted in many a happy marriage. And I know a good match when I see one – where's the harm in putting in a word to help things along?' Then the grin faded. 'But that's not what you came to talk about. What's wrong, Kirsty?'

'D'you think I only come to see you when there's something wrong?'

'No, but you came in that door as if you had the cares of the world on your shoulders.'

Deftly he wheeled his chair round the table until he was beside her. One of the town's carpenters had designed and built the chair for him, and it was Colin's great delight to be able to move about his room, and even to wheel himself outside in good weather. It had taken a lot of skill to master the chair on rough footpaths, but he had persevered and succeeded.

'Tell me, Kirsty.' His voice was calm, reassuring. His hand touched hers, closed over it. Suddenly she found it difficult to meet his eyes.

'It isn't easy to speak of it—'

'Kirsty, when did you and me ever find it hard to talk to each other?'

She stared into the fire. 'Duncan wanted to see you himself but I'd not let him. It's William and Margaret – Duncan thinks they're getting too fond of each other. He thinks it should be stopped.'

His eyebrows climbed. 'You mean they might be falling in love?' he asked with genuine surprise, then laughed softly. 'And here was me thinking of William still as a bairn. God, Kirsty, the years go by too fast for comfort! But why should it bother Duncan? Is my son not good enough for his—'

He suddenly stopped and she looked up to see the animation ebbing from his face, leaving it strangely blank, like a page still to be written on. She started to say something but he lifted one hand sharply, the hand that had warmly covered hers.

'Wheesht now, Kirsty!' The voice was so like Peter's that she almost expected him to add, 'You're letting your tongue run away with you, woman!' as his father would have done. But when he finally spoke it was in his own quiet voice.

'Duncan? It was Lizzie and – Duncan?'

'What do you mean?' Her voice shook, out of control.

'Kirsty, the Silver Bells accident might have robbed me of the use of my legs, but it didn't affect my brain. D'you think you need to tell me anything about my wife that I didn't know already?

Lizzie thought she could keep her own counsel, but I always knew what was going on behind those strange eyes of hers. The only thing I didn't know till now was the man's name. All these years,' he said in wondering tones, 'I thought it was Matt.'

'Oh, Colin—' It was her turn to reach out and take his hand. 'Why did you never say anything? To keep such a secret—'

'It was no hardship,' he said swiftly, briskly, looking more like the old Colin. 'Don't go feeling sorry for me, Kirsty. I've got William and he's my son. I raised him, and I'm proud of him. But Duncan's right – the two of them'll have to stop seeing each other. Tell him I'll find something to say to the boy.'

'You should have told me!'

'What sense would there have been in that?' Colin asked her. 'I didn't know that you knew anything of it. It was Lizzie's secret and I'd not have betrayed her to anyone. Now—' he reached over and patted her hand '—off you go to your bed, Kirsty, and stop worrying. What's done is done. We'll say no more about it – none of us. You can tell Duncan that.'

She got up to go. 'What else d'you want me to tell Duncan?'

Colin smiled faintly. 'Nothing. We've been friends for a long time, him and me. It would be foolish to let a friendship go because of something that happened eighteen years ago.' Then the smile widened a little. 'Mebbe I should be grateful to him for the pleasure William's given me. Now go upstairs and let Billy tell you about the stories in his newspaper.'

She opened the door, then turned. Colin sat motionless in his chair, one finger absently tracing the new design. His head was bent, his hair golden in the candlelight. He looked up and saw her standing there.

'I'm glad it wasn't Matt,' he said.

* * *

When Kirsty fumbled her way upstairs in the dark and stepped into the kitchen Billy, who had just wakened, was shocked to see tears on her round cheeks.

'What's wrong? It's not Colin, is it?' He jumped to his feet.

'No, it's... just—' She went to him and his arms opened to take her. She sobbed on his broad comfortable shoulder and he held her close, stroking her hair, until the tears finally ceased.

Then gently, unsure of his reception but unable to deny the longing that had grown in him over the past weeks, he lifted her face to his and kissed her.

* * *

'But why?' William asked on the following day.

Colin's fingers tightened on the book in his lap.

'You're just an apprentice, and you're young. It's foolish for you to get too friendly with any girl just yet. Later on—'

'To hear you, anyone would think Margaret and me were talking of marriage!' William exploded incredulously. 'I just like her – she likes me – we get on together, that's all.'

'Are you certain?'

'You know Margaret Montgomery well enough! She's not like the other girls – she's not interested in getting wed and raising a family!'

'Still, it's best that you do as I say and leave it at that, William.'

'But why?'

Lamplight cast deep furrows on Colin's face. 'Mebbe you'd be wise not to ask me that again.'

'It's Duncan Montgomery, isn't it?' Bitterness sharpened William's voice. 'He doesn't think I'm good enough for his daughter!'

'It's not that, it's... for other reasons that don't concern you.'

'Don't concern me? You come between me and Margaret then you say the reason's not my concern?' The boy laughed without amusement then threw himself out of his chair towards the door in an awkward tangle of adolescent limbs. 'I'm going to see Duncan Montgomery. I'm going to make him tell me man to man what he's got against me!'

'No!' Colin's body, trapped in the wheelchair, couldn't move between William and the door, but his voice managed to stop the youth in his tracks. He swung round to stare at Colin, his eyes dark angry pools in a pale face.

'William, if you care at all for me and for what we've always been to each other, you'll agree here and now to do as I ask,' Colin said quietly. 'I swear to you that I'd not look for such a solemn promise if I could avoid it. But I can't. For my sake, William!'

And William, who loved his father more than anyone else in the world, gave his promise – against his better judgement.

* * *

It was some time before Margaret realised that William was avoiding her. She was kept busy with her shop duties and hospital visits, and of course Kirsty's betrothal to Billy Carmichael occupied all their minds.

'I thought we'd see it one of those fine days,' Mary said smugly as she sat in Meg's kitchen. 'Billy always had a soft spot for Kirsty, and she needs a man about the house.'

'She's got Jamie and Colin and William,' Margaret pointed out, and her aunt shot her a withering glance.

'I mean a man to be head of the house. Jamie and William are growing up, and Colin always kept himself to himself. Kirsty's the sort of woman who's the better for having a man around.'

'You make marriage sound the same as owning a dog,' Margaret said, to her aunt's amusement and her mother's embarrassment.

'Take that shocked expression off your face, Meg,' Mary ordered. 'The girl's more like me than you – she's got some fire in her. Now, what about the wedding bonnets?'

* * *

It was decided that Billy should take over Colin's room and turn it into a cobbler's shop. The looms were shifted from the Todd house to an empty weaving shop nearby and Colin moved into the loom shop where he had more space for his books and papers.

'Such a stramash – I wonder at times if it's worth it all,' Kirsty fluttered as she supervised the transfer of Colin's possessions.

Jamie flashed a huge grin at her as he staggered across the passageway, carrying one end of his half-brother's bed.

'Of course it's worth it.'

'Here – watch what you're doing and don't break the leg of that thing off against the door!' she shrieked, following them into the room. While the men struggled with the bed she stood alone, gazing round. Without the four big looms the apartment was vast and desolate.

'It's strange to see the shop so empty.' Her voice was suddenly tremulous. Her ears rang with the beat of the looms and the sound of Peter's deep, warm voice. She was grateful when Jamie put his arm about her and gave her a warm hug.

'The looms aren't far away, and Colin's carrying on the tradition in his own way, with his designing.'

'Aye.' Kirsty swallowed hard and smiled up at her tall son. Then her eyes travelled beyond his fiery head to the trapdoor linking the shop with her kitchen above.

'And I'll be able to call down to him whenever I want to,' she added, and Colin, catching the words as he manipulated his chair through the doorway, had the wit to smother his sudden apprehension before he caught her eye.

When the move was completed, William was despatched to fetch a jug of ale so that they could, in Kirsty's words, 'celebrate the wee flitting'.

Drink could be bought at the howff on the ground floor of the new Town House at the Cross. The upper part of the building consisted of the council chambers and offices, and the cells.

It seemed fitting that howff and cells shared the same building, for often enough the temporary inhabitants of the cells were men and women who had overindulged in drink, and it was a simple matter to whisk them upstairs to sleep off their stupor. Everyone thus incarcerated for the night was obliged to pay a fee of four pence – two pence for burgesses – to the jailer.

William had almost reached his destination when someone stepped into his path and Margaret's voice said lightly, 'Good evening to you, Mister Todd. Where might you be bound?'

Colour flamed into his face and he stepped back. 'Margaret! I'm just... just—'

'—Going for ale,' she finished the sentence for him, eyeing the jug in his hand. Then her clear gaze swept up to his face again. 'I haven't seen you for long enough, William.'

'There's been a lot to do at the house, moving the looms out and—' His voice died away and he moistened dry lips with the tip of his tongue.

'I hear Billy's taking you on as his apprentice. And I see you still have that habit of hammering your fingers as often as you hammer the shoes.' She reached out and touched his bruised thumbnail, then it was her turn to colour as he jerked his hand away from her.

'What's amiss?'

'Nothing.' He clutched the jug in both hands as though it was a shield between them. A puzzled frown drew Margaret's neat eyebrows together.

'When are you coming to the hospital again?' Then, as he stood silently before her, she asked with growing suspicion, 'Have you been keeping out of my way deliberately?'

'I'd not do that!' The words poured from him, and were checked. 'At least – I'd not want to!'

Her frown deepened. 'Then you've been told to stay away from me? Was it my father? You don't have to heed him, surely!'

William wished that the ground would give way beneath his feet and let him fall into whatever hell might be lurking under-ground. But the earthen path remained solid and Margaret's eyes were beginning to glint blue fire.

'I – Margaret, don't ask me to explain it, for I can't. It's just that – mebbe they're right, mebbe we were seeing each other too much—'

She gave a short, angry laugh. 'So that's the way of it, is it? You're scared folk might think I've got my cap set at you?'

'Margaret, listen—' It was his turn to put out a hand, with the intention of drawing her into a doorway out of sight while he explained. But she drew back sharply, avoiding his outstretched fingers. Hurt coloured her cheeks.

'Never mind – I'd not want to make a nuisance of myself. I'll wish you good day, Mister Todd – and if we never speak again I'll be well pleased!' she flared at him, then deliberately sidestepped into a pool of dirty water so that she could pass without brushing against him.

He watched her flounce away, back straight, well-shod feet slamming angrily on the path with each step. For the first time in his life he discovered that a heart could ache. He had lost her, and he didn't know why.

Miserable and confused, he stood for a long moment, clutching the empty jug, before turning towards the howff.

10

While Margaret began the long bitter process of struggling with hurt pride, life held few problems for her brothers. Robert, still serving his apprenticeship, had taken to weaving as easily as his father had. It was what he had been born to, and he loved the life.

Thomas, on the other hand, had no wish to take up weaving. Every time his father referred to the day when he would be apprenticed the boy winced inwardly. He loved books and studying, and he had already made up his own mind about his future. He lived in a perpetual dream, and only came to life at school, or studying with Colin Todd, or when he was in his Aunt Mary's house in Oakshawhill.

In the mornings before going to school, as he waited his turn to draw water at the street well, he would stand in a daze, his mind turning over something he had recently read, or memorising some homework. His blue eyes stared unseeingly at the tenements across the road while his lips moved soundlessly.

After school there were errands to run for his mother and then, if he didn't have a lesson with Colin, he was free to scurry up the hill to Mary's house, where there was always a welcome for him. His first five minutes or so were spent in the kitchen, where the cook fed him titbits, then he and Andrew MacLeod would have a deeply satisfying academic discussion in the library, after which they both selected books from Andrew's extensive collection and settled into comfortable chairs to read in contented silence.

Thomas didn't agree with his sister Margaret that big houses were sinful, nor did he share his mother's awe of Mary's home. He simply saw it as a treasure cave filled with literature and he wasn't in the least intimidated by its many high-ceilinged rooms.

When Mary came home from the shop the three of them had tea and then, if Thomas didn't have to hurry home, they all sat in the parlour, Thomas with his homework, Andrew reading or writing, Mary sewing, one or other of them making an occasional remark.

The childless MacLeods developed a genuine affection for Thomas. Mary and Robert got on well enough but saw little of each other. Margaret was so like her aunt in nature that they frequently sparked against each other, but Thomas's placid belief that everyone had a right to live as they pleased made him a relaxing companion.

'Your mother tells me you've had a good report from the school,' Mary said one evening, her needle flying deftly through the material in her hands. Thomas raised his head from the book on the table before him.

'It wasn't bad.'

'You'll soon be finished at the school.'

'Aye.'

'And taking your place at the looms, no doubt.'

There was a pause, then: 'I've no mind to be a weaver,' said Thomas. She raised her eyebrows at Andrew, who had looked up from his accounts.

'Indeed? And what does your father have to say about that?'

Thomas swallowed. 'He doesn't know yet.'

'Have you decided what you want to do with yourself, then?'

'Mister Paterson at the school says I could mebbe get a place in Glasgow Academy.'

'That would take money, laddie.'

'I know. But I'd work hard. I have it in mind to be a physician.'

Andrew dropped the pen he was holding and Mary's embroidery needle stabbed into her hand.

'Tuts, I think this thing's got a life of its own!' she said irritably, sucking the wound. 'A physician, did you say?'

'That would mean going to the university,' Andrew put in gently.

'Aye.' Thomas's dark blue eyes glowed in his round face.

'And that's what you're going to tell your father when the time comes?'

'Aye.' The glow dimmed somewhat.

'It's not just what he has in mind for you, Thomas.'

There was a mild warning in Andrew's voice, and the glow dimmed further.

'I know that,' said Thomas, and sighed heavily.

'Well—' Mary's voice was brisk '—you haven't read all those dry books of Andra's just for the sake of something to do, I'm sure. Plenty weavers read, but I've never seen one that eats books the way you do. You'd probably be too busy with your reading to turn out a decent piece of cloth. Your father'll surely see the sense of that.'

'I hope so,' said Thomas, but without much conviction.

Mary shot a quick glance at him and opened her mouth to say more, but a slight clearing of the throat from the writing desk where her husband sat cautioned her to close her lips again.

Andrew was one of the few people who could tell Mary when it was wise to hold her tongue.

'No sense in worrying the boy further – or raising his hopes,' he said when Thomas had gone clattering home in the warm summer evening. 'He's a clever lad, Mary – but he'd make a poor weaver, for sure.'

'Try telling Duncan that,' she said with a sniff, and Andrew looked at her thoughtfully.

'I'd not dare. It might come better from you. As I see it, my task is to keep my mouth shut and my purse at the ready,' he said; then, elderly and frail as he was, he endured his vigorous young wife's grateful kisses with both courage and pleasure.

* * *

Mary wasn't one to let an idea simmer for long. A few days later she found Meg and Duncan alone by their fireside and settled herself on a chair, untying her bonnet strings.

'Your Thomas wants to be a physician.'

'A what?' Their two faces stared at her.

'A physician. He has it in mind to go to the academy in Glasgow, then to the university to study. He doesn't want to be a weaver.'

'And just who—' Duncan began ominously, then collected his wits. 'Mary, it seems you know more about our son than we do.'

'I should, since he spends so much of his time with me and Andra. He's a fine boy, Duncan, and if you take my advice you'll let him have his head over the matter. Meg tells me he does well at the school.'

'Aye, but—'

'When did you hear this nonsense, Mary?' Meg could never

get used to her sister's habit of organising each and every one of the family without so much as a by-your-leave.

'Just the other day – and it's not nonsense. Thomas never wastes his time talking nonsense – you should know that yourself. Now, Andra and me've been discussing it, and it seems to us that we should see to the cost of it—' she held up a mittened hand as Duncan shot upright in his chair '—since we've no children of our own – Andra being too old and me being too busy anyway – and we're so fond of the boy.'

'Just a minute—' Duncan had rallied and begun to fight back. 'Before you say another word, Mary, I'd always had it in mind to make the lad a weaver, like Robert and myself.'

'I know that, but think about it for a minute. He'd be useless at a loom, for his heart's not in the work and you know better than I do that a weaver needs to be single-minded. Now, Duncan, you'd not want one of your lads to be in a trade he didn't enjoy, would you?'

'Mebbe not, but—'

'Mind you, he still has to prove that he's able, but I'm sure he can do it—'

'To hear you speak anyone would think he's about to open his own surgery already,' Duncan said sourly, and was ignored.

'—So when the time comes for him to go to the academy in Glasgow, and then the university—'

'The university!' Meg said faintly, and was also ignored.

'We'll pay what's necessary. It would be worth it to have a physician in the family.'

'Aye, that would get your nose in the air, would it not?' Duncan said meanly.

'Yours and all, when it comes to it, Duncan, yours and all. You don't have to mention this wee talk to him, by the way. Let him tell you himself when he feels that the right time's come. I'm just smoothing the way for him.'

She rose to leave, and Duncan made one last attempt to assert himself as the head of the house.

'Before you go, Mary – I'll remind you that I've not given my consent for this daft idea you and Andra have dreamed up between you. I'll have to – Meg and me'll have to give it our serious consideration, you understand.'

She smiled sweetly. 'You do that, Duncan. You think about it, and let me know what you decide.'

At the door she turned and beamed on them both again. 'It pleasures me to know that one of my own flesh and blood kin's to be a physician. We'll all be that proud of him!'

When she had gone they sat in a stunned silence for a while, Duncan carefully relighting his pipe, Meg lost in a happy dream. She agreed with Mary – it would be grand to have a physician in the family. But she knew that she daren't get excited about the idea until Duncan had had time to get used to it.

Finally he cleared his throat and spat into the flames.

'I know your sister's always right, Meg,' he said, almost plaintively, 'but does she have to be just as plump and plain about it every time?'

* * *

Margaret's pride wouldn't allow her to look for the reasons behind William's betrayal. Something had been knocked awry in her safe, happy world, and she coped with it by putting the blame squarely on William and slighting him whenever she got the opportunity.

Then her fortunes took a turn that swept William from her

mind. Mary was in the shop with Meg when Margaret burst in, eyes shining.

'The chaplain called me in when I was at the town hospital just now and – and I'm to be taken on to teach the children!' She grabbed Meg and waltzed her round, then collapsed onto a sack of barley. 'Every morning I've to go along and teach them their letters! Me – they asked me!'

'Oh... Margaret!' Meg clapped her hands to her flushed face, giggling like a girl, but Mary was unruffled.

'I don't see why you should look so surprised, Meg. The girl's the best person to ask, is she not? You'll be an asset to the place,' she told her niece warmly. 'I'm right pleased for you.'

Margaret picked up her apron then threw it down again, too excited to keep still. 'Can I go out for a while? There's so many things to think of—'

'Off you go – I can manage for an hour or two on my own.' Meg felt sudden tears at the backs of her eyes as she watched her daughter. It seemed only yesterday that she herself had been on the threshold of adulthood. But in her case it had been the prospect of marriage that brought stars to her eyes.

At the doorway Margaret stopped, darted back and hugged her mother then her aunt. 'I'll work hard – you'll see,' she said, and was gone.

The sisters smiled at each other when they were alone.

'It's good to see her happy again. For a while there she was awful downcast.' Meg shook her head. 'It doesn't take long for moods to change at that age.'

'Margaret's got the sense to know that bitterness is needed as well as sweetness to make life worth the tasting,' Mary said briskly. 'I'm glad she's found the sort of work that suits her temperament best.'

A sudden thought struck Meg. 'Mary, you didn't—?'

'Didn't what? Arrange the post for her? The very idea! Of course not!' Mary lied virtuously. 'Sometimes, Meg, you vex me sorely with your suspicions. You're getting as bad as that man of yours! You can just measure out the pound of meal I came in for, instead of standing there letting your imagination run away with you.'

* * *

Margaret was stifled by the crowded streets. Her feet scarcely seemed to touch the ground as they carried her towards the moors at the edge of the town; then she halted abruptly as William's tall lean figure stepped from a doorway ahead.

Her first instinct was to spin on her heel; she started the move, then checked it. She had to tell someone her news. Until recently she would have gone straight to William. Perhaps this was the time to forget disagreements and start anew—

But even as she began to walk towards him, William glanced up and saw her. His head ducked in an involuntary movement and he swung away, presenting his back to her.

Margaret stood where she was, a red tide surging over her neck and face. Jamie, perched on a passing cart, had to hail her twice before she saw him.

'D'you want to come up the braes with me and walk back down?'

'Yes!' It was just what she needed. He caught her upstretched hand and hauled her onto the cart where, sure-footed, she stood beside him on close-packed bales of linen, above the heads of the pedestrians. The cart lurched and Jamie's arm looped about her waist, holding her securely against him.

'Jamie – I'm to teach the children in the town hospital!'

'Teach them what?'

'Their letters, you daft loon! I'm to go in three mornings a week and – oh, Jamie, I'm going to teach them such a lot!'

As they left the town behind she dropped down onto the lumpy bales and closed her eyes tightly against the sun's light. Her lids seemed to be made of beaten gold. Beside her, Jamie was propped on one elbow, whistling tunelessly.

At the Bonnie Wee Well, where a spring gushed cold and clear from the rock face, the carter stopped and they scrambled down onto the grass. By the time the sun's dazzle had cleared from Margaret's eyes, the cart was disappearing over the slight rise that lay between them and the bleachfields.

She cupped her hands at the spring and drank its icy water, then rinsed her face and arms. Jamie drank his fill and wiped his mouth with the back of one hand.

Margaret opened her arms to the warm air and danced over the grass, twirling like a leaf in an autumn wind, her skirt twisting about her legs. Finally she dropped to the ground, laughing up at Jamie when he reached her.

'Aren't we lucky to be alive and living in a town as fine as Paisley?'

He sat down, arms clasped about his knees, staring down to where the smoke rose lazily from dozens of chimneys. 'You think so? There's a lot more to life than working a loom and going bowling or cock-fighting. The world's out there—' His hand swept the horizon. 'That's what I want to see.'

'Go for a soldier, you mean? Like Matt?'

'Mebbe. I don't know—' he said restlessly.

'Jamie, what would you do if you could do anything in the world?'

'I'd get onto a cart and ride until the horse was too tired to go any further,' he said promptly. 'Then I'd get another cart and another horse.'

She giggled. 'You could go all the way to the end of the world and come back if there were enough carts!'

'I might. I'd not mind coming back as long as I could say I'd seen the rest of the world.'

'Not me – I've got plenty to do right here.' She stretched her arms above her head. 'Oh, I'm so lucky!'

He looked at her, and saw that the sun had turned her hair into a halo about her pretty, happy face.

'And so bonny,' he said, then leaned forward and kissed her, his lips warm and hesitant on hers.

Sheer surprise made her heart skip a beat. As Jamie's lips left hers she stayed motionless, looking at him with startled eyes. Emboldened, he put his hands on her shoulders and kissed her again, a longer embrace this time.

She liked it – but even her first kiss had to take second place to the excitement the day had already brought her.

'Come on, Jamie.' She jumped up. 'We've got a long walk ahead of us and I've to get back to the shop.'

'Margaret, will you—' he began, but she had started running, and only the warm air heard the last few words '—walk out with me again?'

'Come on, Jamie!' She stopped at the foot of a slope, slipped her shoes off, and ran on without waiting for him, down the hill towards the town below.

* * *

The gathering held to celebrate Kirsty's wedding to Billy Carmichael gave proof to the boast that in 1763 Paisley's working class were the best dressed in the country. Most of the women had lace trimming to their vividly coloured gowns and there were plenty of earrings and finger rings in evidence. A few wore the figured silk dresses, which were coming into fashion, and the men were dashing and stylish in ruffled shirts and knee britches, with silver buckles shining on their shoes.

Mary's contribution to the occasion was the finest collection of bonnets ever seen at one gathering. Kate and Margaret were highly amused by her little approving nods each time another of her creations swept into the room atop a head.

'You'd think she'd arranged the wedding just to get the chance to show off her bonnets,' Kate whispered, blue eyes dancing.

'You're right – and you and me are next on her marriage list, so we'd best watch our step,' Margaret prophesied darkly.

'Oh, I don't know about that – I'd like fine to have a wedding,' her friend sighed, and Margaret shook her head in disgust.

The house was packed to the rafters, yet everyone managed to sit down to the wedding feast of broth, beef, mutton and fowls followed by puddings swimming in cream, with bread and cheese for those who still felt hungry. After the food had been washed down with generous mugs of ale, the furniture in Colin's room was pushed back against the walls and the floor cleared for dancing.

The first person Margaret saw when she went into the room was William, leaning against the wall, watching the door. When she appeared, he pushed himself upright and began to ease his way across the crowded floor.

Then: 'Come on, Margaret.' Robert's hand claimed her and whirled her into a group of dancers. Over her shoulder she saw William stop, as though it had been his intention all along, by Kirsty's side.

It was a grand gathering, a testimony to Kirsty's and Billy's popularity. Halfway through the evening, exhausted and hot,

Margaret slipped out of the room and escaped into the coolness of the backyard.

As she walked up the hard earth path by the kail bed a figure stepped out from the shadows under an apple tree. Startled, she gave a cry and stepped back, almost tripping over a brick by the side of the path. A hand held her arm, steadying her.

'Margaret?'

She pulled herself free, embarrassed. 'I-I didn't know there was anyone else out here.'

'You mean, you didn't know I was out here.' William moved back in his turn, indicating the distance between them. 'Don't worry, I'll not come too close.'

'No need to make it sound as if you've got the plague!'

'No?' he said bitterly. 'The way you've been avoiding me I thought I must have.'

She looked fully at him for the first time in weeks. His eyes were shadowed, his mouth unhappy.

'It's you who started this nonsense, not me.'

'And I'd finish it,' he said at once, 'if I only knew what to do.'

She darted a glance at the lighted doorway, wishing she had never come through it. 'Mebbe you just have to grow up, William, and stop letting your father make all your decisions for you.'

Even in the dusk she could see his face redden.

'It's not as easy as that.'

'I don't see why not.' Looking at him, talking to him for the first time in weeks, she wanted so much to knock down the wall that had begun to grow between them. 'All you need to do is face your father and make him tell you why he's come between us.'

'I've tried! He says he can't tell me.'

'Can't, or won't? You're not a child any more – you don't have to spend your life pleasing him! When my own father made a fuss about us, I soon told him what I thought!'

'But I've never gone against him,' William said wretchedly. 'You don't know how things are between us, Margaret—'

She reached out and took his hands in hers. 'I know you're fond of him, but has he the right to expect so much of you? Is it fair to make you turn away from me when I've done nothing and said nothing to anger him?'

'William? Colin's asking for you,' Jamie called from the doorway, and she felt William's hands flinch, then loosen in her grasp.

'Well?' she asked in an undertone. 'Are you going? Or are you man enough to stay here, with me?'

She felt his fingers slide from hers.

'Wait for me – I'll come back and we'll talk about it—'

'We'll talk now or never,' she said angrily, then, as he remained silent, she went on, 'Best run in and see what he wants, like a good little boy.'

She stepped aside to leave the path free. He hesitated, then brushed past her and went down the path and into the house.

Margaret kicked angrily at an innocent cabbage and bit her lower lip.

'What's amiss with him?' Jamie reached her side. 'I've never seen William with such a bad-tempered look. Were the two of you quarrelling?'

'I'd not waste my breath quarrelling with the likes of him!' Margaret stormed, then it was her turn to push her way down the path and into the house, slamming the door in Jamie's surprised face as she went.

* * *

It was late when the evening drew to its close. As was the custom they all stood to sing the 127th Psalm before going off to their own homes, and the wooden beams rang with their voices. 'Except the

Lord to build the house, the builders lose their pain; Except the Lord the city keep, the watchmen watch in vain.'

When the guests had gone, William helped his father back to his room and saw him settled for the night, helping him to undress and easing him back onto the pillow with a woman's gentleness.

'It was a grand wedding,' Colin said contentedly. 'And it's good to see Kirsty so happy again.' Then he looked sharply at his son's closed face. 'What's worrying you?'

William hung his father's jacket carefully over a chair, smoothing the material. 'The same thing that's worried me for weeks. I still want to know what you've got against me seeing Margaret.'

The light went out of Colin's eyes and he slumped back against his pillow. 'I've told you – I've nothing against her! I just think you're both young, and it would be a mistake to see too much of each other.'

'There's more to it than that.'

'I've told you all that I'm going to tell you!' There was an edge to Colin's voice that William had never heard before. 'For pity's sake, will you take heed and stop pestering me!' Then he added sharply: 'Where are you going?'

'Out for some fresh air!' William snapped.

'Wait!'

But the boy had gone. Colin fell back onto the bed, one clenched fist pounding helplessly at the sheet over his useless legs.

* * *

The cool quiet darkness did nothing to ease William's mind. It seethed with pictures of Margaret, laughing as she danced, angry when they faced each other in the garden. And there were bitter memories of that meeting in the street a few months earlier, when she had walked towards him and he, honouring the stupid promise his father had wrung from him, had turned away, only to see her go off with Jamie.

Mebbe you'll have to grow up, William, and stop letting your father make all your decisions for you. Her voice echoed in his head.

Four large, sturdily shod feet blocked his path, and he looked up and recognised two of his fellow apprentices.

'Will! Come and have a wee dram with us,' one of them coaxed. He shook his head. Colin didn't approve of drink, and he himself had never felt the need of it. But the apprentices were insistent. Unwilling to pull away from the friendly arms draped about his shoulders, William allowed himself to be steered to a nearby howff.

The door opened, sending a shaft of light, a cheerful hum of voices, a thick aroma of smoke and alcohol to where he wavered on the threshold. The two youths urged him on.

He compared the loneliness and bewilderment he had known recently with the warm unquestioning friendship of the young men on either side of him. All at once his need to belong somewhere was more than he could bear. Let his own people reject him – there were others.

Without looking back William made his choice, and stepped through the doorway.

PART III

PART III

11

'Paisley—' Mary MacLeod said breathlessly to her companions as she elbowed her way to the front of the crowd '—is for all the world like a drystane dyke. The big stones are the special occasions, and the wee bits holding them in place are made up of the gossip and the scandals.'

She gained a place right on the edge of the road, pulling Margaret and Kate to either side of her, and added with satisfaction, 'Speaking for myself, I have a great fondness for the wee bits. But there's nothing wrong with a big occasion like this now and then.'

Even Margaret, impatient to be back with her charges in the town hospital, felt her blood stir as the shrill piping of fifes and the rumble of drums signalled the approach of the procession. Kate quivered with excitement, her lovely red hair shimmering in the June sunshine.

'I've never seen so many people in the town, even for the Silver Bells race. D'you think King George knows that we're doing all this in honour of his birthday?'

'D'you think he'd care even if he did know?'

Mary's sharp elbow delivered a reprimanding nudge that would have sent Margaret staggering into the roadway if she hadn't been wedged against a stout woman.

'There's an unseemly dryness in your voice, Margaret. Whether His Majesty knows or not it's a grand spectacle for the folk and they've a right to enjoy it.'

'It's too crowded!'

'Havers! A procession's best when you can get a good sight of it, and hear it – and smell it,' her aunt added with relish.

They could certainly smell it. Piles of refuse rotted all along the gutters, and on this day, when the street was crowded, the usual aroma was enriched by the smell of humanity itself. Margaret thought longingly of the braes outside the town, where the air was sweet and fresh and scented by flowers that grew wild among the hedgerows and on the grass and in crannies in the drystone walls.

Then she looked up above the heads of the people opposite and found herself gazing directly into William Todd's serious grey eyes. He was at Kirsty's kitchen window, together with his father Colin, Kirsty herself, and her husband Billy Carmichael.

The other three were craning their necks to see the procession, held as a loyal display for His Majesty King George in this year of his reign 1768. But William stared down at Margaret as though she were the only person in that thronged street.

She looked away quickly. In the past five years she and William had never met informally, never been alone together. Hurt pride and misunderstanding had built an insurmountable barrier between them during those years, but Margaret still regretted the end of their deep friendship, though she would have died rather than let William or anyone else know it.

Mary caught at her arm. 'They're coming! Oh, aren't they bonny lads? See – there's your father!'

The parade was headed by the local militia, their tartan plaids and blue feathered bonnets contrasting with the scarlet cloaks worn by many of the women in the cheering crowd. The officers were on horseback, silver buckles at waist and instep catching the sun.

Duncan and Robert Montgomery walked with the Paisley weavers, the largest contingent in the long procession. They were followed by men from the neighbouring communities – Kilbarchan, Renfrew, Beith and Elderslie, and miners from the Thorn village, each group with its own silken banner carried proudly before it. A breeze caught the banners and filled them till they looked like land-locked sails slashing bold colour against the grey and brown stone tenements on either side of the street.

The men stamped along stolidly to the beat of drums and the chirruping of fifes.

A vivid blue gaze met Margaret's as the Paisley men swept by. Beneath it a wide grin almost split Jamie's face in two, and above it his red head added its own contribution to the colourful parade.

After the weavers came their apprentices, a tousled, cheerful barefoot lot.

'Jackie!' Margaret waved, and her father's new apprentice, a skinny orphan recently hired from the town hospital, blushed with pleasure then stared grimly ahead, sticking his bony little ribcage out in imitation of the older boys.

In the wake of the official parade danced the children, ragged and overexcited, some of them tormenting the apprentices who marched in front of them, others cheering squeakily for a king who, in Margaret's opinion, probably cared nothing at all for them.

Then the parade was by, and the onlookers surged after the marchers to the Cross to hear the speeches.

Once the formalities were over, they were all free to mingle, and meet friends who had come into the town for the big occasion.

Jamie arrived at Margaret's side. 'Come down to the river with us – I'm supposed to keep an eye on Kate and Archie, and they want to go for a walk.' He nodded to where his sister was gazing into the eyes of a young uniformed lieutenant and added hurriedly as Margaret opened her mouth to refuse. 'They'll be wanting to be together, and that'll leave me looking like an old nursemaid if I'm on my own!'

They had no sooner reached the water's edge than Kate and Archie wandered off together on the pretext of having a closer look at an interesting flowering bush. Jamie guided Margaret to a spot where a log by the river made a comfortable seat.

'I thought you were supposed to watch out for Kate? They're nearly out of sight.'

'Ach, she's fine,' Kate's brother said with a sudden lack of interest in her welfare. 'We'll sit here and have a talk, you and me.'

She settled herself on the log. 'Talk? We talk nearly every day – there's nothing left to say.'

'There's always something...' His voice trailed off and he worried at a twig, plucking the leaves from it one by one.

There was a short silence, then: 'You're not saying much,' Margaret pointed out with some exasperation.

'I'm just – thinking it out first.'

'There's no thinking needed. Just open your mouth and let your tongue clack on the way it usually does.'

'Och, Margaret!' he rapped at her in a sudden irritated burst.

'It's not easy to ask someone if they'll wed you!' Then his face flamed. 'I mean – I should have said – d'you have to gawp at me like that?'

For once Margaret found herself at a loss for words. Finally she said weakly, 'Wed? Are you asking me to wed you, Jamie Todd?'

'Well, I'd... if you... I—' Jamie gazed around as though hoping to find the right phrases hanging from a tree, then sat down suddenly on the grass and stared at the slow-moving river, avoiding her eyes. 'Yes.'

'You're daft!'

'No I'm not!' Jamie argued hotly. 'I'm a master weaver now, and we've been walking out together for a good long time—'

'But not like sweethearts – like friends!'

'I've heard of friends who've wed each other before this!' he almost shouted, exasperated. 'I know you've a fondness for me. Every woman has a fondness for someone, Margaret. Kate, there —' he gestured to the two figures a considerable distance away '—she's fond of Archie—'

'I'm not Kate!' Margaret was outraged. 'Just because I like someone it doesn't mean that I want to wed with him. I don't want to wed anyone!'

'Don't be daft, Margaret, every woman wants to get married.' Without realising it Jamie went on adding fuel to the fire. 'Is it William?'

She jumped to her feet. 'Is what William?' she asked in a cool voice.

'Is it him you're fond of? Oh, we all knew you liked each other well enough once, but for years now you've scarcely looked at each other. So I thought that – but mebbe I'm wrong. Mebbe he's the one you care for.'

Then he looked at her face and prudently scrambled to his feet. It didn't seem wise to stay on the ground.

'I've never heard such a foolish notion!' Margaret exploded. 'Of course I've no feelings for William!'

'In that case what's to come between us?' he persisted. 'Margaret, will you wed me?'

'No!' She started to flounce past him but he caught at her hand.

'I'd be prepared to wait while you thought it over.'

'You've got your answer!'

His own temper came to the surface. 'My God, woman, you're stubborn! D'you think I've stayed here in Paisley because I wanted to? It was because I thought you and me might settle down together.'

'I've no intention of settling down with any man!' Margaret snapped, and began to walk back to the town, yelling for Kate as she went.

Jamie fell into step beside her. 'If you turn me down I'm leaving, Margaret. I'll go off to be a soldier.'

'Good fortune go with you. Kate, it's time to go home!'

'I might be gone for years.'

'We'll hold a gathering for you when you come back,' said the light of his life grimly.

'Mebbe I'll never come back. Soldiers can get killed.'

She stopped and gazed up at him as he loomed above her. Jamie was a well-made man, and at that moment, blue eyes aflame and red hair raked by exasperated fingers, he looked invincible.

'Tuts, Jamie Todd, who'd ever be so bold as to kill the likes of you? You'll be back, and we'll all be glad to see you. And isn't it time you attended to your sister instead of leaving it all to me?'

But Kate, pretty mouth twisted in a petulant scowl, was

approaching them with Archie in tow, and Jamie had to bite his tongue and give Margaret the best of the argument.

* * *

Nine people sat down to dinner in the Montgomery kitchen that night. A babble of voices filled the place, led by Mary's. Since Andrew MacLeod's death a year earlier his widow spent a lot of time in her sister's home, rather than 'rattle around', as she put it, on her own in the big house on Oakshawhill. Robert's sweetheart Annie was another frequent visitor, and so was Gavin Knox, a young surgeon who lived in lodgings in Glasgow and often came to Paisley with Thomas, who had attained his ambition and was now a medical student at Glasgow University.

Jackie, the little apprentice, sat at a corner of the table cramming food into his mouth with the dedication of one who was not used to getting enough. Above his busy cheeks he surveyed the company with two round solemn dark eyes, which were hastily lowered whenever anyone looked in his direction.

With his pale face and high-domed head, sparsely covered with fine straight black hair, he looked more like a small middle-aged man than a child of thirteen, Margaret often thought.

She herself had no appetite and no interest in the talk that flew about the table. She pushed a potato about her plate and looked up to find Gavin's clear hazel eyes studying her. She glared back at him and was pleased when he blinked in embarrassment and looked elsewhere.

She didn't have much time for Gavin Knox. The first time he had come to the house he had tripped on a stool and knocked over a pile of pirns she had just spun, and ever since she had dismissed him as a clumsy slow-moving oaf with little conversation. She could never understand why such a ham-fisted man should wish to be a surgeon.

When the meal was over and the dishes cleared away, she escaped to the garden to collect the sun-scented clothes that had been spread out on bushes to dry.

Bees making their final forays of the day droned contentedly as they carved a path through the air between the scented blossoms planted specially for their benefit, and the three skeps sitting in a niche in the stone garden wall. With practised ease Margaret folded the clothes, breathing in their fresh summer fragrance. The tight angry knot within her began to loosen.

'It's a grand evening.'

The knot tightened again as Gavin ducked his dark head under the lintel of the kitchen door and stepped into the garden.

'It was,' she began ungraciously, then added swiftly, 'Mind where you put your—'

It was too late. As they righted the basket and gathered up the spilled clothes she asked in exasperation, 'D'you walk about the wards like that? It's a wonder sick folk ever get better with the likes of you bumping into their beds and knocking them to the floor! Not to mention the harm you probably do with your cutting!'

'So you've got a tongue in your head after all? I was beginning to wonder.' He picked up a sheet and tried clumsily to fold it. 'It's my personal experience that women are only silent when they're mortally ill or already dead.'

Impatient fingers whisked the sheet from his grasp. 'It's well seen you've got no sisters, then! I can attend to the clothes – is it not time you and Thomas were getting back to Glasgow?'

'We're setting off now. Robert and Annie are walking part of the way with us. I thought – we thought you'd like to come as well.'

'I've other things to do. There's been enough time wasted as it is.' She threw the words over her shoulder as she reached for a cravat that had fluttered to the far side of a bush. Gavin's long arm stretched past her and scooped up the errant garment easily.

'The parade? It meant a day off work for the folk – you'd not grudge them a rest now and again?'

'No, but they could surely find a less frivolous cause.' She twitched the proffered cravat from his hand and dropped it into the basket. Gavin fidgeted with a bush that dropped frothy golden sprays almost to the path.

'You think the king's frivolous? So you're no royalist?'

She shook out a sheet, making it crack in the still, warm air. 'I've no objection to the man, but he lives far away in London. We're hard-working folk in Paisley, and it's only other working folk we understand. If the king was to come here and build a house or plant a field or weave a good stretch of linen, I'd see the sense in holding a parade to honour him. But as far as I can make out he does nothing useful at all!'

He was still digesting her comments when she added crisply, 'And you'd best leave that flower alone, for I just saw a bee crawl into it. If the poor thing's forced to sting you it'll be the end of it, and we need our bees. You can carry the basket into the house for me, if you've a mind to be of use.'

* * *

Jamie's proposal of marriage irritated her like a stone in a shoe. She slept badly that night, and her usual enjoyment in her work at the hospital was lacking the next morning. The large gloomy apartment set aside as a schoolroom was even more forbidding than usual; a shaft of sunlight venturing in the high, narrow window only served to emphasise the bleakness of the children's surroundings.

'We'll have a botany lesson!' she announced abruptly, and the solemn, pale faces before her brightened noticeably.

Inside the hospital walls, surrounded by regulations, the children were always solemn and silent, reminding her, as Jackie did, of small careworn adults. But once they were out in the fresh air they started to chatter, and when they reached the fields near the hospital they raced around happily, freeing Margaret, the lesson forgotten, to return to her thoughts.

Instead of hurrying off to help her mother and Janet when her morning's work was done she called in at her aunt's shop. Although the two of them were so alike in nature that they wrangled continually, Mary was the only person Margaret could safely confide in.

She was alone, and in fine fettle, having just succeeded in selling an expensive bonnet to a difficult customer.

'And she took the one I chose for her, not the one she'd have bought herself,' she said smugly. 'A lacy, frippery thing she wanted, and her with a face like a cow looking over a gate at milking time. Not that I told her that, mind you. I put it a shade more politely, and she's fair pleased with what she bought. So am I, for she's a hard one to please. What news is there from the hospital?'

'Alexander Orr's in the cells again, they tell me.' Margaret said absently. 'He's got the madness.'

'D'you tell me?' Mary tutted. 'Poor Alexander, I mind what a fine figure of a man he used to be before the smallpox got him.'

'And wee Geordie Lang's in the sickroom again with a fever.'

Margaret thought of the child as she had last seen him, tossing restlessly in his cot. 'He needs fresh air. The mistress says he gets enough, for he's apprenticed out to run errands for a tailor in all weathers when he's able. To hear her, you'd think these fevers were Geordie's own fault. But what the laddie needs is to run wild for a few years, the way I did – the way you did yourself, living on a farm.'

'We can't all be hearty.' Mary was busy working on another bonnet.

'The hospital mistress would agree with you there. She says he's just suffering from the usual fever, the one that often visits folk in that place.' Margaret felt her mouth twist into a wry smile. 'I asked if she thought it was a sort of poverty fever – and she agreed with me!'

'Now, Margaret, there's a lot done in this town to help the poor – and I should know, for I work as hard at it as anyone.'

'But it's never enough! They need good nourishing food, and more care in the sickroom.'

'And where's the money to come from, may I ask? We all give handsomely as it is. I keep telling you – your grand ideas are all very well, but some folk are born to be poor, just as some are born to be clever, or healthy,' Mary lectured. 'You're only flying in the face of providence when you try to change the natural way of things. Now that we've dealt with the hospital – what's amiss with you?'

'Nothing.'

'I'd like fine to think you'd just happened by to exchange a word or two, Margaret, but you never put a foot inside my door unless you've got something important to say. So out with it before another customer arrives. Besides, the lassie's due back any minute from making the deliveries. And that's a bonnet for a councillor's wife, not a chicken waiting to be plucked—'

Deftly she whipped a half-made bonnet from beneath her niece's restless fingers.

Margaret sighed heavily and shot a sidelong glance at her aunt. 'Jamie's asked me to wed him.'

'Has he, indeed?' Mary asked without surprise. 'And what did you say to that?'

'I told him he was daft.'

'Daft for asking or daft for thinking you'd have him? I could have told him to save his breath, for there's more ahead of you than marriage to Jamie. But he's a fine young man, and there was no need to be hard on him.'

'No need? And him with the impertinence to think I'd fall into his arms and thank him for the honour he was doing me?'

'Men always think that, poor simple creatures that they are.'

'And then he said... he said—' Margaret almost choked at the memory '—that I'd only refused him because I'd a liking for William!'

'Have you?'

'Aunt Mary! You know fine that I've scarcely said two words to him in years. How could I have a liking for any man who spends all his time drinking himself into a stupor?'

'Poor William,' Mary sighed, her fingers smoothing a piece of ribbon. 'Colin's fair out of his mind with worry over him. I never thought the lad would come to this – going from howff to howff with a bunch of ne'er-do-wells.'

'He needn't have, if he'd any backbone at all.'

'You're too hard on him, Margaret.' But Margaret's mouth was set stubbornly, and Mary changed the subject.

'Have you told your mother about Jamie's proposal?'

'And have her planning a wedding? I have not!'

'That was wise of you. Well now, Jamie's proposed, and you've said no, and that's an end to it. Mind you, it's nice to be asked.'

'Hmphh!'

'Is there no romance in your soul at all, Margaret Montgomery? Oh, you'll come to it one day, when you find the right man. Independence is a fine thing – but when all's said and done, there's nothing like the love of the right man,' said Mary with relish.

'I thought you had more sense than that!'

'Oh, Margaret – when the good Lord created you he was short on the sweetness and heavy-handed with the thorns.'

'Mebbe so, but I've the sense not to want to spend all my days sitting by some man's fireside,' her niece said sharply, and Mary sighed, shook her head, and said no more.

12

One afternoon in October, as autumn bronzed the ferns on the braes and the chill promise of winter made itself felt in the evenings, Mary MacLeod made her way up the Waingaitend and past the Town House. Along the High Street she bustled, stepping high to avoid muddy spots and giving a sharp kick to two dogs who tried to start a fight on the footpath just as she approached on her way to see her sister.

Arriving in the grocer's shop she rattled off a list of provisions, finishing with: 'And I've decided to hold a Hallowe'en gathering for the young folk.'

Meg looked at her pityingly. 'Hallowe'en? Who in Paisley would want to know about such daft games?'

'All the young folk. Have you forgotten the times we used to have on the farm?'

'We were just children then.'

'I still recall the state you got into with the three caps, Meg – and so do you.'

For the first time in many years Meg thought of those Hallowe'en nights at home – the smoke-blackened walls of the farm kitchen and the three wooden basins, one holding pure water, one with dirty water, the third empty. And she herself, on the brink of womanhood, standing blindfold with a rod in her hand. She had just started walking out with Duncan, and the game's outcome was vitally important to her.

She remembered her brothers' and sisters' muffled laughter, the scraping sound of the tubs being shuffled about, the slap of water against wood. She remembered her fear, as she blindly pointed the rod, that in the 'best of three' result she would touch the empty basin, which forecast no marriage, or the tub of dirty water, which represented a dishonourable match.

The breathless excitement of that moment held her spellbound for a few seconds, then she came back to the present with a sharp: 'Och, it was only a bairns' game!'

'I mind you picked the dirty water,' Mary said thoughtfully, and was rewarded when her sister flashed, 'I did not – I picked the clean tub!'

'And made a good marriage, so who are you to sneer at Hallowe'en?' Mary seized her advantage. 'As I was saying – there'll be refreshments for the older folk if they care to come along too. We might as well make a proper evening of it.'

'I'm telling you, Mary—'

'No, I'm telling you, Meg – and I'm never wrong. Just one thing – see and get Margaret to come. She needs a bit of magicking to balance that deplorably practical streak she has. I can't for the life of me think who she takes it from,' Mary said airily, and went off to plan her party.

As she had predicted, her house was filled with people on the last evening in October. Instead of turning up their noses at country customs the young folk clamoured to be taught the old courting games.

'The place'll be like a mire in the morning,' Mary said happily as she shooed them all outside into the darkness to 'pull the Castoc'.

They bobbed blindfolded about her kail yard, grubbing up the greens; then they trooped back into the kitchen, pink-cheeked and blinking in the light, to where Mary waited to examine each root. The comeliness of the future partner depended on the amount of earth clinging to the roots, and the shape of each vegetable.

'Well, he might be cabbage in shape and a dour-looking man, going by all that dirt, but he'll have a good heart,' she said blandly as she inspected Margaret's offering. Then she looked up at her niece, a wicked gleam in her eye. 'On the other hand, he'd make a good rich broth, and that'll please your practical heart. Now – if you leave it by the door, you'll find that the first man who comes in'll have the same initials as your future husband.'

'Keep your black-footing for the likes of Robert and Annie, or Kate and her lieutenant,' Margaret told her crushingly. 'They've already chosen their partners. Speaking for myself—'

'There's someone coming in right now—' Mary interrupted, and Margaret dropped the cabbage and fled to the safety of the parlour.

Under Mary's supervision the young people roasted peas on live coals to test the strength of future unions, cast apple peel over their shoulders to find out the initial of their loved ones, and enjoyed themselves to the full.

Even Thomas and Gavin Knox threw themselves into the make-believe with enthusiasm; the only two on the outskirts were Margaret and William, who had forsaken his usual drinking friends to attend the party at his father's urging.

For the final test, Mary bustled the girls into a line in the hall, each clutching an apple and a comb.

'You go into that wee room there one at a time. Comb your

hair before the mirror and eat the apple – mind and hold each piece over your left shoulder before you eat it. Then you'll see your future husband's image in the mirror.'

'I'll not look!' Kate shivered. 'I might see someone I don't like!' But she allowed herself to be pushed into the room, and came simpering out after a few moments, refusing to say what she had seen.

'You too, Margaret—' Mary put an apple and a comb into her niece's reluctant hands when the other girls had finished. 'You have to take your turn.'

'It's all nonsense!'

Mary's eyes widened. 'It takes a foolish tongue to say such a thing at Hallowe'en! This is the night the witches and warlocks have their bit of fun, and who are we to deny them? In you go!' She pushed the girl in, closed the door, and went back to the parlour where all her other guests, young and old, had gathered to hear ghost stories.

The small room was lit by one candle. Shadows flickered in the corners and Margaret's face floated in the mirror like a water lily against a dark background. She heard Mary's footsteps clicking across the hall; a babble of voices rose then sank to a dull murmur as the parlour door opened and shut, and Margaret was alone.

She made a face at her reflected image and decided that she might as well follow the rules of the game and get it over with. She drew the confining pins from her hair and combed it out, letting it drift about her shoulders, then she bit into the apple, daring Mary's witches and warlocks to do their worst.

But no male image, strange or familiar, peered over her shoulder to threaten her future. It was as she had already planned – she would walk through life alone, unencumbered, free.

Margaret pinned her hair up neatly and finished the apple, her mind drifting away from the party and the people waiting for her in the parlour, to the lesson she intended to set the hospital children in the morning.

Then, suddenly aware that time was passing and she would have to rejoin the others, she glanced up – and saw a dim figure reflected in the mirror, hovering in the shadows behind her shoulder.

With a stifled gasp she whirled round, the apple core falling from her fingers to spin into a corner of the room.

'Margaret—' The man halfway between the door and the mirror moved forward. 'I didn't mean to fright you. I wanted to talk to you—'

'William!' She jumped to her feet, one hand clasped to her throat where a pulse hammered against the soft skin. 'You – you daft gowk! Has the drink addled what brains you ever had?'

The thoughtless words, born of fright and anger, were out before she could stop them. In the flickering light from the candle she saw his face twist as though a sharp pain had lanced through him.

'William—'

But he was already turning away from her, towards the door. He stopped as it opened and light from another candle flooded the room. Gavin Knox stood there, looking from one to the other of them.

'I thought I heard you cry out, Margaret—'

'I didn't,' she said quickly. 'We were just... talking.'

William brushed past Gavin without a word. She followed in time to see the front door close behind him.

'Did I do something wrong?' asked Gavin from just behind her. She looked up at his rugged, puzzled face.

'No, but I did,' she said, and led the way into the parlour.

* * *

On the last day of 1768, two months after Mary's Hallowe'en party, Robert Montgomery and Annie were married.

The most striking figure at the wedding feast was Jamie, resplendent in the green tartan plaid and blue feathered bonnet of the 79th Fusiliers.

'Now do you believe I meant what I said?' he asked Margaret belligerently when he first appeared in his uniform. 'If I can't have you, I'll settle for soldiering.'

She smiled sweetly up at him, relieved that at last the matter was settled. Jamie's proposals had begun to be wearying.

'I always believed you – the trouble was that you would never believe me,' she pointed out, and he scowled.

'You'll grow to be a sour-faced old woman if you don't come to your senses!'

'Mebbe so – but if I do you'll thank providence that you're wed to someone else, and not me,' she said but for a fleeting moment, as she watched him moving about the room, tall and broad and handsome, she wished that she could have been an empty-head like Kate, and happy to settle for marriage.

Then she caught sight of William standing behind his father's chair, his eyes on her, and all thoughts of Jamie were swept away in a wave of irritation. Why couldn't William be the one who was leaving Paisley? Life would be easier if she knew that there was no danger of meeting him and being reminded how drastically his appearance had changed in the past year or two.

Habitual drinking had dimmed his clear eyes and given his fair skin an unhealthy sallow tinge. His shoulders were rounded and his brown hair, once touched with rich gold lights, was lank and untidy. His mouth never curled into the crooked grin she remembered so clearly – instead, it had a bitter twist to it.

'Poor William,' Mary said into her ear. 'He looks as if he's in sore need of a friend.'

'From what I hear he's got friends in every howff and drinking den in the town.'

'You know what I mean, Margaret. For someone who cares about folk, you've an awful indifference towards him.'

Margaret's face felt warm. 'The people I care about can't help themselves! William Todd's brought all his misery on his own head. He could easily have decided to live his own life, as Jamie's done, and me – and the rest of us. Instead, he's chosen to do everything his father orders him to! What sort of a man would do that?'

Mary's eyes were surprisingly unsympathetic as she studied her niece. 'Mebbe it takes a special sort of son to follow his father's wishes without question and go against his own feelings. Mebbe you should remember that you don't know the whole story. You're lacking in compassion, Margaret.'

Hurt anger set Margaret's eyes ablaze. 'If you're so sorry for him why don't you go and keep him company instead of wasting your time with the likes of me?'

'Because it's not my friendship he's hungering for – and anyway, he's just gone out,' Mary said calmly, and a wave of relief swept over Margaret. She felt more comfortable when William was out of the way. No doubt, she told herself, still stinging from her aunt's criticism, he had gone to join some of his drinking cronies.

* * *

Outside, William hunched his shoulders against the chill wind and turned towards Pit Land, a tenement in Broomlands Street with a cock-fighting pit at the rear. It was a popular place, and the room was crowded with men when he got there. Weavers and masons and carpenters and merchants rubbed shoulders, for every man was equal at Pit Land as long as he had money to wager.

Here and there were clusters of brawny, unsmiling men with coal dust etched deeply and permanently into their skin – miners from the nearby Thorn village, opting to spend their few hours above ground in this airless room, gambling their hard-won wages away.

Tobacco smoke hung like pools of treacle in the lamplight. In a sanded circle at the centre of the room two cocks danced towards each other, necks and wings outstretched, then in a united movement they locked, a tumble of bronze and blue-black feathers and sharp eager talons.

William dug into his pocket and tossed some coins onto the ground. Then he leaned against a post and watched with dulled eyes, little caring what the outcome of the fight was.

Blood sprayed suddenly from the black cock and sprinkled the men immediately beside the ring. The red bird went in for the kill amid a chorus of jeers from onlookers angry at the speedy conclusion to the bout. A hand scooped up William's wager and he threw down more money. The victor and its victim were removed and two more birds, bloodlust in their glaring eyes, were loosed on each other.

The white cock, owned by an Elderslie man, was well known in Pit Land. It was an undisputed champion, but it was getting old and the challenger had ventured his best bird against it, a gamble that paid off that day.

After a preliminary skirmish to assess its opponent's abilities the other bird, younger and stronger, began to shred its adversary coolly and scientifically. The white cock, covered with blood, retreated almost at once but its humiliated owner, with an angry wave of the hand and a curt 'Let it stay!' deprived it of its right to a swift neck-wringing end. A few minutes later it was a sodden red heap and the owner of the new champion swept up his exhausted bird with a whoop of joy and kissed it, smearing blood from its feathers onto his face.

The scene suddenly came into sharp focus for William. The place reeked of death; the man's bloody face and the bird's bright, hard eyes were demonic in the hazy lamplight. His stomach heaved and he pushed his way out roughly, leaning against the tenement wall and breathing in great mouthfuls of air when he gained the street. Then he wandered into the night, not knowing or caring where he went.

He didn't realise that his feet had carried him out of the town and onto the moors until the splash of a small waterfall reminded him that his mouth was dry. He followed the sound through the dark night, slid down a steep bank and plunged his face into the icy stream, sucking water up greedily.

He was tempted to stay where he was, in that quiet empty place far from the town and its inhabitants. But William hadn't entirely opted from his past. Deep within the bitter shell he had become he still cared for his father, and he knew that Colin would be sick with worry if he didn't go home.

With a sound that was half-groan, half-sigh he resisted the impulse to curl up among the reeds and sleep to the lullaby of the waterfall and began to scramble up the banking.

He was almost at the top when a clump of grass gave way beneath his hand and he slid back, twisting and turning in an effort to stop his descent. His head struck a fair-sized stone by the water's edge; he cried out in pain, then lay still, one arm in the cold water.

* * *

Margaret plunged along the footpath. Chill droplets sprinkled her ankles as she splashed into a puddle but she ran on without pausing to inspect the damage to her skirts.

Behind her she heard Jamie call her name, but she rounded the corner into High Street, unheeding.

'William's hurt bad… bad—' The words pounding in her head kept time with her flying feet. People turned to stare at her as she sped by, wisps of dark brown hair escaping from under her bonnet to blow round her pale face, blue eyes seeing nothing of her surroundings.

'Margaret!' Jamie caught up with her as she reached Kirsty's street door. 'It was your mother I was sent to fetch, not you! You should've stayed in the shop and let her come back with me.'

'D'you think I'd be content to stand there giving out pokes of meal when William's mebbe dying?' she stormed, and pulled away from him, into the passageway. He stood where he was, watching her disappear up the stairs, then, shoulders slumped, he went slowly into the room where Colin waited for news of his son.

* * *

The kitchen was ominously quiet. Kirsty's spinning wheel lay idle, and its owner was bending over the wall bed in the alcove.

'Meg?'

'It's me.' Margaret went to the bed at once, her eyes dark with fear of what she might find there.

William lay motionless, his body scarcely mounding the covers, his face whiter than the pillow and even thinner than usual, as though the flesh had collapsed in on the bones. A bloodied cloth was wrapped round his head. To Margaret's terrified gaze he looked as though he was already dead.

'Is he—?'

'He's still with us, though the dear Lord knows how he survived that cold night on the braes.' Kirsty straightened her aching back. 'A carter found him this morning – his head's cut badly and it looks as though he's been lying in a burn all night. He was chilled through. When's your mother coming? I'll need her help with the nursing—'

Gently Margaret lifted one of William's hands. It lay passively in hers. 'I'll do it.'

'Best leave it to Meg and me,' Kirsty insisted but Margaret's head lifted sharply.

'I said I'll do it – night and day if need be! If anything happens to him it's my fault, d'you not see that?' She stroked the inert fingers that lay in hers. 'If I hadn't been so cruel to him for doing as his father wanted, he'd never have turned to drink the way he did – and he'd have stayed at the wedding party instead of going off on his own. If he should die—' Her voice broke and she bent her head over the still hand clasped in her own grip.

'Margaret Montgomery, your tongue's running away with you! I didn't raise him all those years just to see him put into an early grave.'

'I want to help!'

Kirsty gave her a long level look. 'Very well, but if you're so set on caring for him you'll have to stop crying all over him – he got wet enough last night to do him for a lifetime! Now, dry your face and help me to heat more stones to put against his limbs.'

* * *

It was a long hard fight. In spite of her brave words, Kirsty thought for several days that they weren't going to save William. The soaking he had endured brought on a rheumatic fever, with swelling and tenderness in every joint. Every movement was agony, and Margaret grew hollow-eyed and pale as she listened to him moaning and babbling in a semi-conscious stupor. The physician prescribed one remedy after another and William was bled, purged, treated with hot poultices and cold poultices, and dosed with everything the man could think of.

'I think that man's killing him with his cures,' Kirsty said unhappily. 'What's wrong with warm flannel next to the skin, and good broth – and peace of mind?'

'There's nothing at all wrong with it, for that's what cured me when I was near death's door.' Billy looked down on the grey-faced man in the bed. 'You should try it, Kirsty.'

'You'll have to do something,' Margaret begged. 'I can't stand to see him slipping away from us like this!'

Kirsty hesitated, looking from one to the other. 'If Colin agrees to it, I will. I'll not see William tormented with that man's cures any longer!'

* * *

Slowly, so slowly that it was a few days before they noticed the difference, William began to respond to Kirsty's treatment. Margaret was the first to see it taking effect.

'Speaking for myself, I've viewed healthier corpses many a time,' Mary said bluntly when she called to inspect the invalid.

'He's getting better,' Margaret contradicted her. 'He spoke to me this morning. And it wasn't delirium this time. He's on the mend.'

'I'll just have to take your word for it,' said Mary, but once she was settled by the fire in Colin's room she told him cheerfully, 'The boy's looking better every time I see him. I brought some of my best brandy for him, but he's so well cosseted up there that I decided to give the most of it to you instead. In fact, we'll have a sup of it now to cheer ourselves up.'

His eyes followed her gratefully as she bustled about his room. During the dark days when it seemed as though William was going to die, only Mary had realised how bad the waiting was for Colin, unable to walk upstairs and take his turn at watching over his precious son.

She had taken to visiting the invalid every day and then going downstairs to report on his progress. Now she handed him a cup of brandy then settled herself on the other side of the fire.

'See and enjoy that now. The Honourable James Erskine and his Honourable wife were in for their dinner last night and I opened this bottle for them. My Andra's finest brandy – but d'you think they appreciated it? Not them! "My," says the Honourable, "a real treat, Mistress MacLeod." And down his throat it went in one swallow before I could get a word of thanks out of my mouth. His wife was no better – the two of them were sitting there going at my good brandy as if it was nothing more than water from the street well. So I winked at the maidservant to bring out the claret instead and put the brandy by for you. I'd have been better giving these two the sour-tasting elderberry wine Andra's sister sent from Melrose last year, for all the taste their tongues have.'

For the first time since William's accident Colin's rich chuckle was heard, and Mary smiled down into her brandy, well pleased with herself.

13

Jamie joined his regiment shortly after William began to recover from his illness. On his final day in Paisley, Margaret took time from her nursing to walk with him across the moors where they had all played as children.

'It's a shame, you going away without a proper farewell gathering.'

'I'd not want one with William still so poorly.' He gave her a sidelong glance from beneath his lashes. 'I'll miss you, Margaret.' Then, as she walked on without answering, he asked impatiently, 'Will you miss me?'

'I've known you all my life – of course I'll notice when that red head of yours isn't around!'

'Can you not find a gentler way of saying it?'

'Jamie,' she said, exasperated. 'You know fine I'll miss you, without me having to say it!'

His eyes brightened. 'Does that mean—'

'No, it does not.'

'You don't know what I was going to say!'

'Yes I do. You were going to say that if I miss you and I don't have to say it because you know it already, it might mean that I feel strongly for you and that's why I don't say that either. But it doesn't work that way.'

'Och – Margaret!' said Jamie, thoroughly confused.

Braving the January cold, she sat down on a flat rock and pulled her gloves off. She had picked some reeds on the banks of a burn, and now she began plaiting them as she had done as a little girl. The moors had their own bleak beauty under the winter sun, and the air was sharp and clear.

'How can you bring yourself to leave this place?'

'That's easy enough.' He paced restlessly round her, kicking at dry dead clumps of grass. 'It's the folk I don't want to leave – some of them.'

'You'll meet other folk. The world's full of them.'

'Will you write to me?'

'If you write back.'

'Me? You know I was never one for letters.'

'It's not hard,' she assured him. 'Just let your fingers do the work. If they wag as much as your tongue does you'll have no trouble.'

Then her work on the reeds was finished, and it was time to go back home. Margaret searched the grassy area round the rock, but there was no sign of her second glove.

'I'll keep your hand warm,' Jamie said daringly, taking the ungloved fingers in his. She clicked her tongue disapprovingly, but let her hand stay in his warm clasp.

'Can I kiss you goodbye?'

'You cannot!'

'Surely a soldier has the right to a kiss before he goes off to the wars?'

'What wars?'

'Margaret,' he wheedled, 'I promise I'll bear in mind that we're just friends. One farewell kiss, that's all I'm asking for.'

She couldn't deny a request from someone who might be on his way to the other end of the world. She reached up and put her arms about his neck, her face lifted to his.

Jamie, resigned to the prospect of a swift peck as Margaret's idea of a kiss, was pleasantly surprised. As her lips met his they softened and parted. For a long moment they clung together, and when they drew apart they were both breathless. Before Margaret could move from his embrace, Jamie claimed her mouth again.

Her heart began to flutter and she wondered for a moment why she had so often denied herself the pleasure of Jamie's kisses in the past. Then her practical everyday self took over and she drew back, flushed and breathless.

'Well, that's that,' she observed briskly, as though she had just tossed the dirty dishwater out onto the midden. 'We'd best be getting back now.' And she set off for the town at a rapid pace.

Jamie, striding to keep up with her, was content. He could still feel the soft pressure of her mouth against his, and the warmth of her body in his arms. And her lost glove nestled in his pocket, a fitting keepsake for a brave soldier.

* * *

Once William was well on the road to recovery, a continual stream of visitors tramped up the stairs to see him; Robert and Annie, flushed with the joy and self-importance of their marital status; Kate, perching on the bed and chattering like a bird about her own approaching marriage to her young lieutenant, unaware that each enthusiastic bounce sent waves of pain through poor William's tender joints; Thomas, the gravity of a medical student sitting strangely on his round young face; Mary's sharp, witty tongue bringing the gossip and scandal that made up the 'drys-tane dyke' of Paisley life.

But his favourite visitor, and the most frequent, was Margaret. By some unspoken agreement, neither of them spoke about the misery of their separation. They behaved as if nothing had ever come between them and Colin and Duncan, both shaken by the young man's brush with death, left them in peace.

It was mid-March before William was well enough to go out, walking slowly up and down the garden with his arm about Margaret's shoulders for support, his pale face lifted to the spring sky. The only reminder of the rheumatic fever that had almost killed him was a slightly crooked left elbow.

When he was fit enough to travel, he went down to Beith to convalesce on the farm, which was now owned and worked by Meg's brothers. As she watched him go, Margaret felt a sudden pang that she hadn't experienced when she waved goodbye to Jamie. William was part of her life again, and his going left an empty space in her days.

But an epidemic of influenza in the town hospital soon gave her plenty to do. Hours spent nursing William had given her the patience to work with sick people, coaxing them to take nourish-ment, watching over them in their delirium, soothing them when they were weak and afraid.

Those who died were immediately replaced by new inmates grateful for the opportunity to walk through the big doors even as the bodies were carried out the back door for hasty burial. Poverty was like the River Cart itself – it flowed endlessly, and filled every available space. But while the river gave Paisley new growth and a reason for its existence, the flow of unwanted humanity contributed nothing.

There were plenty who saw the hospital as unacceptable,

humiliating charity and preferred to beg in the streets and sleep huddled under walls rather than apply for a place.

'More fools, them,' Meg said irritably as her way along the footpath was hindered by one of those unfortunates one day. 'Littering the public way when they ought to be in the hospital – I don't know what they think they're about!'

'Have you visited the hospital?' Margaret asked. 'It gives shelter, but it's a cheerless place – and some poor souls still have enough pride left to want to manage on their own.'

'Pity they don't have the pride to look for honest work.' Meg had worked all her life, and she had little time for folk who didn't earn their own way.

Margaret's eyes flashed blue fire. 'There's not enough work for them all – and some of them are sick. Have you forgotten poor old Rab Dalrymple?'

Meg had the grace to look embarrassed. Rab, an old shepherd, had been forced to give up his work during the winter because of increasing blindness. No work meant no home, and Rab had gone to the town hospital. But hunger for the fields and hills where he belonged gnawed at him, and one bitterly cold day he went out, feeling his way along the house walls and out into the countryside, where he was found the next day, frozen to death.

Margaret was haunted by memories of Rab and people like him who were sacrificed because they didn't fit into the community. But there was little she could do about it except work longer hours at the hospital, helping where she could.

During the epidemic she was sometimes joined there by Thomas and his friend Gavin Knox, the 'clumsy physician', as Margaret always thought of him.

The clumsy physician arrived at Margaret's side one evening

as she left an old woman's bedside in the big sickroom, her cloak in his big capable hands.

'Put this on and I'll walk back with you. Thomas'll be a wee while yet.'

She pushed a strand of hair back from her forehead. 'So will I. I've still to—'

'You've done enough for tonight,' he interrupted crisply. 'You'll make yourself ill if you keep working at this rate, and that'll not help anyone.'

She opened her mouth to argue, then shut it again. He was right – her very soul ached with exhaustion. Meekly, she allowed him to put the cloak about her shoulders and lead her out onto the hospital steps, his hand beneath her elbow.

'Lift your chin up and breathe deeply,' he ordered, retaining his hold on her arm. 'I find it the best way to recover when I've been working too hard on the wards.'

'I've not been working too hard.'

'Yes you have. Your colour's gone and your eyes—' He halted suddenly and scooped her chin into his free hand, turning her startled face up to his. 'You've got nice eyes, but they're shadowed. You should pay heed to what I'm telling you. It was foolish to spend weeks nursing William Todd back to health then go straight to the hospital sickroom without giving yourself a rest.'

She pulled her chin free of his grasp, and would have freed her arm too if he hadn't held it in such a grip that it would have meant an undignified struggle.

'No need to lecture me! It's those poor sick folk back there who need help, not me.'

'They're getting it. You're not stepping out as I told you.'

'I'm tired!' she snapped at him, and regretted the words as soon as she saw his eyebrows climb towards his untidy dark hair.

'Isn't that just what I said earlier?'

She could have kicked him. Instead she asked icily, 'Did you never think of joining the militia, Mister Knox? You'd have made a grand officer with your fondness for giving orders.'

He grinned, unruffled. 'You can call me Gavin. I might have gone for soldiering if I hadn't set my heart on medicine instead. Mebbe you're not the only one who wants to help folk. D'you like dancing?'

'Dancing?' The abrupt change of subject took her by surprise.

'Dancing. You've surely heard of it? Folk do it sometimes, to music.'

'Folk that have nothing better to do with their time!'

'So you don't care for it? That's a pity, for there's a public dance to be held in the Saracen's Head in three weeks' time. I'd be honoured if you'd agree to be my partner.'

Sheer surprise brought her to a standstill. As it happened, they were outside the Saracen's Head, the main assembly rooms in the town.

'Well?' Gavin prompted.

'But I-I don't know how to dance.'

'You can learn. I'm told that a Mister William Banks has just opened a dancing school in Waingaitend.'

Panic seized Margaret. 'I'm – I've never felt the inclination to go in for such frippery,' she lied. Part of her wanted to go to the dance, to wear a fine new dress and learn the social arts. But the other part of her was terrified in case she made a complete fool of herself in front of a man who was, after all, a stranger to her. He fell into step with her as she walked on.

'If you feel that you'd not have the skill to master the steps there's no sense in agreeing to go to the dance with me,' he murmured.

'I didn't say I couldn't master the steps if I put my mind to it! I just said that I-I wasn't sure if I'd enjoy the dance.'

'Have you never been to a dance before?' he asked, and she had to shake her head, like a bumbling country girl who knew nothing of society, she thought angrily.

'Then you must let me partner you to this one,' he insisted, and Margaret, afire with mixed feelings, gave in.

* * *

Kate thought that the new formal dances from England were the height of elegance, but Margaret's worst dreams were realised. She was not a natural dancer and she hated every step and every lesson at Mister William Banks' dancing classes.

'I'm not going back,' she threatened each time she came home, but when Kate called to accompany her to the next lesson Meg thrust her out into the street and off she went, tight-lipped. If it hadn't been for the thought of having to admit defeat to Gavin she would never had gone on trying to master the complicated steps.

Her only pleasure in the whole business came when she put on the gown that Kate had specially made for her. Margaret, who had never been overly interested in clothes, possessed a fashionably long, slim figure, and even she was impressed by her own appearance on the night of the assembly.

Her gown was of pale green silk over a hooped white under-skirt embroidered in the same pale green. The over-gown's low neckline was trimmed with white lawn and the sleeves ended at the elbows in a foam of green ruffles. Her shoes were of white satin, and her brown hair was simply dressed and tied with ribbons to match the gown.

When Meg escorted her into the kitchen where Gavin waited, his hazel eyes blazed with surprised admiration.

'You look almost beautiful!' Thomas said in awe, and Jackie, Duncan's little apprentice, stopped in the doorway, mouth agape, the stoup of water he had been bringing in for Meg tilting in his grasp and almost spilling onto the clean floor.

She stood before them, rosy-cheeked under their admiration, feeling strangely unlike herself, yet liking the sensuous kiss of silk against her skin and the whisper of her skirts as she moved.

When they reached the Saracen's Head light was pouring through all its windows, illuminating the area outside, which was crammed with carriages and horses. In the building's main rooms voices and laughter mingling with the lusty music of a Scottish reel.

'Would you care to dance?' Gavin roared over the noise, and led Margaret onto the crowded floor.

At first it seemed that everything was going to go well. The musicians were playing for a Scottish reel, and Margaret began to enjoy herself as she swung round to the beat of the music, her hands tight in Gavin's, her green silk skirt billowing about her. They danced the next dance, a strathspey, then Gavin led her to a seat and went off in search of a cooling drink.

As he came back, weaving skilfully through the crowds, a cup in each hand, she studied him through discreetly lowered lashes. He wore a deep blue coat with silver buttons, a flowered waist-coat, yellow shirt and breeches, and there were silver buckles on his shoes. His own dark hair, unpowdered, was tied back with a ribbon. He was, Margaret had to acknowledge, a fine-looking man. She took the proffered cup and sipped at it. The evening was going to be more bearable than she had supposed.

But the formal English dances proved her wrong. During the first, she managed to be deep in conversation with someone, watching with growing panic as Gavin adroitly steered Kate through the intricate steps, smiling down into her flushed, excited little face. But there was no escape the second time, and her heart sank as he led her onto the floor and the music began.

Three minutes later he caught up with her as she fled outside on to the balcony, to hide her shame in the darkness.

'Margaret?'

'Let me be!'

His hands turned her about to face him. Beyond his shoulder she could see through the lighted window to where dancers circled and bobbed with stylish ease.

'Are you ill?'

'Ill in the head, to try those daft dances!' Her voice shook with humiliation.

'You were doing fine.'

'You didn't think that when I trampled on your foot, did you? I heard what you said then, Gavin Knox!'

'Well – it hurt at the time. But—'

'At the time? You'll probably be lame for a week – and so will everyone else who was dancing near me!' She realised that she was wringing her hands, and pushed them down by her sides. 'I'm going home—'

'No you're not! You came to the dance with me, and I'll take you home when it's over,' he said firmly, his big body trapping her in a corner.

'I'm not one for dancing – I told you that in the beginning,' she wailed. 'Why couldn't you have paid heed then and found some elegant Glasgow lady to go with you?'

'I didn't want any Glasgow lady – I wanted you to be my partner.'

She felt tears thicken her throat and plunged on in an attempt to finish before they choked her altogether. 'It's that dancing class that's to blame! Mister Banks won't teach men and women together, and I'm taller than Kate so I always had to be the gentleman and... and I'd have been better dancing with the girl Thomas invited, for I've... I learned the steps all the wr-wrong way!'

The final words came out in a sort of wail, then there was silence, broken only by Margaret's sniffs of self-pity. Gavin drew in a deep breath and stared over her head at the wall behind her. 'Are you laughing at me?' she demanded to know. It was too dark for her to make out his expression.

'No!' The denial was too prompt, too abrupt. Margaret put her hands on his shoulders and stood on tiptoe, peering into his shadowy features.

'Am I to believe, then,' she said tartly, 'that you always have a silly grin on your face?' Then she released him and stepped back, chin tilted belligerently. 'Get on with it, then – get it over with!' she ordered, as if he was one of the children in the class at the hospital.

She had never heard Gavin laugh so heartily. He roared and whooped and gasped for breath, first supporting himself with one arm about her shoulder – for all the world as though she was one of his drinking friends, she thought indignantly – then gathering her into his embrace.

She endured it stoically, her nose pressed against his jacket buttons, waves of mirth rumbling in his chest and vibrating against her cheek. Finally, just as she was wondering if he was ever going to stop, the peals of laughter eased to hiccups, then slowed.

'Your pardon, Mistress Margaret,' he said at last, his voice still shaky with amusement.

'So I should hope—' she began indignantly, then the words died away as she looked up and saw his face just above hers.

'You look beautiful,' Gavin said huskily and bent his head to hers.

'I-I don't approve of kissing men I scarcely know,' said Margaret weakly when she was free to speak again.

'I should have known that. You'll grow to like it,' he said, and kissed her again.

She should have resisted. Indeed, she fully meant to resist, but somehow time passed and she did nothing about it, other than sliding her arms about his neck and letting her mouth soften and melt beneath his.

* * *

In the two weeks after the assembly, Margaret made a point of being out of the house when Thomas and Gavin Knox came from Glasgow.

Memories of those moments spent in Gavin's arms tormented her. She had lost her head – she had behaved like an empty-headed female, and she was afraid that he, like Jamie, would leap to the conclusion that a kiss meant more than it should. But as the days passed and the physician made no attempt to seek her out, her confusion lessened and the assembly faded into the background.

William came home earlier than was expected. Country air and farm food gave him back his health quickly, and he was soon hungering for Paisley again, for the familiar routine of work and above all for Margaret.

She was wandering alone on the braes, enjoying a rare after-noon's freedom, when a cart rumbled past, bound for Paisley. The man on the box grinned when he saw her perched on the bank of a burn, her skirt kilted about her knees and her bare toes splashing in the water.

'It's yourself, Maggie Montgomery,' he called, and she recognised him as a former schoolmate. 'It's a grand day.' Then he jerked the whip handle over his shoulder. 'William Todd's coming your way.'

She shaded her eyes from the sun and looked up at him. 'William? He's in Beith, surely.'

'I brought him back myself. He got down just over the hill there to walk the rest of the way...' His voice faded as the cart rattled on.

She scrambled to her feet and ran up the rise, not waiting to put her shoes and stockings on. Her heart jumped as she saw a figure in the distance, a man walking with an easy swing, unhampered by the weight of the bag slung carelessly over one shoulder. A warm breeze brought her the sound of a melodious whistle as he walked.

She cupped her hands about her mouth. 'William!'

He stopped, looked round, saw her, and began to run. Her hair was in a curly mass about her face, her skirt caught about her bare legs as she sped towards him, but it didn't matter. As they met he dropped the bag and picked her up, whirling her round as though she was a feather's weight.

'William – put me down! You'll hurt yourself!'

'I will not. I'm as strong and hearty as ever I was, thanks to your aunt's cooking.' He set her down but kept her within the circle of his arms. 'She fed me so well I began to fear that she was fattening me for Christmas.'

'You look so – oh, you just look grand, William.'

He did. His skin had taken on an even gold tan and the gold lights had come back to his soft thick hair. His grey eyes sparkled and the body lightly touching hers was strong and firm.

'And I'm—' She tried in vain to smooth her tangled hair,

laughing up at him. 'I must look like a tinker child. What a way to welcome you home!'

He shook his head, hugged her close. 'You're even more lovely than I remembered,' he said into her wind-blown curls. 'And it's the best welcome a man could hope for.'

Then he scooped up his bag and they turned towards Paisley, his arm firmly about her.

14

Summer blossomed, then gave way to autumn. Weavers with work to do in the late afternoons had to light tapers to see by. Kate married her young lieutenant and in October Robert's wife Annie gave birth to their first child, a son.

Jackie McNab, the orphaned apprentice in Duncan's employment, decided that the time had come to better himself and plucked up the courage to ask Margaret if she would teach him to read and write 'proper'.

'But I taught you along with the others in the town hospital, Jackie.'

His thin little face was crimson, his mouth trembling with the need to say the right things, to convince her of his sincerity.

'But I have to learn more if—' he shuffled his knobbly bare feet and squirmed with self-consciousness '—if I'm to be a proper master. Now that there's drawlooms coming into the town there's a new need for learning—' His brown eyes begged for her understanding.

Despite Meg's good food, Jackie was doomed to carry always the signs of a half-starved infancy. He was small for his age, and rickets, that common childhood ailment, had warped his bones and made him look clumsy, though he was agile enough, with a speed of movement learned from the need to dodge blows and keep out of trouble.

'So you want to learn to work a drawloom, do you?'

His face glowed. Jackie's real idol wasn't Duncan, but Robert, who wove cloth on one of the big new drawlooms with an intricate overhead harness that had to be worked by a drawboy.

'If you'll teach me about letters and numbers I'll learn well,' he said huskily, scarcely daring to hope, and she wanted to take his slight body into her arms and mother him.

'You'll have to work hard, Jackie McNab,' she said instead, with a briskness that was meant as much for herself as for him, and was bathed in a huge smile of gratitude and pure love.

'I will!' gulped Jackie, and was as true as his word. Each evening he studied his books by the light of a taper in the corner of the silent loom shop where he slept. And whenever Robert called at the house, wreathed in the confident aura of a family man with a son of his own, Jackie tried to be there, tucked into a corner of the workshop, devouring the talk that floated round his ears with the blue-grey tobacco smoke from the men's pipes.

'Gauze is on its way out,' Duncan would announce firmly above the thump of his loom.

'If you're right, there's something to be said for cotton, now they've got that new yarn in England,' his elder son said just as firmly. 'I hear it makes for a better cloth.'

'Let England get on with it, then. We've got our own way of working.'

Robert's fist crashed onto the deep windowsill where he sat. 'Listen to me, man – a Lancashire weaver can make seven shillings in a week!'

'And a Paisley weaver can make the same if he puts his mind

to it, without being beholden to anyone. D'you want to see us turning to those manufactories they've started in the south? All the looms under one roof and the weavers working for one employer and not able to call their souls their own? That's not for me!'

'But we have to move with the times!' Sooner or later Robert would come out with Jackie's favourite phrase.

Later, when the day's work was done and he was studying alone in the loom shop, the little apprentice would clamp his slate pencil between his teeth in imitation of a pipe, pace the floor, thump his fist on a loom and tell the silent wooden structures about him, each with its half-made cloth stretched between its rollers, 'Man, we have to move with the times, I'm telling you! Move with the times!'

When all was said and done, Jackie had never been happier in his entire life. Every morning he began his day by cleaning and oiling the looms, sneezing as he removed fluff, spiders' webs and, sometimes, snails attracted by the damp dark places beneath the treadles. Then it was time to have breakfast with the family.

Afterwards he brought in water from the street well and swept the backyard, then he took his place in the loom shop, doing whatever he was bid, and watching the finished cloth gradually take shape between the huge rollers.

If the weavers were keeping pace with the work in hand, they very often took the afternoon off, leaving Jackie free to work on his lessons or run off with apprentices from other shops. They bowled, ran races, went to the braes to paddle in cold, swift-running burns. Sometimes they went swimming at the Hammills, the River Cart waterfalls close to the town centre, or visited the cock-fighting pit behind the Deer Inn in Broomlands Street. There was always something to do. Ragged and mischievous, rebelliously against authority other than that imposed on

them in the loom shops, the apprentices and drawboys often
brought the wrath of their elders down about their uncaring ears,
but Jackie tended to be a follower, not a leader.

The market was another popular venue with the apprentices.
One of Jackie's closest friends was a carrot-headed drawboy
named Charlie, famed for his ability as a sneak-thief. A walk
round the market in Charlie's company usually resulted in some
treat or other – pies or fruit or sweets that had magically slipped
into Charlie's tattered shirt as he passed a stall.

'Want one, Jackie?' he asked one afternoon as he saw the
younger boy's gaze fall on a pile of apples, large and rosy,
promising crisp white flesh and sharp-tasting juice that would
trickle down a boy's chin.

Jackie's mouth watered. 'I wouldn't mind.'

'Easy.' Casually, Charlie sauntered closer to the stall, looking
around, while Jackie watched, his stomach tight with excitement
and his tongue already tasting the fruit. Two scarlet globes
seemed to glide from the stall into Charlie's grasp. One disappeared into his shift, but as the other one was about to follow a
large hand whipped out and caught him by the arm.

'You thief, you! I'll teach you to steal from me!'

Charlie immediately ducked and twisted, but the woman
held on and he only succeeded in ripping the sleeve out of his
worn shirt. The first apple fell to the ground; he threw the other
to Jackie, who automatically put out his hands and caught it. As
soon as its firm roundness slapped into his palms he realised his
mistake, but it was too late.

'Get that one an' all!' the stallholder bellowed above Charlie's
enraged screeches of innocence. Faces turned towards Jackie,
hands reached out to grab him, and he turned and ran for his life.
Head down, the apple still clutched in his hands, he butted his

way across the market, eeling between stalls until he gained the High Street.

He fled across it, miraculously avoiding the carts and carriages, and ran down Waingaitend with some idea of finding a hiding place in the bushes and trees by the river.

Terror squeezed his heart and all but stifled him. He could have thrown the stolen fruit away and run into one of the tenement entries, protesting his innocence if he had been caught empty-handed. But he could no longer think clearly. All he wanted was to get away, to hide, to be safe from pursuit.

He reached the bottom of Waingaitend and ran by the town hospital, too frightened to see Margaret coming down the steps.

She almost fell over him as he fled past, and put out a hand to stop him. Jackie felt her fingers brush his shoulder, and with a thin, choked scream of despairing terror he swerved away, into the roadway and into the path of a large farm cart filled to overloading with refuse collected from a nearby tenement yard.

'Jackie!' Margaret's shriek broke through his panic and he looked up to see the carthorse above him, hooves flailing as the carter dragged back on the reins. Again, Jackie hurled himself to one side, the apple thrown away at last to let his arms curl protectively about his head.

He fell clear of the chopping hooves, which tore lumps of dried mud from the road as they descended, but his bid for safety didn't carry him far enough.

As the cart lurched to a standstill one of its huge iron-bound wheels ran over his outstretched leg, crushing it as if it was a twig.

With a wrenching scream that echoed in Margaret's ears for the rest of her life, Jackie's thin body arched up then fell back, his fingers clawing into the hard-packed earth.

People came running to group around him as he lay there.

Margaret was among the first to reach him, heedless of the unnerved horse's hooves as she dropped to her knees by the boy.

The apple, thrown well clear, had rolled into a puddle of stagnant water. It only lay there for a few minutes before a small child scooped it up and carried it off.

* * *

There was little they could do to save Jackie's leg. The weight of the cart, taking refuse to fertilise the fields, had crushed and mangled the bone beyond any hope of repair. It would have to be amputated.

Nausea swept over Margaret when Doctor Scobie pronounced his verdict. Jackie had been carried into the hospital, where he lay, mercifully unconscious, in a cot in the big sickroom.

'Amputation's the boy's only hope,' the doctor repeated, frustrated by his own uselessness in the face of such terrible injuries.

'And what sort of hope is that for anyone?' Margaret asked dully. 'When will it be done?'

'In the morning. I'll have to find a surgeon willing to undertake it.'

A surgeon. The word penetrated Margaret's misery, bringing with it pictures of a square face under dark hair, a clumsy big body and broad capable hands.

Gavin's one of the finest surgeons you could hope to meet. Thomas's defence of his friend echoed in her head.

'Wait – I think I know of a surgeon who'd see to Jackie,' she said, with rising hope, and fled from the hospital, glad to be out of the place and doing something to help the injured boy.

It was only natural, now, to look to William for help. Within the hour the two of them were huddled in a cart, rattling over the town bridge and through the new streets recently built on the opposite bank, each one called after the trades that had brought prosperity to Paisley. Usually Margaret delighted in those fine names – Silk Street, Cotton Street, Gauze Street – but that day she had no time to spare for them.

William watched her anxiously. 'Margaret, from what you say of his injuries, the boy might not recover even if the king's physicians themselves took on his case. You're mebbe expecting too much of Thomas's friend.'

'I'm not looking for a miracle. I just want to know I've done all I can for Jackie. Gavin might... he might—'

She stopped, fighting back tears, and he put an arm about her and held her close against his shoulder.

Dusk was hovering over Glasgow's fine broad streets by the time they arrived at Thomas's lodging house. Margaret scarcely took time to introduce herself to his landlady before hurrying upstairs with William following close behind her. She rattled on the door panels with impatient knuckles, then burst in without waiting for an invitation.

The little room seemed to be overflowing with books. They fell over each other on a shelf on the wall, sprawled in heaps on the table, lay scattered over the floor.

Thomas, in shirt sleeves, was sitting at the table, and Gavin lounged comfortably in a chair by the fire. The two men looked up, startled, then jumped to their feet.

As Margaret poured out the story of the little apprentice's accident, the medical student and the surgeon exchanged glances. They let her finish without interruption, then Gavin took her over the details of Jackie's injuries again, interrupting her several times, making her describe the wounds as accurately as possible. When she had finished there was a long silence while he deliberated.

'From the sound of it there's not much I can do to save the leg
—' he began and William interrupted him.

'If you're not willing to try, we'll walk the streets of Glasgow
till we find someone who is!'

A muscle twitched in Gavin's jaw, and his eyes seemed to frost
over as they met William's glare.

'I was about to say that I'll do my best. I'll come to Paisley first
thing in the morning.'

'Now! Come back with me now!'

An irritated frown furrowed his brow. 'I'm on my way to dine
with friends right now, and it's an engagement I can't cancel.
Besides—'

She flew at him and he took a step back under the unex-
pected onslaught. 'Be damned to your dinner party!' The oath
sprang easily to her lips in her agitation, though it was the first
time in her entire life she had used it. 'There's a child lying in the
hospital, needing your care right now!'

Appalled by his sister's behaviour, Thomas sprang forward,
but it was William who reached Margaret first, pulling her away
from Gavin and into the shelter of his own arms.

The surgeon smoothed his blue embroidered silk coat.

'The child needs to rest tonight – and so do I, for I've been
working in the wards all day and I'd not trust my own judgement
at the moment,' he said coolly. Then he added, in a kinder voice,
'You have my promise that I'll be in Paisley first thing tomorrow.
Go home now, Margaret, and get some rest yourself. We'll all
need to be strong tomorrow.'

* * *

When Margaret arrived at the hospital early in the morning,
Gavin and Thomas were already there, closeted in a small side

room with Jackie. Clear-eyed and calm, the surgeon gave her a brief nod by way of greeting when they came into the mistress's room with Doctor Scobie.

'There's nothing for it but to take the leg away.'

Despite herself Margaret felt her lips tremble. 'But – all he's ever wanted is to be a master weaver. A weaver needs his two legs!'

'He needs to be alive, too.' Gavin's face darkened. 'It's a matter of trying to save the boy himself now. Thomas, you know what we'll need.' He took his coat off and dropped it on a chair. 'Margaret, do something useful – take the children outside, away from this business.'

Not many people could dismiss Margaret Montgomery as easily as that and hope to get away with it. But Gavin was no longer Thomas's clumsy, amiable friend, or even the man who had kissed her at the dance. He was a professional trained man with an air of authority about him that she had never seen before. Meekly, she did as she was told.

* * *

Thomas felt a stab of envy as he watched his sister lead her charges out of the building. It was the first time he had assisted at an operation under such circumstances, and his skin prickled with apprehension as he went into the room where Jackie lay on a large table. Gavin was setting out his instruments, his face mask-like as he concentrated his mind on the work ahead.

Thomas splashed whisky into a cup and lifted Jackie's head. The boy choked, coughed, then swallowed the liquid that trickled into his mouth. Patiently Thomas fed the cup's contents to him, drop by drop.

When Jackie's eyelids fell and his breathing took on a thick, slow note, Thomas put the empty cup aside and bared the injured leg, drawing in his breath sharply as the shattered mass of bone and bloody flesh was revealed.

The two male inmates who had volunteered their services for payment of sixpence each paled and turned their heads away, but mercifully they both retained their determined grip on Jackie's small body as ordered.

Gavin's eyes were calm and his hand, as it gripped Jackie's thigh just below the groin, was steady. For a second he paused, then the knife descended.

* * *

The small paupers, revelling in their freedom, scampered along the river's banks, noses reddened by the chill wind. Margaret found a sheltered area and paced up and down, tormented by thoughts of what must be happening back at the hospital. Finally, unable to banish the terrible pictures from her mind, she resorted to a childhood trick, thrusting her ungloved hand into a thorn bush, letting the pain of a dozen small scratches shock her back to her surroundings.

The minutes dragged by, and she felt as though she must have aged years by the time the sun indicated that it was midday and she was able to gather up her charges and shepherd them back to the hospital.

They went willingly enough, their appetites whetted by the fresh air, eager for the piece of bread and the small plate of broth that made up their midday meal.

Gavin, Thomas and Doctor Scobie were all in the mistress's room. Thomas, gratefully sipping at a glass of brandy, smiled wanly at Margaret.

'He's survived the operation – and a fine job Gavin made of it,' he added proudly.

'It was that,' the physician chimed in and Gavin, his shirt sleeves and waistcoat spotted and blotched with blood, nodded in offhand acknowledgement of their praise.

'It wasn't a difficult task. But there's many a fine piece of surgery hidden in a grave.'

Margaret's heart was touched by an icy hand. 'You mean he'll die after all?'

He eyed her thoughtfully. 'Don't expect too much, Margaret. The boy's not strong and I've no great hopes for his future.'

Fear for Jackie, the shock of the accident itself, and the surgeon's seeming indifference suddenly welded together within her to red-hot fury.

'So you think you've had a wasted journey? You think we should have got someone else to cut the boy's leg off – or mebbe we should just have left him to die in the street, seeing he's only an orphan and a pauper? I'm sorry if we've taken you away from the important work of tending to a rich man in a fine Glasgow hospital, but you've no need to worry, for I'll pay your fee whatever the outcome. You'll not be out of pocket – not even if your doctoring kills Jackie!'

'Margaret!' Thomas's face was crimson with anger and embarrassment. Doctor Scobie was scandalised, the hospital mistress pursed her lips disapprovingly, but Gavin merely raised one eyebrow.

'You're angered with me,' he said unnecessarily. 'There's no need. I care for the boy's welfare, but it doesn't do to get upset over any patient, rich or poor. If I let myself do that every time I'd not be a good surgeon, you see. And I want to be good at my work.'

'I've no doubt you will be, one day – when you've tried your hand on folk that don't matter to anyone – like Jackie!'

'Margaret!' This time Thomas's voice was a whiplash, cracking across the small room.

'Leave her be,' Gavin advised him calmly. 'She needs to speak her mind. Though you're being hard on me, Margaret. Best prepare your mind for the worst, as I do in these circumstances.'

'Why not?' she asked bitterly, unable to stop the tirade now that it had begun. 'What chance does he have now, in any case – a crippled pauper!'

Gavin got up unhurriedly and crossed the room, 'Just so,' he agreed, and went out, closing the door gently behind him.

Thomas's fingers ground into his sister's arm, forcing her down on a chair.

'Will you hold your tongue, for the love of God – and take a sup of this, for it seems you need it more than I do!' The cup containing half of his brandy was thrust into her hand, and he stormed out of the room.

He found Gavin outside on the steps, leaning against the hospital wall, his hands in his pockets.

'Thomas,' he said thoughtfully when his friend tumbled out of the building and arrived by his side. 'The more I see and hear of your sister, the more I think she'd make a grand wife for some ambitious man.'

'If,' said Thomas, his voice tight with rage, 'anyone'd be stupid enough to want her!'

15

Formally, Margaret proffered Gavin's amputation fee – three shillings and four pence – on the day after the operation, and formally he accepted it.

She watched the coins disappear into his pocket with stunned disbelief. She had fully expected him to refuse payment on the grounds of his friendship with the family. Then she would have been able to force the coins on him and thus ease her troubled conscience.

She glared up at him, and reddened as she glimpsed a sparkle of malicious amusement in the hazel eyes that met and briefly held hers. Then he was serious again, looking down at Jackie.

'He's survived the shock of the cutting, at least.'

'He seems to be comfortable.' She caressed the sleeping child's face lightly with one finger.

Gavin said nothing, and she knew what he was afraid of. Thomas had taught her that gangrene was the surgeon's greatest enemy. All too often infection set into a wound and killed the patient. Nobody knew why, Thomas said, his round face perplexed.

'D'you like tending the sick?' Gavin asked as they left Jackie's bedside.

'I like seeing folk getting better. Thomas is lucky to be going into medicine. I wish I could have done that.'

'Hospital work's not for the likes of you,' he said decidedly. 'They can be dirty places – it's a wonder to me that anyone gets well at all in some of them. I've seen dogs running in from the street to forage round the beds for food. And the women who work in the wards – lazy old hags willing to buy drink for any patient who'll share it with them.'

'Mebbe someone should change things.'

He shook his dark head. 'I doubt if that'll ever happen. The folk who care the most are too busy trying to cure the sick to do anything else, and the rest are indifferent.'

In the days that followed he came to Paisley whenever he could to see his patient. Jackie regained consciousness of a sort, though he was too confused to take in what had happened to him. Margaret was glad of that, for she dreaded the day when the boy would discover that he had lost his leg. In his conscious moments he fretted because they wouldn't let him get up despite his pleas that Mister Montgomery needed him in the loom shop, but Margaret's presence soothed him a little, so she sat by his bed for hours, listening to him babble about the years ahead, when he would be a drawloom weaver with apprentices of his own.

On the fifth day Gavin came to meet her as she went into the sickroom. His face was pale.

'Margaret, before you go in to him, I've changed his dressings and—'

She knew then that the fight was lost. The poison that had crept into Jackie's wound claimed its victim with hideous efficiency, and when the end came Margaret could only be thankful that Jackie's sufferings were over.

Gavin pulled the dirty sheet over his patient's face and walked out without a word, leaving Margaret to tell the mistress the news and beg some brandy from her.

She found Gavin in the empty schoolroom, staring at the wall. She put the cup into his hand, and his fingers curled automatically about it.

'You did your best.'

'It wasn't enough.' He drained the cup in one gulp.

'Gavin,' she said awkwardly. 'I was wrong to speak to you the way I did that first day.'

'You said what was in your mind.' His head was bent, both hands gripping the empty cup as though he was warming himself with it. 'I can never accept a death,' he said, more to himself than to her. 'I should have got used to them, but I never do. This one – it was wasteful. The operation went well. He would have lived.'

'He'd probably have become a beggar if he had, poor boy. He'd have hated that – perhaps it was as well it ended this way.'

'I'm not thinking of that!' Gavin said fiercely. 'I don't care what might have become of him. He died because of something we haven't found yet. Because we know how to cut folk, but not how to care for them properly after the cutting. And I can't for the life of me think what we're doing wrong!'

Then he put the cup down and went back to Glasgow and his duties there, without another word.

* * *

Jamie came home just when Margaret most needed the sight of his cheerful grin and blazing red head.

'You're sure you've missed me?' he asked jealously during one of their moments together.

She beamed at him affectionately. 'The whole town misses you. You're like a stone in a pond, Jamie Todd – you cast ripples everywhere you go.'

'I'm not talking about the whole town, just about you!' He paused, then added, carefully casual, 'I see you and William are as cosy together as a couple of old women gossiping at a street corner.'

'And why not?'

Jamie scowled. 'Mebbe I should have stayed home. Mebbe if I had, you and me would be—'

'Would be quarrelling most of the time instead of enjoying the times we can be together, like this,' she finished the sentence swiftly. 'Admit it, Jamie – you'd not change your soldiering life for anything.'

'I'd not go as far as to say that,' he began, then grinned and shrugged his broad shoulders. 'Well – mebbe you're right. There's things to do and places to see, and the restlessness in me's eased a little now.'

Then, as they rounded a corner and came on a group of sturdy girls, hair tucked under linen caps and round brown arms and legs bared to the chill wintry sun as they gathered water to wash the linen that was spread out to whiten, he added with a wolfish twist to his grin, 'But I'll admit that Paisley has some bonny sights!'

* * *

'This is a bonny pattern.'

William, on one of his many visits to his father's room, lifted a sheet of paper that Colin had left lying on his cluttered work table.

Everything Colin needed lay on that table – colours for his

designs, volumes he used when he taught his young pupils, sheets of paper scrawled with verses, the half-dozen books that Colin happened to be reading – they huddled together in what seemed to be chaos to the observer, though he himself knew exactly where every item was and resisted all Kirsty's efforts to tidy things up for him.

His thin face flushed with pride at William's praise, though his voice was casual. 'I'm pleased with it – but I'll no doubt have to make some changes before it gets to the loom. The weavers are still complaining that I expect too much of them at times. Mebbe one day some clever man'll invent looms that can take my designs as I mean them to be.'

'Nothing surer.' William sat down on the other side of the fire that kept the December chill at bay, and sprawled his long legs over the hearth rug with the air of a man well pleased with himself. 'I've been thinking about my future.'

'Aye?' Colin's loving eyes travelled over the younger man's face, noting with relief how well and happy William looked now that he had stopped drinking and found peace with himself and his surroundings.

'Aye. I like working with Billy Carmichael well enough, Father, but my apprenticeship's long over now and it's time I started out on my own. See.' He held his hands out, laughing. 'Not a mark on them that wasn't put there by honest toil. Mind when I started work? I was never done hammering my fingers or cutting them instead of the leather. I've mastered my trade at last.'

'How's your arm?'

William punched the crooked elbow, the only reminder of his bout of rheumatic fever, with his other fist. 'It doesn't bother me at all,' he said carelessly, intent on telling his news. 'Now, I was out at Renfrew last week, and there's a wee shop there to rent. It would make a nice beginning for a man setting up in business for himself.'

'What would you use for silver?'

William grinned disarmingly, sure of his reception. 'That's why I've come to you – though you'd always be the first to hear of any plans I might have anyway,' he added hurriedly. 'If you could lend me the money to start off with – it'd not be much, just enough for my rent and my materials, I'll work all the hours God sends to pay it back and get myself properly started.'

'It can be a hard life, setting up a new business. I know, for I did the same when I was about your age.'

William brushed the warning aside with a wave of one hand. 'I know that, but I'm not afraid of hard work. It would do me good – I'm getting too lazy working for Billy, for there's not enough to keep me as busy as I'd like. He could manage with another apprentice; he doesn't need a time-served man, to tell the truth.'

He stopped, eyeing Colin anxiously. The older man deliberated for a few moments, eyes fixed on the flames in the grate, then he looked up and nodded.

'You can have as much as I can afford, and welcome.'

William jumped up and shook his father's hand vigorously. 'I'll only take what I need to see me started, and not a penny more. I want to work for what I get.' He paced the floor, the words tumbling out as he planned aloud.

'I could be in business by February at the latest, and my debt could be paid off by next year at this time. By then I'll know how soon I can afford to find a wee house and get wed—'

Colin's laughter, rarely heard, interrupted him. 'Hold on, man!' he protested. 'One minute you decide to set up on your own and the next you're a married man? You're letting your tongue run away with you.'

'Oh, but I've got it all worked out. I'll not ask Margaret until you've got your money back, but by then—'

'Margaret?' his father interrupted, the laughter suddenly wiped from his face, his hands clutching at the arms of his wheelchair. 'What Margaret?'

William stopped pacing. All at once it seemed as though the temperature in the warm room had dropped sharply. A gust of wind rattled at the window.

'What Margaret do you think? Margaret Montgomery, of course,' he said, then his gaze hardened. 'Father, you're not going to start all that nonsense again, are you?'

'Have you spoken to her of marriage? What makes you think she'd have you?' Colin's voice was harsh in its urgency and William frowned.

'I told you I'd no intention of asking her until I've got something to offer her. But I think – I hope – she'll accept me when the time comes.'

'You can't marry Margaret Montgomery.'

The bleak words seemed to take shape and stand between the two men like a barricade. William's young face flinched, then set in a cold mask.

'So you're planning on coming between us for a second time, are you? D'you not think that you and Duncan Montgomery have caused enough trouble between Margaret and me? We're grown now – we don't have to heed our fathers any more.' He leaned forward, each word clear and definite. 'I'll not let you tell me what to do with my life now – and if I have to, I'll find the money I need from someone else – so don't think you can try to buy my obedience!'

Colin's face, youthful in his happiness only minutes earlier, was old and drawn. 'Listen to me, William. Believe me. You can't marry Margaret Montgomery!'

William's hands clenched into fists by his sides. 'I'll not listen! And I'll not let you and her father conspire against us this time. I was willing to wait for another twelve month before I spoke to Margaret, but not any more. I'm going to her tonight, and I'm going to ask her if she'll give me her promise that she'll be my wife as soon as I can offer her a home.'

'And if she refuses you?'

William's mouth twisted. 'If she refuses me of her own free will I'll accept that. But I hope she'll say yes – and if she does, Father, I'll bring her back here with me and we'll throw your small-minded bigotry right back in your face!'

'William – I'm begging you to leave things as they are!'

'I love her, and I've wasted enough time. If you've got good reason for coming between us a second time then for God's sake tell me what it is—' William strode to the door where he paused, one hand on the latch '—or mind your own business from now on!'

For a moment there was silence, then William's tension was released in a long breath.

'You see? There's no real reason at all, is there? Just some bee you and old Montgomery got in your bonnets. I'm going to Margaret.'

His thumb pushed the metal tongue down, releasing the latch. His wrist tensed to pull at the door.

'She's your sister.'

Even the flames in the hearth seemed to stop moving. William's fingers tightened on the door handle but he wasn't aware of its edge cutting into his palm. He felt as though he had been pushed off the edge of the world and was cartwheeling through space.

'What?'

Colin's voice was bleak. 'Margaret Montgomery is your sister.'

William opened his clenched hand with difficulty and walked across the room to the window. Kirsty was spreading her washing over bushes to dry. Her rounded arms, damp from the washtub, seemed impervious to the bitter wind.

Billy came from further down the garden, a muddy spade in his hand, and said something to her as he passed. The two of them laughed together.

William turned away from the scene, avoiding Colin's gaze, and picked up the design he had been looking at earlier.

'How can she be my... my sister?' he asked through stiff lips.

'Because Duncan Montgomery's your father.'

There was a pause, then: 'Go on!' William's voice was rough, ugly. 'Or am I supposed to try to guess what happened? D'you want to turn this nonsense into a child's game?'

'It isn't nonsense, William. I wish to God it was. Your mother, Lizzie, was my wife, but it was Duncan who fathered you, not me.'

'How did it come about?'

'I don't know the full story of it. I never wanted to know.'

'Well, I do!' The design was crushed into a ball, thrown aside. 'It's my existence we're talking about! Why wait till now to tell me?'

'I thought you were my own flesh and blood until a few years ago, when Duncan saw the danger of you and Margaret becoming too close. It makes no difference to me. You were never his – always mine!'

'"When Duncan saw the danger—"' William repeated, stunned. 'Duncan saw it? But it was you who came between us – you who used my affection for you to get my promise that I'd not see Margaret again.' He ran a hand over his hair, bewildered. 'You damned near killed me, to cover up what he'd done to you – and to me?'

'He wanted to be the one to speak to you, but you'd not have listened to him, and neither would Margaret. D'you not see that? It had to be me. It was the only way I could think of to protect you and her from the truth!'

'But you've kept your friendship with him! With the man who betrayed you with your own wife!'

Colour flooded Colin's face but his voice didn't waver. 'What's the sense in raking up the past and hurting innocent folk who know nothing about this?'

'It was all right to hurt me, was it? To put me through hell and then do this to me when I finally come out the other side and try to make something of my life?'

'If you hadn't fallen in love with her you'd never have had to know—'

William laughed bitterly. 'I might have realised the fault would lie with me at the end of it!' Then he asked, low-voiced, 'Is there anything else I should know while we're about it?'

Colin's fingers had teased a thread from the blanket about his knees, and twisted it about his index finger until it was a livid white.

'Lizzie – your mother – she didn't die when you were small. She went off with another man. I've no idea what happened to her after that.'

'The bitch!'

'You'll not speak of her like that?' Colin flared at him. 'When all's said and done she's still my wife and your mother!'

William's laugh sounded as though it had been blessed in Hell. 'My mother? An hour ago I had no mother! An hour ago I was a happy man!'

'William, it's breaking my heart to see you like this!'

'Is it? Who else knows about – about me?'

'Only Kirsty.' Fear jumped into Colin's eyes. 'You'll not tell Margaret or her mother? It would kill Meg if she knew—'

'You think I'd want to tell anyone about this? You think I'd want anyone to know that I'm the fool who was going to ask his... his half-sister—' William choked the words out '—to be his wife? They'd all have a good laugh over that one in the drinking houses and the loom shops!' His hands clenched on the back of a chair.

'Go and see Duncan,' Colin urged, at his wits' end. 'Talk to him. Ask him all you want to know—'

'No! If I found myself alone with Duncan Montgomery I'd not be able to keep my hands off him. He's made a bastard of me – he'll not make me a murderer as well.'

'William, listen to me,' Colin implored, but the hard young voice flowed on, each word striking at Colin's heart.

'"The sins of the fathers shall be visited on the children." Is that the way it goes? I could never believe the Almighty would be cruel enough to make that come true, but He has. My Heavenly Father! That makes three fathers I've got today – and not one of them able or willing to give me any comfort!'

He lunged towards the door.

'Where are you going?'

William looked back at the man huddled in the wheelchair, a look so devoid of feeling that Colin's breath caught in his throat.

'As far from Paisley as I can,' he said, and went out of the house where, after a lifetime, he felt that he no longer belonged.

* * *

'But why go away now, just when – when everything's all right again?' Margaret asked, perplexed.

'Because I'm tired of Paisley, the way Jamie got tired of it. There's other places to see.'

'William Todd, you'd hate soldiering and you know it!'

William's face was set in a stubborn scowl. 'There's more than soldiering.'

'What, then?'

'All sort of things. Don't nag at me, Margaret! I'll go to Edinburgh first, to Unc—' he stopped abruptly, then went on '—to Matt's farm. Then I'll find work in the city, or mebbe I'll take ship for some other country.'

Matt Todd had left the army years earlier and was farming outside Edinburgh.

'There's something you're not telling me,' Margaret said suspiciously. Then her face darkened. 'Your father's not starting his nonsense about us again, is he?'

'No!' William exploded, then drew a deep breath. 'No, of course not. I just want to stretch my legs. Leave it at that, Margaret – a woman can have no notion of the way a man's mind works!'

There was a ruffled silence while she eyed him narrowly and he glowered at a beetle struggling up a blade of grass.

'I know how your mind works,' Margaret said at last. 'I know you'll not be able to stay away from Paisley for long. You'll be back soon enough.'

The toe of William's boot flicked the beetle off the grass stem. It soared through the air and disappeared from sight into a clump of reeds.

'I'll never be back,' said William. 'Never!'

PART IV

PART IV

16

Rain fell steadily from a grey sky. It pattered on the earthen streets and, with the help of horses' hooves, cartwheels and feet, turned them to quagmires. March of 1770 had come in like a lamb, blue-skied and rich with the promise of spring; now it was going out like a lion, laying down a grey, damp carpet to welcome April.

Even the red tents sheltering the kail wives and their wares at the open-air market looked drab and colourless. Customers hurried through their business and turned homewards without stopping to talk. The place was almost deserted.

'You should have stayed by the fire,' Margaret told Gavin as they splashed along the High Street and turned towards the market. He pulled his hat more firmly over eyes half-shut against the rain.

'A wee bit of water never hurt anyone. And it looks as if it might be easing,' he said optimistically.

If it had been up to Margaret she would have stayed at home, snug and dry, but her mother needed some vegetables for the evening meal. At least she and Gavin were warmly dressed and well shod.

She went from stall to stall, prodding the merchandise with an experienced finger, bargaining with the kail wives who were, for the most part, bare-armed and bare-headed in spite of the rain. Gavin followed her patiently. Living in lodgings as he did, he enjoyed the domestic side of life in the Montgomery household.

Margaret finally decided between two large solid cabbages and paid the woman.

'That'll please my mother. You'll be staying for your dinner, I suppose?'

'I will. I enjoy your mother's cooking.'

'I've noticed,' she said dryly, and stopped at a stall to peer at some cheeses.

Gavin stepped across a puddle. 'Mistress Peterson feeds me on herring and potatoes every day. First thing in the morning, then again in the evening with a mug of small beer.'

She looked up at him, blinking against the rain. 'You seem to be thriving on it.'

'I am that,' he agreed cheerfully. 'It's a fine nourishing diet, but a change now and then's more than welcome.'

'Mistress!' An old woman wrapped in a greasy, tattered cloak that had long since lost its original colour and warmth tugged at Margaret's sleeve. 'Mistress, have you mind of Beth Lang?'

'Beth? I mind her fine.'

'You've to come to her right now, for she needs you,' the woman said, and scuttled off over the wet slippery ground like an aged crab. Without any hesitation Margaret pushed her basket into Gavin's hands and followed her down one of the narrow lanes leading to the maze of alleys and closes and tall houses by the river.

The area was the oldest part of the town and its tall buildings had long since deteriorated into dirty, neglected slums. This was where the poor who could still afford some form of shelter congregated. Rubbish was piled high on footpaths and streets, the gutters flowed with stinking water, many of the windows were empty holes in the walls, open to the wind and rain.

Margaret followed the old woman into a lane so narrow that her shoulders almost brushed the walls on either side. Something squelched underfoot and she recoiled instinctively. When she looked up again her guide had vanished. Just ahead was a doorway, two crumbling steps up from the street. She went through it into a dark ill-smelling passageway, felt her way along the slimy walls, and almost fell through an opening. The stench of the small room caught at her throat.

The place was lit by one tiny window. Half its panes were broken and the gaps stuffed with rags in a vain attempt to keep the wind out. The existing glass was too thick and too dirty to allow much light to filter through.

As Margaret's eyes accustomed themselves to what there was she made out a rough table and a bench. The old crone stood beside a younger woman who held a whimpering baby in her arms. A man snored in one corner, his face to the wall. A pile of rags in another corner moved, and she realised that several children were lying there in a heap.

'There she is.' The old woman pointed to the darkest corner of all, where someone shuddered and trembled on a heap of straw.

'Beth?' She dropped to her knees, heedless of the filthy floor. The girl, in the grip of a spasm that made her entire body shake violently, groaned as Margaret tried to take her into her arms.

'Margaret! In the name of God, where are you?' With a wave of relief she heard Gavin's voice from the passageway.

She called to him, and saw the shock on his face when he arrived in the doorway.

'Gavin, it's Beth from the town hospital. She's sick.'

'She's been taken with the fever,' the old crone said, though by now Beth's teeth were chattering so hard that they could all hear her, even above the man's snoring and the wails of the baby.

Gavin knelt, brushing Margaret's hands aside with an impatient: 'Out of my way till I see to her.'

She stood up. The last time she had seen Beth, the girl was employed as a servant in one of the big houses, and doing well.

'What brought her to... to this place?' she asked the women, who shuffled uneasily.

'She'd need of a roof over her head, and enough to pay for her keep,' the younger woman said reluctantly, her voice hoarse and slow. 'But now the money's gone and she's sick. You'll have to take her back to the hospital.'

She began to cough, a bubbling cough that racked her body. The baby, fearful of falling, caught hold of her hair with tiny grasping hands and cried louder.

'She told us about you.' The old woman took over the story. 'She'll have to get out of here.'

The other woman straightened, spat, and sucked air into her lungs, the coughing fit over. The sick girl's breath whistled in her throat.

'She'll have to get out of here,' Gavin agreed, his voice grim. 'What's wrong with her?'

'She's dying.' He straightened up and tore his coat off. 'And it's no wonder, in this place.' He wrapped the coat about Beth then lifted her in his arms. 'Out of here, Margaret, if you value your own life!'

He pushed past the two women, Beth's tangled fair hair swaying as her head lolled against his shoulder. The old crone, her good deed done, spat an oath at him, but the younger one allowed herself to be elbowed aside without complaint, her gaze fixed avidly on the table where, Margaret saw, Gavin had put the basket containing her mother's cabbage.

'Here, make the children some broth with this,' she said before she followed him out, thrusting it into the grimy hand that was already reaching out to claim it.

Gavin was waiting in the street, breathing deeply to flush the fetid air from his lungs. In the grey light of day, Beth looked as though she was made of grey-blue wax.

'Show me the way out of this rabbit warren.'

'Gavin, will she—'

'Hell's teeth, woman, stop chattering and do as I tell you!' he roared at her.

They made an incongruous trio: Margaret in her good warm clothes; Gavin, his waistcoat and shirt black with rainwater; and Beth, unconscious in his arms, her ragged gown half-covered by the elegant bottle-green coat he had wrapped about her. But few people turned to stare as they passed, for they were in a part of the town where folk minded their own concerns and it was not wise to be too inquisitive.

As they turned into New Sneddon Street, a passing carriage stopped and Mary MacLeod's sharp nose appeared at the open door.

'Margaret! What in the world are you up to now?' she demanded of her niece.

'She's saving a life,' Gavin snapped back, wrenching the door open and stepping up into the carriage as though the girl he held weighed no more than a rag doll. 'Drive us to the town hospital.'

'No!' Margaret scrambled up behind him. 'I don't want her to wake up and find herself in the hospital sickroom. That's where her brother Geordie died of the poverty fever.'

'The what?' he asked, bewildered. Then Beth began to cough in great harsh spasms that twisted her thin body, and he said tersely, 'I don't care where we take her as long as she finds a warm place to rest.'

'Then we'll go to my own house,' Mary decided promptly. As the wheels began to turn she sat back and murmured to her niece, 'He's mebbe a bit on the sharp side, but I like his style!'

* * *

'You might not be able to save the girl, Mistress MacLeod.' Doctor Scobie's long sad face looked longer and sadder as he walked into Mary's parlour an hour later.

'I'll make a brave try at it, though. What ails her?'

He pursed his lips in a way well known throughout Paisley. 'Well, now – her brother was never strong, as I mind. And it seems that she has the same tendency to be affected by humours in the atmosphere—'

'She's half-starved and worn out,' Gavin interrupted from behind him. The older physician looked ruffled.

'Mebbe, mebbe, but even so—'

'But why was she in that place at all, when she left the hospital to work in Councillor Brodie's household?' Margaret wanted to know.

'Why is anyone in a hovel like that?' Gavin's face was dark with anger. 'Who owns the place?'

'I'll... I'll be on my way,' Doctor Scobie said uneasily, picking up his bag and giving one last regretful glance at the cupboard where Mary kept an excellent Madeira. 'I'll call tomorrow morning, Mistress MacLeod – that is, if the girl's still with us by then—'

'I'll let you know if she should leave,' the lady of the house assured him graciously, and rose to accompany him to the door. 'And I'll make sure Beth's still alive tomorrow,' she added when she returned, 'for I don't believe in giving in to doctors and their opinions. Now, you were asking about these tenements down by the river. All the property down there's owned by Councillor Johnny Brodie.'

'The man who employed Beth?' Margaret asked, stunned.

'The very one. A bad-tempered, greedy wee runt of a man, he is – but a great one for making money and keeping it.'

'Come on, Margaret.' Gavin's hand clamped round her wrist. 'We've got things to discuss with Councillor Brodie!'

'Now don't go upsetting the man,' Mary squawked primly after them, a glint in her eyes.

'I've a feeling poor Johnny's in for a shock,' she added to her late husband's portrait, hanging above the ornate fireplace. 'And it serves him right!'

* * *

Councillor Brodie lived in a large and comfortable house only five minutes' walk from Mary's. His thin eyebrows rose at the sight of Gavin's dishevelled appearance.

'You find my wife and I enjoying a quiet hour at home. You'll take some claret?'

'Thank you, no.' Gavin ignored the chair he had been waved to, and stayed on his feet. Margaret declined an invitation to sit on the sofa by Mistress Brodie, so the councillor was forced to remain standing with his guests. He was a small man, intended by Nature to be thin but blessed, because of his wealth and self-indulgence, with a pot belly which, together with his skinny limbs, gave him the look of a beetle that had learned to walk on two legs.

Gavin swept aside the usual formalities. 'We're looking for a girl named Beth Lang. I believe she's in your service.'

Brodie's jaw dropped and his wife looked up briefly from her embroidery. 'I mind the name, Johnny. She came from the town hospital, did she not?'

'To take up employment in your house.' Margaret's voice was angry, and Gavin laid a restraining hand on her arm.

'That's her. I dismissed her,' said Mistress Brodie serenely, and returned her attention to her work.

'There you are, then. She was dismissed.' The councillor was clearly beginning to wish that they would go away and leave him in peace.

'Why?' Gavin turned his attention to Mistress Brodie. She looked him up and down, decided that he was a fine-looking young man, recalled that she had two daughters as yet unmarried, and smiled on him.

'Theft.'

'Never!'

'Hush now, Margaret,' Gavin reproved. 'And when would this be, Mistress Brodie?'

'Some two weeks since. I thought you'd have seen her back in the hospital, Margaret, and got the whole sorry tale from her.'

Margaret kept her voice under control with an effort. 'She didn't go back. What's she supposed to have taken?'

'I recollect it now,' the councillor butted in, annoyed at being ignored in his own parlour. 'She's the one who took the ribbon from Liza's room.'

Margaret turned to him. 'You found it in her possession?'

'No, but she must have taken it, for it disappeared and the only other servant's from a good Paisley family, so it wasn't her.' The councillor's wife nodded complacently.

'You turned a girl into the street because of a missing ribbon?' Gavin asked slowly.

'It was our Liza's best new ribbon!' Mistress Brodie pointed out.

'We could have sent the girl to the cells and had her flogged for theft,' her husband chimed in. 'But we were generous. We just told her to go.'

'Where did she go?' Gavin pressed.

'That's not our concern.'

'I'll tell you anyway. She took lodgings in a house you own by the river, and now she's mebbe dying. There's a whole family still there, living in a way you'd not force on a pet dog.'

The councillor retreated a step or two towards the sofa. 'The girl's a thief – no responsibility of mine. And if you can't be civil to me in my own house I'll thank you to leave!'

'Civil!' Margaret began, but Gavin's fingers clamped onto her wrist and she stopped.

'D'you ever visit the houses you own by the river, Councillor?'

'I've no need. A man sees to collecting the rents for me.'

'Would you come with us now and see where we found Beth Lang?'

'I will not, for I've important town business to attend to. And I'll have no more of your insolence, Mister Knox!' Brodie retreated right behind the sofa. His wife, who was easily his height and plump all over, rose to her feet as though prepared to defend him with her embroidery needle if necessary.

'We'll leave, since you request it in such a civil manner.' Gavin's voice was suddenly silky. 'Come on, Margaret.'

* * *

'That was a fine performance!' she snapped at him when the councillor's door closed behind them. 'Why didn't you let me speak? I'd have given him something to think about!'

'So will I, in my own way. Best leave him to me, for I don't live here and he can't harm me the way he might try to harm you or your father.' Gavin looked up at the afternoon sky, which was beginning to clear, then said again, 'Come on, Margaret,' and set off along the road, her hand clasped firmly in his. 'We've got work to do before night falls. We'll go to the hospital first.'

In the next hour, working with an air of efficiency and authority she had never seen before, he hired a cart and persuaded the hospital mistress to find room for the family living by the river.

'The youngest'll be dead in a matter of weeks, and the mother's in a bad way too, so they'll not take up room for long,' he told her with cruel honesty. 'But we might be in time to save the rest of the family.'

When they returned to the room where they had found Beth he marched in and pulled the man to his feet, ignoring his fuddled protests.

The women and children began to cry in fear and panic as he half-carried his feebly struggling burden out to the waiting cart. Before he could re-enter the room the younger woman slammed the door and started to drag the table against it. Margaret tried to stop her and the woman clawed at her, hissing like an enraged cat; then she shrank back as the rotted wood of the door exploded under the weight of Gavin's foot.

'For pity's sake, can't you see that you're being saved, not murdered?' he roared in exasperation, and the children's sobs redoubled.

'You're frightening them! Why don't you try kindness?'

Margaret shouted at him over the din. 'How would you like it if a stranger burst into your home and began to drag you out?'

'I'd like it fine – if I lived in a sty like this!' he retorted, and threw a handful of coins down on the table. The noise stopped at once as the women and children stared at the money. Then, as if by magic, the table was bare and the children were being hushed and gathered together.

Gavin grinned at Margaret. 'You see? Money can do more than kindness,' he said smugly, and ushered his charges out to the waiting cart.

'Mister Brodie'll easily find more tenants to replace them,' she said helplessly when the family had been driven off, clutching their few possessions.

'Not in this room.' He led her back into the building. 'Look at it – the walls are running with water—' His fingers sank into crumbling plaster and with a short sound of disgust he rubbed his hand on his coat and moved to the window. Tall as he was he had to hoist himself up to peer through what glass remained. The breeze ruffled his dark hair. 'The river runs right by this wall. It's oozing in through the foundations.'

He dropped to the floor, then went down on one knee to examine the boards. After a moment he stood up and stamped hard. A plank crumbled under the weight of his foot and the room smelled worse than ever.

'I thought so.' He looked round and his eyes fell on her. 'Give me that thing you've got round your neck – I'll buy you another!' he added as she hesitated. Dumbly she handed over her small head shawl and watched as he wrapped it round one hand then began to rip the floorboards up. The stink in the room was indescribable now, and she clapped a hand over her mouth and ran to the door. Outside, she breathed fresh air in deeply before venturing back into the room.

'Stay where you are,' Gavin rapped as she arrived in the doorway. He was examining the large cavity he had made in the floor. Rotten boards were piled by his side.

'A sewer runs right under this floor. It's a wonder these folk didn't fall through the rotted boards. Well, if Mister Brodie won't come and see it for himself we'll just have to take the proof to him.'

Gingerly, he tied a rag round a piece of flooring and dipped it into the hole he had made. It came out saturated with thick, stinking slime.

'Now – we're going to pay another visit to the Brodies,' said Gavin coldly.

17

When the councillor's maidservant answered the door, Gavin shouldered it wide and marched through the hall, Margaret at his heels. Straight into the parlour he went, ignoring the maid's cry of: 'But the master has callers!'

Councillor Brodie and three other men sat round the table; Mistress Brodie and one of her daughters plied their needles diligently on the sofa. Six pairs of eyes looked up as Gavin swept in. Six noses wrinkled as the smell from the rags reached them.

'There—' he dropped his unpleasant burden on the table before Brodie '—is your lodging house, Mister Brodie.'

The man's face paled and he stood up, pushing his chair back so violently that it crashed to the floor. His wife and daughter squealed.

'Don't go, gentlemen,' the surgeon added smoothly to the other three men, scrambling to their feet. 'You're welcome to hear what I have to say. This rag comes from a bed used by children in a house owned by Councillor Brodie here. A sewer runs under the floor. The river seeps into the building through the walls, and wind and rain have access through broken windows.

You can judge for yourself what the stink's like. The children's mother's dying and their father drinks all the money that comes in – apart, I'm sure, from Mister Brodie's rent – to forget the misery of it all.'

Mistress Brodie fainted onto her daughter's shoulder. The colour had flooded back into her husband's face, and his eyes had begun to bulge. His companions were discreetly melting across the room and out of the door.

'I'll have the law on you!' the councillor raved, pointing a shaking finger at Gavin.

'You do that – and I'll see to it that the whole town knows how you treat your tenants. I'll make you a laughing stock in this place.'

'I'll set the militia on you – the pair of you!' Brodie screamed. Dirty mud from the rag oozed over his polished table and the papers strewn across it. Gavin leaned over to prod at the man's fat belly.

'You're welcome to try,' he said with quiet menace, his finger forcing the councillor a step back at each word. The man almost tripped on his overturned chair and only an undignified skip kept him upright.

'I just wish,' Gavin said with real regret as they stepped out of the councillor's gate, 'that I could have pushed him into that sewer. He belongs in it.'

Margaret was almost dancing with glee. 'You did enough! Oh, Gavin – I was proud of you!'

Then her smile faded. 'But your clothes are ruined – and look at my skirt! We're like a couple of tinkers!'

He examined a jagged tear on his coat sleeve and shrugged. 'Mebbe my landlady'll be able to mend it.'

'Come on home – I'll see to it.' She walked on, thinking about the family who would be trying to come to terms with their new life in the hospital at that very minute, and had got to the end of the lane before she realised that Gavin wasn't with her.

He had perched himself on a low wall and was staring intently at a small and ugly pig that was nosing happily round a pile of refuse. Gavin had broken off a twig from a branch overhanging the garden wall behind him and was twisting it absentmindedly between his fingers.

She went back to see what was of such interest to him but could find nothing – only the contented pig.

'I've been thinking, Margaret,' Gavin said, his eyes on the black twig with its tight-curled sticky buds. 'I've been thinking it would be a good thing if you and me were to wed.'

'You're daft!'

When she had said that to Jamie by the river he had angrily defended himself. But Gavin, lounging on the wall in the day's dusk, merely said, 'I think I must be. What's your answer?'

'But – why should marriage come into your head in a place like this?' She indicated the lane, the muck heap, the rooting pig.

'I didn't plan to mention it here,' he said with a hint of exasperation. 'But I suppose one place is as good as another for the purpose. We get on well enough and I like your sharp way of treating folk, though I realise that most men wouldn't. And there's a lot of sense in that pretty head of yours. I'm ready to settle down – and I have no wish to settle with anyone but you.'

'But I scarcely know you!'

'I've been coming to Paisley with Thomas for a good year now. Besides, we can get to know each other better when we're married, and living in the same house,' he pointed out. 'The more I think of it the more the idea pleases me. You're going to refuse me, aren't you?'

She glared at him. 'If I am I'll do it myself. No need for you to stick your nose in!'

He rubbed the offending feature and grinned. 'You're free to make up your own mind, and you always will be. But as your brother's closest friend, I feel it's my duty to advise you to give my proposal some thought. I'm a good catch.'

Then he got up, scratched the pig behind one ear with the branch, and walked on down the lane, saying over his shoulder, 'Come to that, it would be a fine match for both of us.'

It was a ridiculous proposal – unromantic, ill-timed; never, surely, had a woman received a more disinterested offer of marriage, Margaret thought angrily. She ran after him and caught him up as he reached the corner.

'We'd fight – all the time.'

'Well – most of the time, perhaps. I'm counting on that, for I never wanted a dull marriage.'

'If I wasn't happy I'd not stay.'

'I'd hold the door open for you myself. Well?'

Exasperation, disbelief, bewilderment milled together in her mind, together with the dawning realisation that her life would never be the same again, now that Gavin had walked into it. And the further realisation that she didn't want him to walk back out of it.

'Well?' his maddeningly calm voice prompted.

'But Gavin – you've never said you love me!' she almost shrieked at him, stamping her foot. 'Why can't you say you love me?'

His expression, polite interest with just a hint of anxiety underlying it, wavered and crumbled as though it had been a mask, giving way to a look that made her heart flutter and her head spin. She swayed, and might have fallen if he hadn't swept her into his arms.

'And risk the rough edge of your tongue? Oh, Margaret,' he

said against her neck, 'are you entirely blind? Don't you know that I've loved you since that night you danced all over my feet?'

'I didn't—' she began to say before his lips stopped hers.

'Don't you know how impatient I've been, and how afraid that you'd send me away if I spoke at the wrong moment?' he asked when he finally lifted his head. 'I thought I'd lost you when William Todd came back from Beith, for the two of you were together so much.'

She ran her fingertips from the corner of his mouth to where his hair curled on his temple, and the sensation brought a melting joy she had never known before. 'William's one of my closest friends, nothing more.'

Her fingers buried themselves in his hair, sliding round to the back of his head, pulling him down to meet her eager lips again. The pig found a choice morsel and nibbled at it happily, its little eyes fixed on the couple who stood, locked in each other's embrace, at the corner of the lane.

'My mother,' said Margaret shakily, when she was free to speak again, 'will be pleased.'

He grinned down at her, his tawny eyes openly alight with happiness. 'She will. But d'you think our news'll be enough to take her mind off the loss of that fine cabbage we were supposed to bring back?'

18

By the time Margaret and Gavin married, three months later, Beth Lang had recovered from her ordeal in the slum by the river, and had been taken on as Mary MacLeod's companion.

'It's pleasant to have a young person about the house again,' the milliner said on one of her visits to Margaret's new home. 'I've been lonely since Thomas went off to Glasgow. Though I'm right glad,' she added with more than a touch of malicious pleasure, 'to have you two so near me now.'

Margaret flushed crimson and thumped the teapot down with more energy than necessary. Gavin had agreed to her wish to stay in Paisley, where she could continue her work in the town hospital, but only on condition that they took a house fit for a surgeon. Despite her protests, he had bought a house on Oakshawhill, almost the twin to Mary's.

'And that's a nice respectable maidservant you've got,' Mary went on mercilessly.

'It was Gavin employed her, not me,' her niece snapped. 'I could have managed the house fine on my own!'

Gavin gave up trying to hide his amusement. 'Poor Ellen has

to run morning, noon and night, trying to get through the house-work before Margaret does it for her. I found the two of them nearly at each other's throats yesterday over who was to get to scrub the kitchen floor.'

'I can't sit still and let someone else clean my house for me!'

'Now, Margaret,' he said with that air of calm possessiveness that both maddened and warmed her. 'You do plenty, what with the hospital and helping your mother in the shop and enter-taining our visitors. That's more than enough for someone in your—'

He stopped short as his wife glared at him.

'—condition,' Mary serenely finished the sentence, setting her cup down and brushing a crumb from the lacy ruffles at one wrist.

'I told my mother in confidence!'

'Tuts, Meg never said a word – it was the smug look she's had on her face for the past seven days that gave it away. Gavin's right, though – you'll have to learn to let other folk take on some of your work.'

* * *

A wet, cold October left Colin with a heavy chest cold, and Meg with an agonising bout of rheumatism that forced her to stay at home. That same month the widow who lived with her family in the rooms behind the shop remarried and moved with her family out of the town altogether, leaving the burden of the shop on Margaret's shoulders.

'Colin'll have to find someone else!' Gavin insisted, worried about her health. 'What about the girl who worked there before?'

'Janet? She's gone from bad to worse, married to that lout of a husband,' Meg fretted. 'She's got a family by his first wife to see to, and her own children – not that I'd be able to trust her on her own now.'

'William!' The worried frown cleared from Margaret's brow, to be replaced by a broad smile. 'He's the very one to look after the shop.'

'He'll not come back,' Meg scoffed. 'He's happy working for Matt. He wouldn't even come home for your wedding.'

'But he'll do it for his father's sake. And there's no denying—' the cloud drifted over Margaret's face again '—that Uncle Colin's getting frail now. I'm sure William'll come home – and I'll go to fetch him myself!'

* * *

There were moments, during the bumpy carriage ride to Glasgow and the bumpier coach journey to Edinburgh, when Margaret regretted her decision. When they reached the capital, Gavin had to carry her in his arms into the coaching inn, where he coaxed some brandy and water between her ashen lips.

'But don't ask me to eat, for I never will again!' she said miserably into his comforting shoulder, her stomach heaving at the aroma drifting from the kitchens.

By the time the brandy was finished she felt a little stronger, and after a night's sleep and a good breakfast the following morning she was herself again and impatient to make the final short journey out to the farm where Matt lived with his wife Mirren.

Their visitors got a warm welcome. Matt, strong and handsome as ever in spite of his greying head, sent a boy to fetch William, who was out in the fields.

'I think he'll want to go back with you, for Colin's sake. But he'll be missed here, for he's a good worker.'

'You should come back yourself, for a visit,' Margaret urged, but he shook his head.

'This place won't run itself. And to me, Paisley was never the same after my father died. I'd see his ghost everywhere. Have you had news of Jamie?'

'The last we heard he was in London, and wondering if he might be sent out to the Americas.'

Matt's big body heaved in a nostalgic sigh. 'There's nothing like soldiering to set a man up,' he said, then grinned at Mirren and added, 'Mind you, there's something to be said for a settled life and the right woman to share it.'

'You're right,' Gavin said from the window seat, his gaze reaching across the low-ceilinged kitchen to enfold Margaret in its warmth.

Then he looked out of the window and saw a tall, lithe, well-muscled young man come into the cobbled yard, two farm dogs twisting round his feet as he walked.

'What is it? Is it him?' Margaret saw his change of expression and hurried to the door. Then with a glad cry of 'William!' she was running across the yard.

Gavin watched from the window as William stopped in his tracks; surprise, disbelief, and something else that was controlled so swiftly that Gavin hadn't time to register what it was, chased each other across his tanned face. Then Margaret threw herself into his arms, almost knocking him over, and he caught her and held her close.

In that moment, as he saw his wife's dark brown head blend with William's short, loose curls, bleached by an outdoor life into a tumble of bronze, Gavin knew a stab of uneasiness, and something even stronger. Something that had until then been alien to him.

Jealousy.

* * *

'There's nothing in Paisley for me. I'm better where I am.'

Margaret put her spoon down, her face stiff with astonishment as she faced William across the table. 'But your father's not well! He needs you!'

'Did he ask for me to go back?'

'You know he'd never do that. He doesn't even know we're here.'

'That's all right, then.' William kept his head bent over his plate, though he wasn't eating. 'He can get a woman in to tend the shop. There's plenty'd be pleased to get the work. I've my own life to live here.'

'But we all want you to come home, where you belong,' Margaret persisted, and his head was suddenly thrown back, the gold lights in his hair catching the lamp's glow, his eyes angry.

'I don't belong there! I never did!' he said, and pushed his chair back.

'William! Tell him,' she appealed to Matt as the door to the yard slammed behind William, but the older man shook his head.

'He makes his own decisions. I don't know why he's so bitter, but it's deep in him. Best not tamper with it.'

She rose from the table and followed William out to the yard, stumbling as her eyes tried to accustom themselves to the change between lamplight and darkness. A dog growled at her and William's clipped voice silenced it.

'William? Stop this nonsense and come back to Paisley with us!'

'It's not nonsense!' he rapped back in the same tone that had dealt with the dog. 'I'm not one of your hospital children to be ordered about!' Then he added, his voice changing, 'Why did you have to come here and meddle in the life I've made for myself?'

'I just want you to come back to your father – to all of us—'

She reached out to touch his arm and felt the stuff of his coat slide by her fingers as he pulled back. Then a soft gold light spilled over them as the farm door opened. The glow touched his eyes and gave them the same tawny light that Gavin's had. She saw them move over her, stop at the spot where pregnancy swelled her gown.

Gavin, silhouetted in the doorway, called at her, and William said, low-voiced, 'Go to him, Margaret. Go back to Paisley with him and leave me to my own devices!'

Then he was gone, merging into the shadows, the dogs at his heels, and she was alone.

* * *

As Robert Montgomery had predicted, silk was becoming one of Paisley's main cloths, though linen was still of considerable importance. On her return from Edinburgh, Margaret managed to get a small inkle loom set up in the hospital so that some of the women there could weave ribbons, another popular new product.

She also found a woman to work in the grocer's shop, and Meg herself was soon back behind the counter, wincing when she had to stoop to ladle grain from the sacks on the floor.

Colin couldn't shake himself free from his chest cold. It settled, and they were all reminded, as they heard his harsh cough, of his father's chronic bronchitis.

Margaret persuaded Beth Lang, Mary's companion, to take over her work at the hospital temporarily. She and Gavin battled over her decision to return to teaching once her baby was born, and she won.

'But it's not seemly for a woman to leave her child to someone else's attentions!' Meg fretted.

'I'm needed at the hospital. I'll not be away from the house all that much, and Ellen's well able to watch over the baby when I'm not there.'

'Isn't it a blessing,' said Mary slyly, 'that you've got a maid-servant?'

'Since Gavin insists on employing one, Aunt Mary, I might as well make use of her,' her niece said sharply, and Mary smirked into the ribbons and lace of the hat she was making.

It was a relief to Gavin when Margaret stopped going to the hospital and the shop every day. He worked hard, and it made all the difference to him to find her waiting for him when he came home.

Their marriage was very happy, for all its minor storms, and they looked forward together to their baby's birth.

The tranquillity he prized so much was shattered when he arrived home one evening in late November to find Margaret pacing the parlour floor, shaking with rage, while Mary sat by the fire and watched her with a worried frown.

'I'm glad you're back. See if you can talk sense to this woman,' she appealed to him. 'It's not good for her to get herself into such a state.'

'Gavin!' Margaret clutched at him, her bright eyes and the tension that almost sparked from her body alarming him. 'You'll have to make them see reason! You're a surgeon – they'd surely listen to you!'

'Who? For the love of God, Margaret, sit down and tell me what's amiss?' He pushed her gently down onto the sofa and sat beside her. 'You'll do yourself and the baby no good!'

'That's what I told her. But it's the society—' Mary began, and he groaned.

'Not the Society for the Reformation of Manners again! Margaret, haven't I advised you to keep well away from them?'

'D'you think that would make any difference? Looking the other way's not the answer!'

'Sometimes it's the only thing a sensible person can do!'

The Society for the Reformation of Manners was a group of well-to-do Paisley people who took it upon themselves to seek out and chastise the sinners in their midst. Compassion and understanding were not emotions that they recognised, and both Margaret and Mary had clashed with them on more occasions than Gavin cared to remember.

'You think we should just let them get on with their foul work unhampered?' There were tears in her eyes. 'Gavin, they're going to flog Janet through the town tomorrow if we don't stop them!'

'That's the woman who used to work for Colin and Meg,' Mary offered. 'It seems she took some cloth from a loom shop and sold it.'

'But surely that doesn't warrant a flogging?'

Margaret took a deep breath, then said in a flat, calm voice that worried Gavin more than her former hysteria, 'It does as far as the society and the council are concerned. Janet's to be driven through the town tomorrow, and given ten lashes at each end of New Street, then another ten lashes at the Cross. Then she'll be put out of the town to fend for herself.'

'And her children,' Mary finished the story. 'That no-good man of hers got out of harm's way the minute he heard that she'd been taken.'

'You've spoken to the society, Mary?'

'We both have – Duncan and Meg too. But Johnny Brodie's in control of them now – and he's waited for nearly a year to get his revenge for that business over his house down by the river.'

Gavin groaned again. 'Councillor Brodie!'

'They've hired a man from outside for the work.' Margaret's voice was still flat. 'They're paying him three guineas.'

'What? That's more than I'm paid to amputate half a dozen limbs!'

'The society seems to think it's worth the cost,' Mary said dryly. 'Well, I've done all I can – I'll have to get back home. Take my advice, Margaret – tell yourself that you can only do your best and no more.'

When she had gone, Gavin gathered Margaret into his arms.

'Mary's right – what more can anyone do?'

'You're a surgeon,' she repeated. 'They might listen to you.'

He gave in. 'I've little hope of succeeding, but I'll try – after I've had something to eat.'

* * *

She was in bed, wide awake, when he got back. He sat on the bed and took her hand.

'Councillor Brodie's done his work well. Not one of them would change his mind. They as good as told me to mind my own business.' The humiliation he had suffered at the hands of Brodie and his cronies choked him. 'Make up your mind to it, Margaret – you can't always expect the whole town to dance to your tune, and that's a fact.'

Without another word she threw herself over in the bed, turning her head away from him, listening to the sounds of him undressing.

For the first time, they slept without holding each other.

* * *

'I wish I could stay with you today, but I'm needed in Glasgow,' Gavin said after a silent breakfast on the following morning. He hesitated, then took her into his arms. Her lips were cool and unresponsive to his kiss.

'Stay in the house today. Don't go out.'

'That won't save poor Janet from her flogging, will it?'

He shook her gently. 'Margaret, nobody can help Janet now. Can you not see that?'

She could, and she would have been happy to stay at home, closing her mind to the day's events. But it was impossible. When the crowd gathered to witness the flogging she was on its outer fringes, watching as Janet was driven up in the back of a cart, her wrists lashed to the rail before her.

The woman, younger than Meg and Mary, looked years older than either of them. Her face was lined; her straggling lifeless hair was grey. Margaret, who hadn't seen her for years, was shocked by the effect life had had on the girl who used to work behind the grocery counter. A carriage bearing some of the society's members, Councillor Brodie among them, followed the cart.

As the man paid to administer the punishment raised his whip, Margaret suddenly came to her senses. Gavin was right – she couldn't help Janet this way. She was only adding to the mob that had come to jeer and gawp and be glad that it wasn't happening to them. She turned, and would have hurried back to Oakshawhill if the crowd hadn't surged forward to get nearer to the cart, closing round her and carrying her with them.

The whip descended. Janet's curses rose to a scream, and to Margaret, fighting to keep her feet as she was carried forward, it became old Hector Lyle's public hanging all over again. She felt her throat constrict and closed her eyes against the faces round her, especially the sight of Janet flinching as the whip came down again and again on her back.

The darkness behind her lids flashed red lightning and threatened to draw her down into its depths forever. Afraid that she might lose her footing and be trampled, Margaret opened her eyes again and saw a crimson thread of blood run down Janet's chin as the woman sank her teeth into her lower lip. Her face, turned towards Margaret, was knotted with pain as the lash landed for the tenth time. Then the whip was laid aside and a small cup of spirits held to Janet's lips. She sucked at it greedily as the cart jolted into motion down the slope that led to the foot of New Street.

Jostled by the crowd, unable to fight free, Margaret was forced to follow and witness the next ten lashes.

'For God's sake have some mercy!' she heard herself scream at the men in the cart as Janet's thin shawl was torn to shreds and fell, wet and red, from her back. But nobody heard her in the noise of the crowd, half of them jeering at the victim, the other half shouting encouragement to her and abuse to the stony-faced society members in their carriage.

When at last they reached the Cross, and the final ten lashes were administered Janet's defiance had gone, and she slumped over the cart's rail, her body jerking as the lash hit it. The man who wielded it was clearly softening the blows, for now that the sport of it was gone the crowd's mood towards him was becoming threatening.

Then it was over, and Janet was released and allowed to fall to the floor of the cart. The militiamen in attendance kept back the crowd as her friends lifted her and carried her away. The society officials hurriedly left the scene, and the crowd dispersed, leaving Margaret free, at last, to go home.

All she wanted was to go to bed, to hide herself from the day's events in sleep. But when she reached the front door Gavin opened it, his face a mask carved out of ivory.

'Where have you been?'

She dragged her shoulders straight, walked past him to the parlour.

He followed her in and shut the door as she sank down onto a chair by the fire. 'You went to the flogging, didn't you?'

'Of course I did.'

He was white to the lips. 'I knew fine you'd disobey me. I came back as soon as I could – I was out of my mind with worry!'

'I'm not a child! I can look after myself!'

'I wish I could be as sure of that! Listen to me – the woman stole from a weaver. In this town that's a sin, and she knew it. She was punished according to the law and it's not your business to interfere. D'you hear me?'

'I do – and you sound as twisted as Johnny Brodie! I'll not stay in my own parlour to listen to such talk!'

She stormed to the door, anger revitalising her exhausted body. But he was there before her, his hands on her shoulders, his face twisted with rage.

'You'll not mention me in the same breath as that man!'

'Take your hands off me,' she ordered coldly, and his arms dropped to his sides. Choking with rage, they glared at each other. It was Gavin who made the first move towards reconciliation.

'Margaret – you know well enough that if the law's broken there has to be a punishment.'

'So Johnny Brodie can make money from other folk's misery and get away with it, while the likes of Janet are beaten until the blood runs for trying to find the money to feed their children?'

'I'm not proud of the way the law works. There are changes needed, but it's up to the men who run the country to see to that, not you and me. I've got enough to do, worrying about my own wife's well-being, and my child's well-being too.'

She swept away from him, back into the centre of the room. 'Your wife – your child!' she mocked, anger flaring again. 'No need to worry about your possessions, Mister Knox. Your child'll do fine, for he's to be born to folk with enough money to buy food for him. We won't have to steal to keep him alive!'

'Margaret—' He reached for her, but she evaded him.

'I wish you'd stop talking about your precious child as if I've nothing to do with him at all – as if I'm nothing but a... a box to hold your son!'

Hurt grimaced across his face then the anger flooded back again. As he advanced towards her, the door behind him opened cautiously and Ellen poked a scared head in.

'Mistress Knox—'

'What d'you want?' Gavin rounded on her and she recoiled before the look on his face.

'A visitor to s-see the mistress. Will I tell him?'

'Tell him to go to He—'

'Tell him to come in, Ellen,' Margaret ordered grandly.

'You'll do nothing of the—' Gavin began, but the embarrassed visitor had already been scooped into the room by Ellen and was hesitating in the doorway, his country clothes and weathered brown face giving him a strangely alien look.

'I decided I should come home—' he began.

'Oh! And a welcome sight you are!' Margaret's anger melted into tears of joy as she brushed past her husband and went forward, hands outstretched.

Gavin stayed where he was, his eyes as cool as his voice when he said formally, 'Welcome back to Paisley, William.'

19

It seemed as though Margaret's marriage sailed into a sheltered harbour with the birth of her daughter in March 1771.

There had never been a bonnier, better-behaved baby than Christian, who had her mother's neat-featured face and Gavin's thick dark hair and gold-flecked hazel eyes.

At last Margaret settled happily into domesticity, even deciding to share the hospital work with Beth so that she could spend more time at home caring for Gavin and their daughter.

With William back, Paisley was its old self. The only person she missed now was Jamie, whose letters were few.

'Kirsty's worried about him,' William said on one of his frequent visits. 'When he does manage to put pen to paper, he says very little. There's something amiss.'

'I've no doubt he'll weather anything that comes his way,' she said comfortably, knitting wires flashing between her skilful fingers, one foot rocking Christian's cradle. 'How's your father today?'

'Keeping to his bed. I was shocked to see how he'd changed.'

'He'll be the better for seeing you. You were right to come home.'

'Mebbe.' Then he changed the subject. 'I've ordered a good stock of snuff for the shop. I hear the men at the hospital are to be given their snuff penny again.'

Her face lit up. 'Poor souls – a penny a week's not much, but a wee bit snuff gives them such pleasure.'

* * *

Two months after William came home Colin Todd died in his sleep. It was as though, as Kirsty said, he had been waiting to see his son home again before he let go.

Margaret paced the parlour restlessly on the evening of the funeral day. Gavin was closeted in his small study, Ellen was entertaining a friend in the kitchen, Christian slept peacefully, and none of them needed Margaret's presence.

She picked up her knitting wires, but tossed them down again almost at once. Her spinning wheel was discarded just as promptly. She went to the window, but the darkening street outside was empty, with nothing to fix her eyes and her mind on except trees tossing and bending in the rising wind. Finally she fetched her cloak and put her head round the study door.

'I'm going to see William. Ellen'll listen out for the baby.'

'You're going out on a night like this?' The first spatter of rain on the glass underlined Gavin's words. 'Kirsty and Billy are there – he doesn't need you.'

'I'll not be long.'

'If you wait five minutes, I'll walk down with you.'

But she had no wish for his company on her errand. 'You get on with what you're doing. I'm able to walk down the hill on my own. I'll not be long,' she said again, and went out before he could argue.

By the time she reached the High Street house, the rainstorm had started in earnest and the sky was black. The door had been left on the latch and she slipped into the passageway, a sixth sense leading her to Colin's room instead of up the stairs to the kitchen.

The room was dark, but she could see William, sitting in the wheelchair, silhouetted against the window. His head turned briefly as the door opened and closed.

'Margaret?'

'I'm here.' She sat down at the table.

'I'm glad you made me come home for... for the end.'

'You'd have come anyway.'

'No.' After a long pause he said, 'I went away because of a quarrel we had.'

Surprise sharpened her voice. 'You and your father? But you've never ever said a harsh word to each other!'

'He didn't – but I did. The thing about words is that you can't take them back.'

'But it was all right in the end, surely?'

'I think so,' he said. 'We never spoke of it again. I was too shamed, and mebbe he didn't feel that there was time for further bitterness in his life. God knows he'd supped more than his fair share of it.'

'You came back, and that's all that would matter to him.'

She heard his breathing check and then change to a soft, uneven rhythm, and guessed that he was crying. Her hands fluttered in her lap hesitantly before folding about each other. Comfort was for hurt children; men needed solitude in their grief.

She waited until, a full ten minutes later, his breath steadied and he scrubbed a hand over his face, then she got to her feet and touched his shoulder.

'I must go home now.'

He turned his head and she felt his lips brush her fingers before she went as quietly as she had come, leaving him alone in the dark.

Lamplight spilled from under the parlour door when she reached her own house again. Gavin was hunched in a chair before the dying fire.

'So you're back.'

'I said I'd not be long.' She knelt on the hearth, sifting powdery ash from the fire with the poker then lifting coals from the gleaming brass scuttle to lay on the embers.

'Did you see him?' Gavin's voice was sullen.

'William? Yes, I saw him.'

'And comforted him, I've no doubt.'

She laid down the tongs, sitting back on her heels. 'Nobody can give him much comfort at a time like this. He'll have to get over his loss in his own time and in his own way.'

'That's what I tried to tell you – but you insisted on going to him all the same.'

She got to her feet. 'Of course I did – as I'd have gone to anyone who's suffering as much as he is just now. And if you're going to make such a fuss about it, I might as well go to my bed as stay here.'

He was out of the chair and at the door before her.

'Was Kirsty there? Or Billy?'

Irritation began to edge her voice. 'What has that to do with it? Gavin, what's come over you? Every time William's as much as mentioned you begin to jump about like a cat that's fallen into a washtub!'

'It's not me who does the jumping – it's you! When he's here you fret about his comfort, when he's not here you wonder if he's all right.' Then his angry tirade stopped as she began to laugh. 'What is it now?'

'It's just you... you should see yourself, like a wee boy who's been left out of a game! Gavin, you're surely not jealous of William? He's like one of my own brothers – the best of them, for Robert was a bully and Thomas too fond of his books for my liking. William was the gentle one, the one I felt safe with. But you're the man I wed, Gavin. If you think of William as a threat, you've as much notion of common sense as your daughter has of Latin right now.'

Gavin eyed her doubtfully. 'Did he ever ask you to marry him?'

'Never.'

'If he had, would you have accepted?'

The laughter was still in her voice. 'I've no idea, for I never intended to marry, as you know yourself. And as he didn't ask me, the thought was never in his mind either. Oh, Gavin.' She slid her arms about his neck, drew him close and spoke against his throat, feeling his skin warm and pulsing beneath her lips. 'I'll make my own friends where I choose – just as I chose my own husband. And I'm too well pleased with him to look elsewhere.'

Then she squeaked as he lifted her off her feet and turned to the door.

'Put me down – I've just built up the fire!'

'You have that,' he agreed huskily, carrying her out of the room and across the dark hall to the stairs. 'And now you'll have to take the consequences!'

* * *

Kirsty's kitchen was warm, noisy and filled with the smell of broth and fresh-baked bread. Meg and Mary, Kate and Robert's wife Annie had come to take tea, and the patchwork rugs on the floor were lively with babies – three-month-old Christian propped up on cushions, Kate and Annie's older children crawling and toddling near their mothers.

Margaret took a moment to wonder, as she often did, at her own presence in the middle of such a domesticated crowd. Motherhood must addle the brain – but it was a pleasant affliction, she admitted to herself, poking Christian with a gentle toe and watching the smile that was so like Gavin's break over the baby's face.

Then she lifted her head, listening, thinking that she had heard the street door open, a familiar voice calling. But it was impossible to be sure of anything with such a clatter of tongues vying with the whir of Kirsty's spinning wheel.

So it came as a complete surprise to them all when the kitchen door flew back on its hinges and a tall figure appeared in the doorway. He looked drawn, and considerably older than when they had last seen him, but there was no mistaking the fiery hair, the wide grin, the blue eyes.

'Now then,' said Jamie Todd, 'here's a bonny sight to welcome a man back home among his own folk!'

* * *

'Prison!' Margaret said, aghast. 'Jamie Todd – I always knew you'd fall into bad ways! Haven't I said it time and time again?'

'Not to my knowledge.' Jamie, sprawled comfortably in the Knox parlour, was unrepentant. 'It's not as if it was a real jail, Margaret. Just an army one. Insubordination, they said.' He rolled the word around his tongue with relish. 'The truth of it was, I got tired of being ordered about by namby-pamby officers who didn't know what they were talking about half the time.'

She eyed him closely. For all his joking there was a new awareness at the back of his eyes, deep lines etched into his face, a cynicism that had never laced his smile before.

'There's a lot more to it than that. Something bad happened to you, Jamie.'

For a fleeting second she saw bitterness chill his eyes, then it was gone.

'I'll just say that I wanted to see the world – and there are some things out there that I'd as soon not have seen,' he said lightly, and she knew that that was as much as she or anyone else would get out of him.

'And what do you plan to do next? There's plenty young men in the town talking of going to the Americas to find a new life.'

He stretched his legs out and contemplated the toes of his boots. 'No, I've had my fill of travel for the moment. And it's time the looms were back in my father's shop. After all, weaving's what I was trained to do.'

He hadn't lost the ability to surprise her. 'You'd settle down here and be a weaver?'

'I'm in the mood for that. Paisley has its attractions for me now—' a sly smile sparkled at her '—and that bonny Beth Lang who stays with your Aunt Mary's one of them.'

'Just you watch yourself, Jamie Todd! I've already decided that Beth would make a fine wife for William.'

'Let William look out for himself, then,' said Jamie, half in fun, half in earnest. 'The girl I wanted belongs to someone else now – and a weary traveller's entitled to find his comfort where he can.'

20

'Please God, no!' Margaret prayed aloud as she threw herself out of bed and ran, sure-footed in the darkness, to the crib. By the time Gavin had lit the lamp the baby was in her arms, still making those terrible choking, wheezing sounds that had wakened the two of them.

'Give her to me—' Gavin took Christian over to the light. Her face was congested, her frightened eyes stared up at him, her small fists flailed at the air. 'Go and boil a kettle, Margaret!'

She ran barefoot, terror choking her throat just as the croup was choking her baby. Through her mind, as she poked the glowing kitchen range into life, splashed water into the kettle and swung it on its hook over the fire, tramped a never-ending list of names of infants who had died in the town from the dreaded illness.

Throughout that long night she and Gavin took turns to walk the floor with Christian, filling every pot they could find so that the kitchen became humid with steam to loosen the mucus in the little girl's lungs. Slowly she improved, and by dawn the immediate crisis was over and she slept, exhausted.

It happened again on the next night, and the next. Before their eyes Gavin and Margaret saw their baby sicken and lose ground.

'If anything should happen to her—' Margaret said fearfully one morning when dawn's grey light found Christian slipping into her first sleep of the night, her dark hair wet with sweat, her mouth blue-tinged. Gavin reached out and drew her close.

'Nothing's going to happen to her – nothing!' he said fiercely, but when she looked up at him she saw her own terror mirrored in his tired face.

'Gavin—'

'Sshhh.' He led her back to bed, though it was almost time for him to get up and go to Glasgow. 'I've been thinking, Margaret – some folk say that sea air can be beneficial. I've a cousin living down in Ayr – we could take Christian to spend a few days with him.'

'D'you think it would help her?'

He shrugged helplessly. 'I don't know – but I'll try anything.' Then he lifted her face to his and kissed her gently. 'Leave Ellen to see to the wee one today and go out for a while. You'll make yourself ill if you stay in all the time with her – and I couldn't bear it if something happened to you as well.'

Against her own wishes she did as she was told, turning her steps towards her parents' house. But Meg was out somewhere, and Margaret couldn't face Kirsty, who had lost a baby to the croup herself. Without making any conscious decision she found herself walking into the grocer's shop.

William was serving a customer. She nodded and went through to the back. The rooms where she had been born and raised were sparsely furnished, for he had few needs. There were a lot of books, two chairs flanking the fire, a rag rug, and little else. The mantelshelf was bare of ornaments.

Shivering, she knelt down to stir the fire into a blaze. The shop door closed and she heard William come into the room behind her.

'Margaret?'

She kept her eyes on the fire. 'William, my baby's going to die.'

He drew in his breath sharply, knelt down beside her so that he could look into her face. 'No!'

'She is... she is,' Margaret insisted, and the tears that had been aching to flow for the past three days finally surfaced in a passion of grief and fear beyond her control.

To her relief he didn't try to stop her. He gathered her into his arms and rocked her as she would have rocked Christian, holding her against his shoulder, letting her sob herself into hiccuping silence before he mopped her face, eased her gently into a chair, and bent to lift the kettle that simmered all day on the range.

Then he wrapped her hands round a cup of tea and made her sip the hot liquid.

She sniffed and gave him a watery smile. 'I've wanted to cry for days now – but I couldn't, in front of Gavin and Christian.'

'Who told you she was going to die?'

'Nobody. I just know. William, if you saw the state she gets into just trying to draw a breath—'

'Hush.' He leaned forward and put a hand against her cheek, his grey eyes holding her own. She felt as though his strength was flowing into her. 'Hush, Margaret. She'll not die – not Christian. She's not the dying sort – and I should know, for I was close to it myself a few years since and it was you who drew me back from the edge.'

'It was Kirsty's skill, not mine.'

'Mebbe, but you gave me a reason to get better – then,' he said quietly, but her mind was on Christian and she scarcely heard him.

'We're taking her to Ayr for a while. Gavin says the sea air might help her.'

He nodded, memories clearing from his eyes. 'Mebbe. It's been a bad summer here. All that rain – the burns are rushing down from the braes and the Cart's risen well up its banks. The air's damp and chill.'

The shop door rattled and he had to leave her. She took advantage of his absence to finish the tea and wash the tearstains from her face. When she heard the customer go out she went into the shop, clear-headed and calm again.

'I'd best get back to Christian. Thank you for being such a good friend, William. There's nobody I can turn to as easily as I turn to you.'

A muscle jumped in his face but he said nothing, busily shifting a new sack of meal into position and opening it.

'When I get back from Ayr, I'm going to give those rooms of yours a good clean-out,' she added briskly. 'Oh, they're neat enough, but they need a woman's touch. We'll have to think of finding a nice wee wife who'll look after you properly.'

He looked at her, opened his mouth to speak, closed it again – then the door rattled once more, letting in three women laden with baskets, and Margaret left him to his work and went back home, comforted and refreshed.

She never found out what he had been going to say.

* * *

Ayr was a revelation to Margaret, who had lived inland all her life. Situated on the Firth of Clyde, it had its own harbour and fishing fleet, rich farmland around it, and beaches where waves rolled majestically in to break on great stretches of sand.

At Gavin's insistence the three of them spent almost all their time out of doors. They collected shells to take home, and when Margaret kissed Christian her skin tasted of the salt-laden winds that blew in from the sea.

All day and every day, no matter what the weather was like, they walked for hours. She and Gavin talked and talked, played with the baby, grew closer together – and best of all were the nights, when Gavin made love to her in the big comfortable bed, and together they listened to the murmur of waves breaking on the shore, and to the easy, regular breathing of their healthy, contented little daughter.

* * *

'You'd think the sky would have run out of rain by this time.' Margaret peered from her parlour window at the dripping trees. The rain, driven by a wind, lanced at a sharp angle, and the few people to be seen were almost bent double as they battled along against the worst bout of September weather in living memory.

Meg, waiting by the fire for Duncan to come and escort her home, bounced Christian on her knee. 'There'll be damage done to roofs and chimney pots tonight,' she prophesied. 'It's not a night for man nor beast to be out.'

'Gavin's supposed to take his turn at the night watch tonight.'

'You tell him to stay by his own fireside – even the robbers'll stay home if they have any sense.'

It was a town rule that all the able-bodied men had to take their turn at patrolling the streets at night. Many of them paid others to do the work for them, and as often as not this led to more law-breaking, for substitutes had been known to turn a blind eye, for a share of the profits, to any crime they came across.

'Here he is,' Margaret said as Duncan's burly figure bowled along the road at a brisk pace and collided with the gatepost.

He refused her offer of refreshment. 'We'd best get back home, for it's getting worse outside,' he said, and took Meg off, the two of them clutching each other as the gale whirled around them.

Gavin insisted on going through with his town watch duties. Well fed and warmly wrapped up against the worsening weather, he stopped her protests with a kiss.

'You're the one who's always going on about duty,' he said, then the door slammed behind him on a gust of wind, and she was alone.

When Christian was put down for the night, Margaret settled by the parlour fire with a novel borrowed from the town's new book-lending club. The wind's whistling round the eaves and the warmth of the fire began to lull her to sleep, and she jumped when Ellen showed William in, his clothes and hair dark with rain. He shook his head when she urged him to take his coat off and get dry.

'No sense in settling down, for I'm off in a few minutes.'

'Off where?' she asked, with sudden foreboding.

'To Edinburgh, for a start. I've come to make my farewells.'

'But why, William? You're settled here again!'

He picked up her book, riffled through it without glancing at the pages, set it down, fidgeted about the room. 'Now that my father's dead there's no reason for me to stay.'

'But your friends are here! And there's the shop.'

'You're all busy with your own lives, and I'd sooner farm than be a shopkeeper.' He went to the window, parted the curtains to peer out at the wild night.

'How long have you been planning this?'

William let the curtains drop and turned to face her. He looked very tired. 'I've known for a while that I was wrong to come back. I've told Kirsty and Jamie. It's best that I go.'

'But not tonight!' The words broke from her in a cry. 'Not like this, without giving me time to say a proper farewell. You can't be so cruel!'

'Sometimes being cruel's the best way. Goodbye, Margaret,' he said, but she moved before the door, blocking his way.

'William, you've been special to me all my days. It was you I went to when I thought my baby was dying. It was you who gave me the strength to go on. Have you forgotten already?'

'No, for that was the day I knew that I had to go away.' Then, as she stayed where she was, back against the door, his voice hardened. 'Margaret, stop this nonsense and let me by!'

'Not until I find out why you're leaving us!'

For a moment she thought that he was going to pull her clear of the door, and one hand reached behind her back to anchor itself to the handle. Then the anger went out of his eyes, leaving a dull hopelessness echoed in the slump of his shoulders as he walked over to lean on the mantelshelf.

'All right, I'll tell you.' His voice was empty, lifeless. 'You'll not rest until you know, and it's my last chance to say it aloud. And when I have, you'll be glad to see me go.'

Suddenly she was afraid for him. 'William, whatever it is that's bothering you, you must know I'd never think ill of you!'

He turned, looked at her, and said clearly, 'You think not? You see, Margaret – I love you.'

Rain beat at the window. A puff of smoke eddied round his legs as the gale gusted down the chimney.

'It isn't a brotherly love. It's the strong love a man feels for a woman, and it's destroying me. Every time I hear your voice or see you smile or watch the turn of your head it tears the heart out of me. I want to hold you and have you for my own, but I can't do that – I never could. So I'm going out of Paisley, to a place where I'll not be tormented with the nearness of you.'

'But... you never said anything in all the time before Gavin—'

'I told you,' he said harshly, 'I couldn't! That's why I went away. I was contented enough until you came after me and told me I should come back. So I did – just to be near you. I should have had more sense.'

He moved suddenly, but she was faster, her hands on his shoulders, holding him.

'William, don't just leave me like this, without—'

His eyes moved to a point above and behind her and she turned, her hands sliding from his wet coat, to see Gavin in the doorway, his eyes dark and expressionless as he surveyed them.

Wet hair was plastered to his forehead and rainwater ran down his face and dripped to his shoulders. As he moved into the room and dropped heavily onto a small chair, mud dropped in sticky clumps from his boots.

Margaret was too agitated to think of the picture she and William must have presented to him. 'Gavin, he's leaving tonight for Edinburgh! Tell him he can't just go away like that!'

Gavin's voice was tired. 'He'll not go anywhere tonight, for the river's in spate and that wind would blow anyone off the bridge if they were daft enough to venture onto it in the first place.'

As he reached for the claret, which stood on a small table, lamplight caught the side of his face and she saw a broad ribbon of blood from hairline to chin.

'Gavin!' William was forgotten as she ran to her husband. He put his hand to his cheek and looked at the blood on his fingers with disinterest.

'Pour some claret, for pity's sake, for I'm weary to the bone. It was – a chicken, as I mind. It was trying to roost under a roof and the gale blew it off just as I was rounding the street corner. It struck me in the face.' He took the proffered glass, drained it, managed a twisted grin. 'For a minute I thought it was the Devil himself attacking me, for it's a night when a man can believe in Hell. The poor bird must have got as big a fright as I did.'

She explored the wound with gentle fingers. The panicky bird's beak and claws had gashed his cheek in several places between the corner of his eye and the angle of his jaw. A few drops still oozed from the deeper scratches. She refilled his glass and thrust it into his hand.

'I'll fetch water and some clean rags.'

The front door banged as she was coming out of the kitchen with a bowl of water, but she didn't give it a thought until she got back to the parlour and saw that Gavin, still huddled in his chair, eyes closed, was alone.

'Where's William?'

Gavin started and looked up. 'I didn't see him go.'

She set the bowl down and ran back to the hall. The heavy front door flew open as soon as she turned the handle, hurling her back into the hallway. Wind and rain surged in, wrapping her skirts about her legs and soaking her. She screamed William's name into the night and the sound was blown back down her throat, almost stifling her. She put her shoulder against the door to close it, but it resisted until Gavin's weight was added to hers.

He shot the bolt across, locking the wild night out. 'Leave him be. He'll go nowhere tonight, I told you!'

Later, in bed, her head pillowed on his shoulder, she listened to the storm outside and thought of William.

'You don't think he would try to go away in this, do you?'

He cupped one breast, kissed its soft curve. 'Of course not. He'll have had the sense to go back home.'

Reassured, she gave herself up to his loving.

21

'You're never intending to go out of Paisley tonight, surely?' the stable owner asked as his final customer appeared from the storm. 'Man, you'd be daft to try it!'

But William was adamant, and an extra coin or two showed the man the sense of his argument. He led out a sturdy, reliable horse, saddled it, and vanished back into shelter.

The animal was reluctant to leave its stable and William, an indifferent rider, had difficulty in persuading it to move out into the street. The force of the wind, once they were clear of the protective house walls, sent the horse staggering before it managed to brace itself and go forward.

Gavin was right – the Abbey Bridge would be an impossibility in such bad weather. But there were two fords, one at the Sneddon, near the town hospital, the other at the Saucel, on the other side of the Cross. William checked a move on the horse's part to go back to the stable and dragged on the reins, turning its head towards the Saucel.

Rain sluiced in sheets against his face, making it difficult to keep his eyes open. He seemed to be completely alone – even the beggars that usually slept against the house sides had managed to find better shelter that night. The wind shrieked like a pack of enraged ghouls and tried again and again to pluck him from the saddle. He gripped tightly with his knees, determined to get out of Paisley that night.

Clumps of roofing thatch, slates, tatters of cloth and small twigs whipped by him as he rode. His hat was torn from his head and his hair flailed about his face. The wind changed direction and now the rain stung his face like a thousand tiny needles.

He heard the river long before he saw it, roaring defiance to the night as it plunged dementedly between banks that could scarcely contain it. The ragged, racing clouds let the moon through for a minute just as he reached the ford, and William saw that the normally slow-moving river, swelled by weeks of rain and fed by a hundred little burns running down from the braes, had become a maddened foam-flecked thing that seemed to be trying to toss the bulk of its water back into the sky.

His terrified mount threw its head up as he urged it down the banking. William's teeth sank into his tongue and he tasted the salt of his own blood.

'By God, you'll go on!' he roared, consumed with terror at the thought of being trapped in Paisley for another night. It was as though the town was a living entity, reaching out to pull him back as he tried to escape for the second time.

The horse backed into a tree and thin branches whipped painfully about his wet, uncovered face. Enraged by the stinging pain he caught at a branch and tore it free, more pain scalding through his crooked elbow as he did so; then he used the weapon to whip the horse back into the water, screaming curses that were torn away by the gale the moment they left his lips.

The animal went forward, its hooves slipping in the mud. As the river foamed round its legs it panicked and swung round, scrambling up the soft banking, throwing William off. He managed to get to his feet and found himself thigh-deep in water. Free of his weight, the horse gained the bank and disappeared, headed purposefully back to its stable.

William fought the river's pull, rubbing rain from his face and trying to judge the distance to the opposite bank. In normal weather it wasn't far and the water was no more than knee-deep; in earlier days, before the bridge was built, sturdy women had earned their living by carrying people on their backs across that same ford. Now, swollen and angry, it was an unknown element.

He planted his feet firmly against the riverbed, peered across the tumbling white-flecked water, and saw a light ahead. Someone had set a lamp in a window in the New Town. The sight cheered him. If he could keep moving towards that light he would be safe. He could, if necessary, find shelter on the opposite bank for the night and leave for Glasgow early in the morning before the town was awake. He went forward slowly, tensing his muscles against the pull of the river, testing the riverbed with each step before going on.

Suddenly his foot slipped and the torrent was on him like a hungry dog, bowling him over, bruising him, burying him beneath the surface.

He came up choking and spitting, treading water in a futile attempt to find something solid beneath his feet. He couldn't see the lamplight any longer and he had to fight down panic as he thrashed about, his feet reaching desperately for the riverbed and failing to find it. Then he realised that he must have been carried over the Hammills, the small waterfall between the Saucel ford and the bridge. Now he was in the deep pool where he had often gone swimming as a boy.

Weighted down by his clothing, he kicked out and managed

to swim, letting the current carry him for the moment while he concentrated on clearing the pool and reaching shallower water.

But before that happened the Cart wrenched free a mass of flotsam caught between two boulders and hurled it angrily over the Hammills into the pool. A heavy piece of timber hit William with great force on the back of the neck.

His body relaxed, gave up its struggle, and let the river take it, turning over and over as it went.

* * *

William Todd was found early next morning, wedged among a pile of debris that had lodged at the Sneddon ford, on the New Town side of the bank.

Jamie came running up Oakshawhill with the news, his boots splashing through great puddles, his face so white that the untidy mop of hair above it looked as though it had been set on fire.

As soon as she opened the door and saw him, Margaret knew what he had come to tell her.

Gavin's smart new carriage bowled along the road that led from Barrhead to Paisley. On the wide driving seat beside him, Margaret smoothed the skirt of her handsome new green silk gown then braved the sun to look up at her husband, his hands steady on the reins. Happiness enfolded her as snugly and neatly as the long-sleeved gloves on her hands.

Gavin had been visiting a patient, and she had left Christian, now a busy toddler, with Ellen, and gone with him in order to spend some time with Kate, who lived in Barrhead. Beneath the seat, protected from the sun, was a mass of red and pink and white and yellow roses specially picked from Kate's garden; her husband Archie, now retired from the army, was a keen horticulturist in his spare time.

From the road she could see burns splashing demurely downhill to join the Cart, neat within their banks and bearing no resemblance whatsoever to the undisciplined torrents of the great storm nine months earlier. White and pink flowers massed the hawthorns, frothy elderflowers had come into bloom, ragged robins clustered in red clumps by the roadside, creamy-white honeysuckle held out inviting blossoms to the bees and butter-flies, who were not slow to sample the heady nectar offered to them.

The air was thick with scented warmth, and even when they came into the town, passing the riverside area where the manu-facturers had their warehouses and then taking the turn into New Street, they were bathed in the perfume of the roses near their feet.

'Stop here a minute,' Margaret said suddenly and Gavin drew the carriage up without comment at the gates of the Laigh kirk-yard, then jumped down and lifted her from her seat as though she was as light as Christian, instead of a grown woman and almost seven months pregnant.

The Todd family plot was at the back of the graveyard, away from the comings and goings of the street. Colin's and William's graves still had a new look, though the summer had covered them with fresh green grass to take away the stark rawness of brown earth.

Clumsily, Margaret bent and laid a spray of white rosebuds on the mound that covered Colin, then a second spray on William's resting place. She stood for a moment, head bowed. She often came here to talk to William and be comforted by the memory of him. She missed him sorely. She always would.

'Come on,' Gavin said quietly from behind her. 'They'll all be waiting for us.'

They were – Jamie and Billy, Meg and Duncan and Robert. Margaret stopped short in the doorway of the High Street loom shop, astonished.

'It looks just the way I mind it as a wee girl!'

Almost all the floor space had been taken up by four looms. The floor had been freshly swept, linnets chirped in a cage hung at the sun-splashed window, a great box of the pinks that many Paisley men grew in their weaving shops stood on the sill.

'Now then—' Jamie's grin spilled over them all as he went to his loom, which stood just where his father's had been. He settled himself on the 'saytree', the long bench, and ran his fingers lightly over the wood before him. Then he looked up at the open trapdoor above.

'Are you ready?'

'I'm more than ready!' Kirsty called from the kitchen, where she was seated at her spinning wheel. 'It's long past time for this house to hear the beat of a loom again. Get to your work and save the chattering till later!'

He winked at the others. 'Aye, Mother.'

His foot pressed on a treadle. A set of warp threads lifted and Jamie sent the shuttle flying through the gap to the other side of the machine. Then he moved his foot to another treadle, and another set of threads lifted to form an arch in their turn. The shuttle sped back through it and Jamie warmed to his work, swaying to a steady rhythm beaten out by the thump and clack of treadles and shuttle.

Margaret felt Gavin's arm go round her, and leaned her full weight back against him, secure in the knowledge that he would always be there.

She stood within his embrace, watching as the good strong cloth on the loom began to take shape and grow, inch by inch.

* * *

MORE FROM EVELYN HOOD

Bonds of Friendship, the next instalment in Evelyn Hood's The Paisley Women Series, is available to order now here:

https://mybook.to/BondsBackAd

BIBLIOGRAPHY

The Paisley Shawl, Matthew Blair
The Paisley Thread, Matthew Blair
From Cottage to Castle, Andrew Coats
Paisley Weavers of Other Days, David Gilmour
Paisley Weavers, Pen Folk, Etc., David Gilmour
Vanduara, William Hector
Edwin Chadwick. Public Health Movements 1832–1854, R. A. Keats
Statistical Account of Scotland, Volume VII
'The Paisley Pamphlets', Renfrew District Libraries Services

ABOUT THE AUTHOR

Evelyn Hood is a *Sunday Times* bestselling author best known for her Scottish family sagas set in her hometown of Paisley, and the 'Prior's Ford' series set in the modern-day Scottish borders. Throughout her distinguished career, she published more than 40 novels, numerous short stories, plays, pantomimes, and musicals. Evelyn Hood passed away in Ayrshire in 2023, but the legacy of her writing continues, inspiring a generation of saga writers and touching reader's hearts worldwide.

Sign up to Evelyn Hood's mailing list for news, competitions and updates on future books.

ALSO BY EVELYN HOOD

Sixpence Stories

Introducing Sixpence Stories!

Discover page-turning historical novels from your favourite authors, meet new friends and be transported back in time.

Join our book club
Facebook group

https://bit.ly/SixpenceGroup

Sign up to our
newsletter

https://bit.ly/SixpenceNews

Boldwood

Boldwood Books is an award-winning fiction publishing company seeking out the best stories from around the world.

Find out more at www.boldwoodbooks.com

Join our reader community for brilliant books, competitions and offers!

Follow us
@BoldwoodBooks
@TheBoldBookClub

Sign up to our weekly deals newsletter

https://bit.ly/BoldwoodBNewsletter